I0720938

SAN JUAN SUNRISE

Ed Lehner

Jennifer Morse Series: Book 1

ALKIRA
PUBLISHING

San Juan Sunrise by Ed Lehner is about a young woman's journey to finding herself and letting go of the past. From a young age, Jenny's life has been filled with abuse and neglect, and because of this, she has chosen to live a secluded, albeit empty, life as an adult. But her past keeps rearing its ugly head, threatening to engulf her within its murky depths. On one particularly harsh night camping, Jenny is forced to seek refuge from a stranger. However, Will turns out to be caring and sweet, and the two form a close bond, Jenny, although still skittish with those around her, slowly learns to trust again. But Jenny still has a long way to go if she is going to live a happy and normal life and that includes facing the past. Forgiveness can only come from within. Is Jenny strong enough to put the past behind her once and for all?

Beautifully written and engaging, *San Juan Sunrise* offers readers a wonderful learning experience. The novel perfectly depicts how everybody has different issues and that true healing comes from how we deal with them. The characters were well-developed and engaging, especially Joan, whose caring nature and stellar advice were exactly what Jenny needed. Forgiving is hard and trying to move on can seem nearly impossible, but allowing pain to overshadow one's life is never the answer. The story was touching, delivering insight into cycles of abuse and the heavy impact and sad repercussions it has on its victims. *San Juan Sunrise* will leave a lasting impression on young and older readers.

—Danelle Petersen for Readers' Favorite

After a traumatic childhood, Jenny is emotionally disturbed. She trusts no one and is fearful of everyone she meets. Beset by unresolved anger and ongoing depression, she prefers the loneliness of desolate places - the mountains, the desert - and spends much of her time hiking alone.

Jenny's erratic emotions and slow, difficult progress to healing, are brought into high relief as she struggles to shake off the lingering effects of her abusive past. Her character is well drawn, showing her to be volatile and spiky, wary and vulnerable.

Meeting William changes her life and through his friendship and the friendship of others she meets through him, she begins to find a way to deal with her psychological damage. Jenny is forced to face what she would rather shy away from - and she must do it herself. The prose is intense and descriptive, allowing the reader to experience the events of Jenny's life in close up.

San Juan Sunrise is a compelling novel about trauma, recovery and redemption, which keeps the reader involved throughout.

— **Barbara Scott-Emmett, author**

Author Ed Lehner offers an effective and well-written story about childhood abuse that can be dark and triggering. The protagonist Jenny is convincing in her internal struggles to deal with her severe trauma. Readers can understand how her past has led her to mistrust people and her deep-rooted issues. The character development of the friends that enter Jenny's life is robust and rich. The subject of child abuse is sensitively explored within a compelling storyline that gives hope to survivors by showing that it is possible to overcome traumatic childhood experiences. *San Juan Sunrise* takes readers on a courageous and healing journey that offers light at the end of the tunnel with the promise of trust, friendship, love, and self-discovery.

— **Christine Nguyen for Readers' Favorite**

"I can either choose to continue to ignore my past and stay stuck in my fear, and mistrust, and continue to be isolated, or face it and deal with it." In *San Juan Sunrise* by Ed Lehner, we start to understand Jenny's character whose past traumas shape her present decisions. Jenny's distrust stems from her memories of "The Farm," which sounds like a comforting community but the context for her wariness becomes clear as she opens up about it. Lehner tackles themes of trauma and abuse through Jenny, while also emphasizing personal empowerment through self-expression. Joan's suggestion for Jenny to keep a journal offers her a safe place for private introspection and a return of agency to her narrative. Chris, who is vouched for by Amanda so we trust as a reader, is a sweet turn when he enters the story. The shared experience of meditation in the desert where they discover a deeper, spiritual connection is heartening. I liked the spiritual elements the most and this makes the healing journey feel organic. The book is simply written and does occasionally get lost in its minutiae, but, overall, it is a good work of literary fiction with a deep nod toward the holistic.

— Jamie Michele for Readers' Favorite

San Juan Sunrise
Ed Lehner
Copyright © 2024
Published by Alkira Publishing, Australia
ABN: 32736122056
http://www.alkirapublishing.com

All characters in this publication are fictitious and any resemblance to real persons, living or dead, is purely coincidental.

All rights reserved. No part of this publication may be reproduced, stored in a retrieval system or transmitted in any form or by any means electronic, mechanical, audio, visual or otherwise, without prior permission of the copyright owner. Nor can it be circulated in any form of binding or cover other than that in which it is published and without similar conditions including this condition being imposed on the subsequent purchaser.

ISBN: 978-1-922329-71-4

Sometimes, one must face his or her fear of the unknown and venture forth into the abyss. So it was for the young woman looking out over the vast mountain landscape, arms wrapped around herself, trying to stay warm under a cold, bright sunrise unfolding over the San Juan Mountains. She inhaled deeply, filling her lungs with the thin mountain air.

She had stood at the edge of this ridge many times over the past years, at eleven thousand feet, high above the valley below, never tiring of the expansiveness that seemed to let her heart sail free. Being completely alone comforted her. But it was only for the moment; her memories remained. All of it was still there, haunting her, following her, surrounding her, like a hungry mountain lion that never quit stalking her.

CHAPTER 1

Jennifer Kathryn Morse, twenty-five years old, five foot ten, exuded a lean fitness from a summer of backpacking and living in the San Juan Mountains in southwestern Colorado. With her gray eyes, dirty-blonde hair—ragged and shaggy from bathing all summer in cold mountain streams and waterfalls—and her tattered and worn clothes, she presented quite a figure.

Jenny had spent another summer living in the high country, loving the solitude and freedom of the mountains which consoled her, like the mother she'd never known. But now, late in the season, nights were getting colder, the chill warming in the high mountain sun during the day. Her gear was adequate for summer, but not for cold. She chastised herself for prolonging her trip down to the cabin where she'd spent last winter; where she planned to spend this winter. She would again hate the confinement of the four walls. The hike down would require two long days over rough terrain.

She liked her solitary life where nobody knew her whereabouts, hidden away in the mountains. If she died up here, nobody would ever know. Nobody would miss her, except maybe her brother and her grandparents, the only people who knew she still existed, and they probably wondered if she still did, since she'd barely been in touch the past two years.

She ambled slowly back to her camp, had a quick breakfast of a Power Bar, and packed up her small camp, which was about half a mile off any trail at around nine thousand feet in elevation. She shouldered her backpack and headed out, leaving no trace.

Two long days later, she took a breath and smiled, happy as she stumbled out to the north end of the Animas River Valley, a glacial plain that extends from Durango, a small mountain town in southwestern Colorado, up about fifteen miles to where the river narrows into a rocky canyon.

Exhausted after two long days of rigorous hiking, Jenny stumbled along the trail toward the clearing that held the cabin. But something was wrong. She should see it by now.

A few steps further on, she stopped and stood rooted to the earth, staring, eyes wide. Instead of the cabin, she saw only a pile of burnt rubble, the old cast-iron wood stove, the stone foundation, and the old outhouse.

A wave of panic rolled over her. Fear seized her gut. *Crap! Now what am I going to do?* She thought about camping by the burned-down cabin for the night, but she wanted to be inside someplace warm and cozy with a hot shower for a good night's rest.

Perhaps the out-of-the-way mom and pop motel in Durango. She'd stayed there for a night or two in winter when she hitchhiked into town for supplies. She turned and headed back out to the road toward Durango, hoping to hitch a ride.

She hiked two miles down the road but found no cars and no ride. The sun disappeared behind the mountains, clouds moved in, and the temperature fell.

She forced herself on for another two miles, now so tired she could barely keep moving. Her feet and legs hurt so bad she knew she couldn't keep going much longer.

She stopped for a moment and looked around, seeing a ranch house on her right. There were lights on. The house sat about a hundred yards down a gravel drive surrounded by some groves of pine trees. In the dimming light, she could see a two-car garage, an open outbuilding with an old pickup inside, and what looked like a cabin off to the left. Everything around her was private land and posted as No Trespassing. While hating to even think about it, she realized she had no choice other than to ask permission to camp there. She stumbled down the drive, dragging her feet. She almost had to crawl up the six steps onto the wide porch.

She knocked timidly on a solid door that appeared to be made of old, weathered boards. The large brass lockset clicked with the sound of a precision mechanism as it opened.

A tall man with soft, dark eyes, graying hair, and a well-trimmed beard stood facing her.

He looked her over and frowned. "Yes, how may I help you?"

"Hi. I'm so sorry to bother you. I'm Jenny. I was trying to hitch a ride to town. No luck, and it's getting late. I'm totally exhausted … been hiking down from the mountains the last two days. Would you mind if I pitched my tent somewhere in your yard for the night? Please? I promise not to disturb you or make any mess, and I'll be gone in the morning. Promise." Her voice trembled, revealing how scared and close to tears she felt.

The man still stared at her. She hadn't had the advantage of a hot shower for four months. Her clothes, secondhand when she'd bought them, were now frayed and torn.

"Are you homeless or what?" he asked. "I really don't want to start having any homeless people around here. Maybe you should just move on."

She smiled a sad smile with tears threatening to slide down her cheeks. "Please, mister, I've been on an extended backpack trip for a few months in the mountains, and I'm headed back down to town for the winter. I've been gathering material for a book I'm writing. I'm not homeless. I couldn't catch a ride. I'm really exhausted and just need a place to camp for the night. I'll be seriously gone in the morning. You won't even know I was here. Promise," she said, desperately trying to stop the trembling in her voice.

The man looked at her for another few moments, contemplating her words and appearance. "I suppose you can camp out in my yard as long as you're out of here in the morning. I don't want to start letting folks think that they can start camping here. My name's William, by the way. Make yourself at home."

"Sure, William. No problem. Thank you so much. You're so great. I really appreciate your kindness and understanding. Would over there be okay?" She pointed to a grove of pines, as she started to back away.

"Yes, sure, that'd be fine. Have a good night." He turned and closed the door with a soft click.

Relieved that was over and she had a place to camp, she turned and headed to the grove of pines about one hundred yards away and pitched her tent. She crawled inside and ate her remaining trail mix. At last she crawled into her sleeping bag for some welcome sleep.

The next morning, she awoke cold and shivering. The temperature had gotten much colder than normal for early October. She checked her watch. It was eight o'clock, but it still looked to be almost dark. Then she saw the tent was sagging. *No, no, no.*

She sat bolt upright and unzipped the door flap. A pile of wet snow tumbled into her tent. At least a foot of new, wet snow had fallen, and it was still coming down heavily. She'd known from seeing the clouds building in the west at sunset that there was weather coming in, but she'd never expected snow at this lower elevation this early. Rain she could handle but not this.

It had been pleasantly warm when she crawled into her summer-weight sleeping bag last night wearing only shorts and a T-shirt. Now her teeth were beginning to chatter. The weather wouldn't warm up until the sun came out, whenever that might be.

She pulled on her leggings, a light fleece, rain jacket, and boots, then waded through the snow up to the house. Frightened to bother this William again, she knocked with great hesitation, then waited for what seemed like an hour, shivering. Her now-chattering teeth sounded like castanets. It was, in reality, only two minutes before the door swung open, and there stood William, staring at her.

"What do you want now? You said you'd be gone."

"I'm so sorry, William, but have you seen how much snow there is out here? I hadn't expected this. I'm so unprepared and so cold. I should've come down two weeks ago. I know better. I screwed up. I'm really scared. Please. I just need to warm up, just for a little while, please. I'm so very sorry to bother you, but I'm really scared that I might be close to hypothermia."

He stared at her for a moment, noticing her shivering, and then looked out and saw the snow. "Oh my! I hadn't really paid much attention. I didn't realize there was this much. Okay, come in and get warm. I have some fresh coffee. Are you hungry? I'll make some toast if you want. Eggs? I sure don't want you freezing to death in my yard. I doubt there'll be anybody along now until after this quits."

"Thank you, thank you, thank you." She brushed the snow off herself, kicked off her boots, and entered what would be a new part of her life.

CHAPTER 2

A fire blazed in the fireplace. William told her to go over and warm herself, which she did, languishing in the heat. She savored the aroma from the burning pine logs mixed in with the smell of freshly brewed coffee. He brought her a large cup of the steaming brew and two slices of toast slathered with butter, along with a jar of peanut butter and a knife. She smelled eggs and ham frying. Jenny began to think this man was truly an angel in disguise, but she didn't trust anyone, especially men, and was extremely wary of being alone in this house with a man she'd just met. She fingered the six-inch sheath knife she wore on her belt.

"This is nice of you. I'm sorry I'm bothering you, but thank you so much. You're a life saver."

"It's okay. I don't usually have people at my door. You're not a bother. I'm happy to help a woman in distress. Get yourself warm. Have a seat here by the fire. Please. You don't have to stand."

"I'm just going to get warm and get out of your way, try to hitch a ride to town."

William gave her a sarcastic smile. "As I just said, there

won't be anybody out on the roads now. Wait until it quits snowing and the road's plowed. Just relax. I'm not as bad as I sometimes seem to be. I'm just used to not being bothered by anyone. It's okay. I want you to stay in here where it's warm."

Jenny eyed him, suddenly realizing her predicament of being trapped in here for the duration of the storm. If she decided to bolt, she could freeze to death.

She looked around the house, seeking ways to escape if she needed to, and noticed walls lined with bookshelves filled with books. Soft chairs were available in which to read them. The house was old but updated. It had a great room consisting of a modern kitchen, a dining table with six chairs, along with this very cozy sitting area, all trimmed out with darkened pine woodwork and off-white walls. She heard classical music coming from somewhere. Where there weren't bookshelves, modernist art hung on the walls. It was warm and inviting, like a small, intimate library, like a place where she could feel comfortable under different circumstances.

She suddenly let out a little scream. "William, there's a cat rubbing against my legs. I'm afraid of them, William. I really am."

"That's just Cat, Jenny. She's harmless and really loves people. Not to worry."

"That's not the point. I just don't like them, or dogs for that matter … I was attacked when I was a little girl and don't like them. Please can you get this cat out of here?" she implored.

"Hey, all right. Just a second, I'll get her."

"And you named your cat 'Cat?'"

William came in and picked up Cat, who yowled mildly in protest. "I named her after Holly Golightly's cat in *Breakfast at Tiffany's*. Cat was a stray that moved in with me several years ago. She's really a nice cat. I guess someone just abandoned her."

He petted her while he talked, and Cat purred contentedly. He took her away, put her in another room and closed the door.

The cat gone, she considered her options, but there really weren't any. Maybe she could try some of the social grace her grandparents had taught her. "You have a nice house, William. I'm admiring all your books."

"These are only a small part of those I've read over the years. I'm a prolific reader with a bad habit of buying books until I'm out of space and then have to do some trading with the used bookstores in town or donate to our library.

"I'm an author and have a number of books published. Probably not anything you may have read unless you read trashy novels like the airport or vacation throwaways. I inadvertently got into that genre early on and never was able to get out of it. It has made me wealthy, but I'm not very proud of them. You said that you're a writer?"

Ignoring the question, she said, "Oh my God, you're a writer. Do you have any of your books here? I'd love to read something you wrote. What's your last name? Maybe I've already read one of your books. I've bought a lot of books from the used bookstores in town when I used to hitch in from my cabin to town for supplies in the winter."

William motioned her to a shelf. "Everything I wrote is over there on the shelf, all in chronological order. Have a look, but unless you like books with the covers showing busty women with torn bodices and hunky guys, let it be said, that's the genre, easily read schmaltzy romances, all formulated stories my publisher wanted, knowing they could market and sell. They're a far cry from being any sort of literary works."

Jenny went over and saw there were over a dozen. She pulled a few from the shelf and looked at the covers. He was right about the torn bodices and hunks. And there was his name emblazoned on every one, William Brighton. She'd never heard of him.

While looking through one, she said, "I'm embarrassed that I told you I was a writer last night. Let's just say that, ah, I want to be a writer. I wrote some poetry and short stories in college and some since I graduated, but I thought they were all fairly lame. All my college professors liked my work and thought I had great potential, potential I certainly haven't realized for sure. I entered some short stories and poems into some contests when I was in college. Several were accepted which made me feel good and more confident, but I haven't done much since.

"I hang out in the mountains during the summer and winter in an old cabin a few miles north of you, writing in my notebooks, hoping something might click, but nothing ever does. I keep thinking that if I just keep writing, the muse might shine her light on me someday. I try not to get discouraged. I just try to keep going, hoping I might be able to write something decent, some good story." She trailed off into silence, looking down at the floor, then adding, "I just can't seem to focus on anything that I think might be interesting."

"I know that cabin," William said. "I knew that someone was staying up there in the winter. That was you? It burned down last July. Everyone thinks someone torched it." He shot her a look. "You told me last night you had a condo in town? But you stay in a cabin out here in the winter? What's that about?"

"I'm sorry. I lied to you. I was desperate and didn't want you to think I was homeless. Truth is, I guess I am. I have some money in the bank and could afford a place if I wanted, but I choose solitude instead. Please understand. You said you like your privacy. I guess I do too.

"That sucks about the cabin. I asked around before I ever moved in, and no one seemed to know who it belonged to. Everyone said to just move in for as long as I wanted or until someone kicked me out. It was rustic, but it had a good wood-burning stove, a decent roof, and it was pretty comfy … after I got rid of all the critters that lived there. I bought a saw and axe and used deadfall for heat, hitching to and from town for provisions. It was good."

He accepted her answer and didn't pursue the subject as he brought her a plate of scrambled eggs and ham with more toast and butter, setting it on the breakfast counter. "Here's some food for you. Sorry for not asking you how you like your eggs prepared."

"Thanks, William. They're fine. I haven't eaten a feast like this in months."

As hungry as she was, Jenny found it hard to eat because of the nervousness in her gut. She kept her eyes on him all the while. The hot coffee and food were helping her warm her body, and she liked being in this beautiful, warm house, comfort she hadn't allowed herself in several years. She still watched him like a cat, prepared if anything should happen. But she found herself slowly, reluctantly, warming to this man, but, remembering her past, she kept her guard up.

Still trying to be social, she asked, "Are you from around here?"

"No, I'm originally from New York City where I earned an MFA in Creative Writing at Columbia. I wanted someplace away from the busyness of that city, some place quieter, and moved here about twenty years ago. I came down here after a book signing in Denver and fell in love with the area. I bought this old house and ten acres, once part of an old ranch. I remodeled and modernized it, and have lived here off and on through two wives. I've been here permanently for the last six years."

He thought for a moment. "Maybe I'm like you, sort of a recluse, looking for the muse to strike and give me an idea for a truly meaningful novel, not the crap I made my living on. I sold a zillion of those schmaltzy reads and had two turned into mildly successful movies. They made me a lot of money, but I feel far from successful. I'd like to be known for at least one decent book of what might be thought of as actual literature.

"Hey, I have some work to do. The weather is starting to clear and the roads should be okay in a few hours. Then I need to go into town and I'll be happy to give you a lift, save you from trying to hitchhike."

She responded quickly with "That would be great," feeling a gush of relief knowing she'd be out of here.

William then ignored her, cleaned up the dishes and excused himself to go to his office. "Stay cozy. There's more coffee, so sit, relax. We should be able to go in a few hours."

With him in another room, she relaxed a bit and pulled one of his books from the shelf and started to read. She read the first few chapters, then skipped through some later chapters. From what little she read, she thought the writing was good, but the story, like he said, was trash.

Bored, she put the book away and wandered over to the window. The sun was fully out, snow melting off the porch roof. She found her fleece top and jacket and went out. The sun was warm, making the day pleasant to be outdoors. She waded through the snow to her camp, gathered and packed her things, and took down her wet tent, carrying it all to the porch. She spread the tent over the railing in the sun to dry. It felt good to be out of the house and free, not feeling trapped.

By two thirty, her tent had dried, and she had everything

packed. But no William. She went to his office and knocked quietly on the door. "William, sorry to bother you, but the sun is out. If you're still planning on going to town, I'm packed and ready to go whenever."

She heard a rustling from inside. "Thanks for reminding me. I wasn't paying attention to the time or what was going on outside. Give me a minute."

She paced nervously, wanting to get to town.

The door opened. "Okay," he said, pulling on a jacket. "I'm ready."

She followed him to the garage and put her pack in the back of his Subaru hatchback. The four-wheel drive car got them out of his unplowed drive to the paved county road, which had been plowed, and he headed south toward Durango. By the time they got to the north city limits, the snow had disappeared, and it looked like it had rained instead. Such was Colorado weather.

As they approached the cheesy motel where she'd stayed before, she said, "Right here's good." He pulled in, and she retrieved her pack and closed the hatch.

"Are you sure this is where you want to go?"

"It's fine, William. Thanks. Thanks for everything."

"Well, I'll be off then. Good luck and nice to meet you."

"Yeah, thanks again for everything."

Knowing their cheapest rooms were $39.00, she checked to see how much cash she had. It was only fourteen dollars. She hurried to a trolley stop to catch a ride the twenty blocks to downtown to get to her bank before it closed, but she'd just missed it. The next one wouldn't get there for an hour. Now she regretted not getting the bank card her banker kept wanting her to have. The more she thought, the more she felt like a complete waste, a derelict.

Out of desperation, she walked toward downtown. After ten blocks, a car pulled into a driveway right in front of her and stopped.

It was William. "Hey, you okay? I thought you were getting a room, but then I saw you walking, heading toward downtown."

She explained her dilemma, and by the time she'd finished, she was on the verge of crying.

"Why don't you get in," William said, "and come back to my place for the night? You can use the guest room. Things will be better in the morning, and I'll bring you back to town. What do you say?"

Jenny felt panic form in her gut, felt her knife, hesitated, then reluctantly accepted, wanting a warm bed in a warm house rather than the alternative of sleeping out who knows where with who knows what.

Back at the house, William showed her the guest room. "The guest bath is right over here; there are clean towels. Please make yourself at home. Anything in the fridge is yours for whatever you want or need for your dinner. Be comfortable, and please call me Will. All my friends do."

"Thank you, Will. You're a kind man. But please stay out of this bedroom. I don't want any funny business. Just to let you know, I sleep with this under my pillow at night." She brandished her knife.

William, wide eyed, held up both hands. "Hey, no need for that. I'm not that kind of man. Seriously, please trust me on that. You're perfectly safe. Promise." With that, he backed out the door and left.

She felt her heart pounding in her chest.

After she calmed down, she noticed the room had the same woodwork as the great room, but the walls were painted in light-gray green. Two large prints of mountain scenes decorated the walls. An iron-framed queen bed and two pine end tables with matching lamps sat against one wall, with a small matching dresser against the wall facing the bed. A closet opened next to the doorway to the hall.

She took a long hot shower that she wanted to last forever. After washing her hair twice, rinsing out her clothes, and hanging them on the shower rail to dry, she found a soft terry cloth robe in the closet. It was early evening now, and she was hungry, so she sneaked through the house, making sure William wasn't around, and raided the fridge for a cold dinner of salami, cheese, an orange, and some iced tea. She found some crackers in a cupboard, ferreted everything back to her bedroom, and locked the door.

CHAPTER 3

William had apparently disappeared into his office. She thought about him. What struck her was how kind and gentle he was with the cat. Then she recalled her friend Annie from when she was growing up in the commune in California, a place called "The Farm." Annie had two cats, and Jenny remembered how kind and gentle she'd been with them even though Jenny was afraid of them. Annie had been the only person she ever felt okay to be around. She'd always asked her in for tea and cookies, always talked with her, and treated her so kindly. Annie also helped with home schooling. She grew herbs, and her cabin always smelled so wonderful from them drying inside. Jenny wistfully wondered how Annie was, her one ray of sunshine during growing up.

Her mind drifted to the ugliness she'd experienced when twelve years old, out at her favorite place on the top of a secluded cliff that overlooked a valley below. Engrossed in a book she'd scrounged, enjoying her quiet, she felt annoyed when Old George, one of the Farm's founders, interrupted her solitude.

He sat down beside her, wanting to talk, but she ignored

him and continued to read. He went quiet. She glanced over and saw he had his pants down and was masturbating. He noticed her looking at him and asked her to do it for him. She screamed and ran away from him, back to her yurt, and told Dory about what had happened.

Dory, the woman her father lived with, looked at her with a blank expression and told her that all men wanted to have you suck their cock, fuck you, or beat you. And if she wasn't careful, she'd end up with two kids like her and her brother. Jenny, ashamed and afraid, never told anyone else.

Back in the present, having finished eating, she took her plate and glass back to the kitchen and placed them in the dishwasher, then she went to check out William's books and found *Nightwood* by Djuna Barnes. She read the first page. It looked interesting, so she took it, along with a chair from the dinner table, back to her room. Not trusting the lock on the door, she placed the back of the chair under the doorknob.

She curled up in the luxurious bed and stared at the opposite wall for a long while, wondering what she had gotten herself into. She wanted out. Tomorrow morning couldn't come soon enough.

Then, afraid of sleep, she read until her eyelids started dropping. She dropped the book and fell asleep, her knife tucked under her pillow.

She awoke to what sounded like a motor running softly somewhere. She opened her eyes to see Cat snuggled in next to her, her head sharing her pillow. Tentatively, she reached over and touched the cat, which ceased its purring to open one eye and look at her, then it stretched, curled in closer, and resumed purring, now much louder.

Jenny rolled carefully away, ready to get up, and the cat yawned, calmly did some morning cat stretches, had a little bath, and then began purring and moving toward Jenny. She put her hand up and said, "Stay!" like she'd seen people do with dogs.

Cat stopped, sat, cocked her head, and looked at her. Jenny cocked her head and looked back, not sure what to do. The cat then turned and found the warm place where Jenny had been sleeping, curled up, and went back to sleep. She considered the creature for a moment, wondering how it'd sneaked into her bedroom, then she remembered she'd left her door open when she'd gone out to raid the fridge. She backed away and quietly went to the bathroom.

After fetching her now-dry clothes, she got dressed and walked out of her room to the inviting smells of fresh coffee, bacon, eggs, and toast. Cat jumped up off the bed and accompanied her, going to her food bowl. Jenny quietly replaced the chair at the table, hoping William hadn't noticed it missing.

CHAPTER 4

"Good morning," William said, "see you have a new friend. Wondered what happened to her. I was just about going to come wake you up for breakfast. Have a seat. There's some fresh juice poured for you. Sorry I left you on your own for dinner last night. I had a ton of emails I had to answer and two phone calls to the West Coast. Hope you found something to eat."

Feeling a little overwhelmed and unsure of herself, she responded, "I, ah, yeah, I had a wonderful night. Thanks, William, I mean, Will. Cat was in bed with me when I woke up."

"I'd put her in my bedroom, but cats can be sneaky when they want to be. Are you okay?"

"Yeah, I'm fine. Sorry I overreacted last night." Surveying the food, she said, "Wow, another wonderful breakfast. I haven't eaten like this since I was at my grandparent's place. Susan, my grandmother, pampered me to death. It's a wonder I don't weigh seven hundred pounds. Thanks so much."

"No problem. Sleep okay? That knife didn't jab you, did it?" he said with a laugh.

"I slept great, and no, I didn't stab myself," she said sarcastically. "I appreciate your hospitality and everything. When're you going to town?"

"Ah, Jenny, I was thinking. I might have an offer for you. The old bunkhouse out back is in decent shape. It has indoor plumbing, is furnished, and has central heating, plus a good wood stove. If you'd like to stay there for the winter, it's yours.

"And another thing. if you'd like, I could maybe help you with your writing. Maybe I could help you to focus in on an idea, help you develop it. Maybe write a few short stories."

Her wariness radar blipped loudly in her head. "William, you know nothing about me other than that I'm a homeless drifter who knocked on your door. Just why would you do this? You said you like your privacy. Now you want me living here? I'm not at all sure I understand. Thanks for the offer, but no thanks."

"Listen, Jenny, I see an opportunity to help a young writer. Maybe give you some support—which I never had when I was starting out. I could mentor you, be your coach and critic. I'd just like for you to be comfortable and able to spend time writing. Don't say no until you think it over. I wouldn't bother you. You'd be on your own. And that bunkhouse will be way, way more comfortable than that old cabin ever was."

She studied him, her head cocked to one side, coldly responding, "So what's in it for you? Nobody offers a complete stranger something like that. I don't think so."

"Essentially, I'd like to have someone in the bunkhouse, if for nothing more, so I wouldn't have to worry about it, about the heat going off, pipes freezing, and so on. So you'd really be doing me a favor. And, you seem like a nice young woman who needs a break. And I need a caretaker for the bunkhouse. So … want to go and have a look after we eat?"

"Yeah, maybe," she said, still wary of his offer. "I'll take a look."

Breakfast finished, she followed him out to the little bunkhouse. He explained on the way that at one time, it had been an actual bunkhouse for the hired hands or cowboys.

William said, "I had it updated as a guesthouse for my kids when they came to visit. As it turns out, they never do, except for Peter, who's in law school in Denver. He stays in the guest room, so this remains vacant. It may need some work to make it decent."

He opened the door for her, and she went in and looked around. She saw it as a smaller version of the main house with a smaller great room and a fully furnished modern kitchen. It had one bedroom with a queen bed, dresser, and closet, along with a nice bath and tiled shower—a dream come true for her, and she loved it. As for "a lot of work," no, after some cleaning it would be perfect.

"You'll have to furnish sheets, blankets, and such," William said. "There're towels, dishes, silverware, pots and pans, some cooking spoons and spatulas." He showed her a small washer and dryer off the hallway. "So … what do you think?"

After looking around and inspecting the place, she said, "Okay, maybe I'll try it, but I want my privacy. Complete privacy. I don't want you pestering me. And I can pay rent. I'm not destitute. I have money for rent."

"No rent is necessary. I don't need the money, and as I said, you'll be doing me a favor. Okay?"

Not knowing how else to respond, she turned and, reluctantly, reached out to shake his hand. "Deal."

He gently returned her handshake. "I'm happy you like it. Please enjoy."

"Is there a Walmart or something so I can get bedding? I

also need to get some decent clothes and burn these old rags I'm wearing. I hate to bother you, but would you give me a ride?"

He smiled and said, "I was going to go in, but I've some more business I need to take care of. Tell you what, why don't you take my car and go in?" He reached into his pocket and handed her the keys to his Subaru.

She looked at him incredulously. "Really? You'd trust me with your car? You don't know me or if I can even drive or if I even have a driver's license … which, by the way, I do."

He laughed. "You'll be fine. Just bring yourself and the car back in one piece. Okay?"

Jenny thought of her driver's education course when she was working toward her GED in Denver and earned her license and how she'd only driven a few times since in her grandparent's car. She was hesitant when she carefully started out toward town, but after a few miles, she found William's Subaru to be great fun to drive.

Off she went to town thinking, *I could just drive into New Mexico, abandon the car and hitch down south somewhere.* She stopped by the post office to check her box to see if she had any mail, not surprised when there was nothing. Then she walked to her bank, where she withdrew $300 and applied for a bank card. The sports exchange store was next, where she found some warm things for winter. She topped off her shopping spree with a stop at Walmart for some underwear. Going commando for the last few months had gotten old. She also got sheets and blankets. She began to feel a little extravagant but was careful not to get carried away. Her total expenditures came to $175.39.

On her way out of town, she stopped for some groceries and bought William a nice bottle of wine.

CHAPTER 5

She returned safe, sound, and smiling. "Thank you so much, Will. I bought you a bottle of wine as a thank-you present. You're smiling at me. Want to see what else I bought?"

"By all means. Will you be modeling?" he teased.

"No!" She shot him a glance, bordering on fear and anger, then gathered her bags and left.

Knowing him for only the last two days, she was being extra careful. He seemed kind, kinder than anyone she'd ever known, other than her grandparents. He left her alone, didn't bother her, and didn't seem threatening—so far, anyway. He treated her like an adult. She enjoyed talking with him. He listened and seemed to be interested in what she was saying without any judgment or advice. He'd given her a warm place to stay. But somewhere down in her deepest place, a little voice kept telling her not to trust him, he would turn out like all the rest, he would want to get into her bed at some point. He would try to take advantage of her.

As she was leaving, William said, "There're some cleaning supplies under the kitchen sink. Want some help?"

"No! You've got things to do. I can take care of whatever

needs to be done."

"Oh, I almost forgot, here're the keys."

With that, she turned and left without another word and went to unload her purchases into her new little house. After she'd locked all the doors and checked the windows, she felt safe, warm, and cozy.

That night, William came to her door and invited her over for some homemade pizza. Even though she was still unsettled about his "modeling" remark, she reluctantly accepted the invitation.

William opened the wine she'd brought and offered her a glass, which she refused, afraid that if she drank it, she might let her guard down, which was still on high alert.

"No wine?" he asked.

"Not tonight. Just water."

She helped to clean up the kitchen, and once finished, William asked her to sit down to talk. She warily accepted, opting to sit as far away from him as she could.

"What do you like to read, Jenny?"

"Well, I started reading *Nightwood*, from your library, that first night. Read 'til I couldn't keep my eyes open anymore. Love it. I'll probably finish it tonight. Poetic, sweetly written, like I'd like to be able to write someday."

"Then do it. Read her, study her style, read her poetry. She was mainly a poet, you know. There were many great women writers in her era. Check out Gertrude Stein, Alice B. Toklas, Natalie Barney, Renée Vivien. Of course, they aren't as well known or popular as the men like Joyce, Hemingway, D. H. Lawrence, F. Scott Fitzgerald, and other male writers of that period. But, nevertheless, these women were great. Read and study those you're drawn to. Study their styles. Then write your own stories, your own poems."

Jenny sat quietly for a moment. "I've read Hemingway, Lawrence, Fitzgerald. I can't write like they did. They were good. They had great stories. They lived in a time of great stories. I have no stories, no stories like they had."

"No, you don't have their stories. That was their time. This is your time. You have your own stories. Let your heroes guide you. Check out these women. Some had their demons which they tried to conquer with their words. The night you first came here, you told me a little about your early life. I can't help but believe that there's much more you haven't told me, which is fine. I don't need to know. But we can become whole by telling our stories. Let your words come out unhindered and try to conquer your own demons."

They sat and talked for another hour about writing and said good night around ten o'clock. Jenny went back to her new abode, locked the doors and went to bed. Rather than read, she lay awake and thought about what had happened the last few days. She had a feeling of being secure, which was new for her. She was warm, comfortable, had food, and a secure roof over her head. She thought of Cat and, as much as she disliked cats, almost wished she were in bed with her.

CHAPTER 6

The next day, Jenny asked William if she could borrow his car to go to town again. She went back to the bank and checked on her account, which was increasing by the usual $7,500 per month from her trust fund. Her savings had accumulated to over $200,000 over the last few years. She felt financially secure, but having so much money was foreign to her. Her banker had advised her numerous times on what to do to make this accumulating wealth grow more than in a low-interest savings account, but she'd ignored his advice. She withdrew $3,000 cash and transferred another $5,000 to her checking account.

After the bank, she went to her storage unit and gathered her boxes of books. Then off to the Apple store, where she bought a new laptop computer. Her final stop was a sports store, where she bought new running shoes, socks, a pair of winter running tights, a light running jacket, a new yoga mat, and a few other necessities for running and doing yoga.

Back at the bunkhouse, she unloaded the car and returned it and the keys to William.

"Are you getting settled?" he asked.

"I'm getting very settled, yes. Thanks. I'm starting to feel comfortable and safe. Give me a few days, and I'm going to get on with writing. I want to impress you."

He smiled. "We'll see. Take your time. No rush. And feel free to use my library, so long as you make sure to return my 'friends.'" He turned and walked away.

Jenny walked back to her place and put away all her new possessions, made her bed, then organized and put her few books up on the empty bookshelves. She looked around, realizing she was accumulating things. Never having had many possessions, she had confusing thoughts about it.

The only other nice house she'd ever been in was her grandparents' large downtown penthouse in Denver. It'd been wonderful, though it seemed cold with hard modern furnishings. It had never been as comfortable there as she already felt in this little house.

That night Jenny had a deep, restful sleep with dreams of people around her, loving and caring for her, and she was able to feel love toward them, feeling warm, secure and trusting. When she awoke in the morning, that sense of security remained with her. But Jenny didn't trust that feeling, not at all did she trust it, and quickly pushed it aside.

Cat had somehow managed to sneak into the bunkhouse and lay curled up by her, purring loudly. Jenny languished a moment, watching the peacefulness of this creature, then coaxed her to the front door and outside, wondering how it'd managed to sneak in.

Then she did the yoga routine she'd learned from Annie back at the Farm. She made coffee, sat down in front of her new computer, and froze, having no idea what to write about. She got up and found a half-filled notebook and a pencil, curled up on the couch, and began to write a poem about her new adventure.

The morning slipped away without much success with the poem. Frustrated, she ended up killing an hour fooling around with her new laptop. Discouraged and feeling restless, she decided to go for a run. The sun was out, the roads were dry, and the snow was almost melted under the Colorado sun. The weather was again seasonably warm. Running always cleared her head. She changed into shorts, a long-sleeved top, and her running shoes. Then she went out, only to run into William, who looked like he was about to do that same thing.

"Hi, Will, I'm going for a little run. Looks like you have the same idea. Want to join me?"

"Sure, but you'll leave me in your dust, I'm afraid. I'm pretty slow these days."

"Well, I haven't done any at all lately. Let's start, and we'll see how it goes, okay?"

She started out at a slow jog, and William had no trouble keeping up. The air was cool, fresh, and sweet.

"Don't get off your pace just for me," William said.

"Nah, this is a good pace for me right now. I'm feeling a little slow myself."

They ran a mile or so without talking, then William asked, "Do any writing this morning?"

"Well, I started a poem, but my head wasn't in it."

"Just start writing words. Don't worry about what you're writing or where you're going with your words. Just write. Write about anything, like your experience the last few days, about something that inspired you when you were in the mountains this summer, what you saw, what you felt, encounters you may have had, the cabin that burned down. You never know what stories might be lurking there; every writer has times when there's nothing. We've all faced it one time or another. But writers write, and sometimes when we get started, a story can take us to places we never expected. Get rid of that critic in your head…" He trailed off, a little out of breath from talking and running at the same time, and his pace slowed a bit.

She replied, "Thanks, Will. By the way, I still feel like I should be paying you some rent. You're providing me with real comfort like I've never had before; I can afford rent, I truly can."

"No, we talked about that already, and that wasn't our agreement. Royalties still roll in every month, and I've more money than I know what to do with. I can't spend everything I have, and I really don't care to. I don't need or want rent money from you." Breathing hard, he slowed again.

"But William, it would make me feel better, okay? How about five hundred dollars per month?"

"Tell you what, take that five hundred dollars a month and buy yourself a car," he said between panting. "It'll give you freedom to come and go as you wish without having to depend on me. I'm gone once in a while for several days, even weeks at a time, leaving my car at the airport sometimes. Then what?"

Car, license, insurance, gas, service. More stuff, more responsibility. "Maybe. Let me think on it."

At two miles William was ready to turn around. Jenny had had enough as well, and they headed back in silence, the only sound their breathing.

She got to her bunkhouse, still thinking about it. A car? *Maybe I should do it.*

After a shower, she walked over and knocked on William's door. "Sorry to bother you. Could I borrow your car again to go into town? I thought about what you said, and I want to look at cars."

William smiled. "Better yet, let me take you. I know some guys at the used car lot and might be able to get you a good deal."

"Not sure that I want a used car. I'm thinking new."

"Can you afford new? They're expensive."

"William, I have money, a lot of money. I can afford new."

"Well, then, let's go see what we might find."

They drove to the south end of town where all the dealerships were located. On the way William veered left off the main highway onto Main Street, pointing out where his recent ex-wife, Helen, had her yoga studio. He also showed her one of the local bookstores, restaurants, and other points of interest.

Jenny said she'd walked down Main Street a number of times, mainly to the used bookshops to load up on books during the winter months when she stayed in the cabin. She'd never paid much attention to the other stores, restaurants, and such.

"My ex, Helen, and I are still good friends, but we just couldn't live together. She wanted her space and was committed to her studio, and I was too controlling, wanting all of her time with me. I've since come to realize how hard I was to be with."

Jenny found it interesting that he was sharing this information with her. It was another thing to consider.

They came to the dealership, which had Subaru, Jeep, Chevrolet, and GMC models. Walking around the lot, Jenny spied a gun-metal gray Jeep Cherokee Trailhawk. "That's the one."

A trim forty-something man with a big salesman's smile approached them and greeted William by name. He introduced himself to Jenny as Tom Anderson. "Want to take this Cherokee for a drive?"

"Sure, I'd love to if it'd be okay."

"Of course it's okay. Let me get the keys."

After Tom left, she asked, "How do you know Tom?"

"He's sold me several Subarus over the years. After a while, it seemed like everybody knows most everyone in Durango."

Tom returned with the keys and opened the door for Jenny. She climbed in with Tom getting in the front and William in the back.

Jenny drove out of town, went down some back roads, came back, drove around town, and headed back to the dealership.

Tom explained all the Jeep's bells and whistles as they drove. "This is a used vehicle with 5000 miles on it. The original owner decided they didn't like it and came back and traded for a Rubicon. The car has a new-car, extended Jeep warranty. So it's really like a new used car and is a great deal. Also, this Cherokee is rated for serious off-road travel. It has skid plates and everything you need for back roads."

"This is exactly what I want. What do I have to do?"

"Oh. Okay. Let's go in and get the paper work going. When do you want to pick it up?"

"Now."

"It will take at least an hour to get both the Jeep and paper work ready."

William pulled Jenny aside. "Are you sure about this? There're others you might like also. It's a big decision? Look around?"

"No, William, I know this is the one I want. It's perfect for everything I want to do."

"Maybe you should do some research on this Jeep model. See what others think? Check out consumer reports?"

"You've bought cars from this man, and I trust your judgment on that, and I trust this car. I don't want to spend time doing research. If I wait it may be gone by tomorrow."

"Okay, then. It's your decision."

William pulled Tom aside and held back as Jenny proceeded on. They had a quiet discussion out of reach of Jenny's hearing. Then they all went into Tom's office.

"William tells me this is your first car. Let me work on some numbers."

Tom left, and William asked, "Are you sure about this, Jenny? That Jeep is a lot of money."

"Absolutely sure, Will. Thanks for the concern, but maybe it's time I started to grow up and quit avoiding my life. I love that Jeep. It will take me into places in the mountains and deserts I would never be able to get to. I love it."

Tom came back and quoted some numbers, which both Jenny and William went over carefully. They looked at each other and nodded in agreement. William posed a number of questions and seemed satisfied with all of Tom's answers.

Tom asked, "Will you want financing?"

"No, I'll bring you a check for the full amount, if Will will drive me to my bank." She looked questioningly at William.

Tom looked at her, and then at William, with a raised eyebrow. Jenny just smiled, and William shrugged, rolled his eyes, and nodded. "Let's go, then."

Jenny got the cashier's check and headed back to get her new car. Her heart was about to explode with anticipation and excitement. She got the car with a full tank of gas, and instructions on all the intricacies of a four-wheel-drive high-tech machine.

"You'll need insurance," William said. "I'll call my agent and see what we can do." He called his insurance agent, explained what was happening, and introduced Jenny who talked to the agent, answering her questions, some of them needing William's help. Since it was now five o'clock, she promised to be in tomorrow morning to pay her premium and sign the necessary papers. The agent told Jenny she'd already activated a policy and that Jenny was covered.

Jenny smiled and turned to Will. "I want to go driving for a while. Thanks for all your help." She almost called him "Dad" but caught herself. "See you later."

She drove around for a while, checking out some of the outlying roads and then the town itself, enjoying her newfound freedom. Around six she was ready for dinner. She spied a pizza place downtown on Main Street, parked, went in, and ordered a small pizza and a glass of wine. While waiting, she checked the place out.

Only a few tables were occupied, but more people came in right after she'd sat down. A group of four women about her age sat at a table close by, talking and laughing. At another table sat two young couples who talked seriously for a while and then broke into laughter. A twosome near the back of the room held hands across their table.

Though surrounded by other people, Jenny felt alone. She had no friends or anyone. She got up, quickly paid her bill, and went to her car, where she put her head on the steering wheel and broke into sobs.

CHAPTER 7

Friday: Jenny got up, went for a five-mile run, returned home, and began to write. Four hours later, she hit "Select All" and then "Delete," thinking it was all just shit. Frustrated, defeated, and sad, she went to town for coffee and a few groceries, remembering to also stop by the insurance agent's office and pay for her auto policy.

She went to Raven's coffee and newsstand, got a latte, found a place on a nice sofa, pulled out her notebook, and began to write about buying a new car which somehow moved to writing about being alone. She realized the only person she knew in this town was William. She thought it might be all right that fate had introduced them. He'd taken her in and given her a wonderful place to live for the winter. But she didn't know how to deal with all of it, having no experience of trusting anyone other than her grandparents.

Tears came again. She got up and left, bought what groceries she needed, and went back to her bunkhouse.

She heard a knock on her door. William was there with his usual congenial smile and said he and Helen were having dinner the next night in town, and they would like her to join them.

"Ah, wow … I don't know. I don't want to intrude. Where?"

"A nice restaurant we like. You wouldn't be intruding. We'd love to have you join us. I've told Helen about you, and she wants to meet you."

"Oh, man. I've nothing to wear. Ah, maybe not, but a rain check?"

"Oh, come on. Go and get yourself something nice tomorrow. You can afford it," he said, with a knowing smile.

"You really want me to join you in a nice restaurant? I've never been to a 'nice' restaurant except years ago with my grandparents. I don't think so. You and Helen have a good time."

"Oh, come on. Get over it. You'll be fine. We're really informal in this town, nothing fancy. Maybe one step above dirty jeans, but not much."

"Let me sleep on it, and I'll let you know tomorrow."

"Good, I already made reservations for three." He turned and walked away.

She had a dream that night of being a beautiful princess in her own fairy tale. When Jenny awoke, Cat was by her head, purring.

After a short run, she went to town, stopped at her bank, got some cash, and went for a stroll down Main Street. She came upon a little boutique that had clothes in the window she liked, so she went in.

A young woman, about her age, came to help her. Together they selected a nice outfit. After she paid for it, she asked for a recommendation for a hair salon. The saleswoman gave her the names of two places nearby. She left and proceeded to the closest salon. She'd always cut her own hair ever since she left the Farm. She was pampering herself by going to a hair salon, something else she'd never done before, and it made her feel uncomfortable. She was living in a really nice place, she'd bought a new car, and now this. *What the hell am I doing?*

She found the salon and went in. After waiting for twenty minutes, a young woman greeted her warmly and led her to the chair. As soon as she was seated, the stylist fluffed Jenny's hair with her fingers. "Wow, who did your hair the last time? Looks like it was cut with a chainsaw. Sorry, don't mean to offend."

Jenny chuckled. "Actually, it was a knife, and I was the cutter. This is truly my first-ever time getting my hair cut by a real professional."

"Oh my God. I'm so really sorry. Open mouth, insert foot."

Jenny laughed. "Hey, no offense taken. It's just the way it was. Hopefully this will turn out better than my efforts. Can you do anything for me?"

"Absolutely. Let's get started."

After the stylist got her ragged hair straightened out, Jenny found that getting it cut professionally was an enjoyable experience. She liked having someone give her a shampoo. The young stylist then gently cut her hair into a manageable length, still long enough for a ponytail.

When the stylist had finished, Jenny looked in the mirror. "Wow, you made me look great. Thanks so much. I can't believe how nice it looks. It's really nice. Thank you, thank you so much."

"Thanks. Really I just got it untangled, evened it all out and gave it a little shape, is all. Glad you like it."

Jenny paid for the cut, thanked the woman, Claire, and said she'd be back. She walked down the street to her Jeep feeling special.

Back at William's house, she knocked at the door. When

he answered, she asked, "So what time, and do we go in together or separately?"

He stared at her. "My God, you look different. I hope you realize just what an incredibly beautiful young woman you are. Sorry, excuse me, but you are, ah, okay, ah, let's go in together, and reservations are for six. I'll pick you up at five thirty. Helen will meet us there."

A warmth rushed to her cheeks as she responded with a laugh "No one ever said I was beautiful, just got a nice haircut, is all. Did I look that awful before?"

"Of course not. You just look different, a good different."

"I'll be ready at five-thirty."

Jenny spent the rest of the afternoon browsing through her many notebooks and trying to write, trying not to be anxious about the dinner. William knocked on her door precisely at five- thirty.

"Wow!" was all he could say. "Ready?"

"Totally." She walked to his car in her new tight jeans, a silky top, and a nicely blinged-out denim jacket.

William scampered around to open her door for her. Jenny realized what it was like to be a grown-up woman. It was a new feeling, a good feeling. It was all new to her, and it felt nice.

They drove to the restaurant, making small talk with no mention of writing, for which Jenny was grateful. They arrived shortly before six, walked in, and as they were led through the quietly lit restaurant—about half full of diners who were talking and laughing, eating and drinking—the food aromas lit up her taste buds.

Jenny followed William to a table where a beautiful older woman with dark, bobbed hair streaked with gray and intense blue eyes was already seated. She got up to greet them, her smile radiating warmth and self-assurance. Tall, elegant, and graceful in her movements—like a ballerina—she was impeccably dressed in stylish jeans, a silk blouse that matched her eyes, and a denim jacket with floral embroidery on the collar and sleeve cuffs.

"You must be Jenny. I'm so happy to meet you. Will has told me so much about you. I'm Helen."

Jenny couldn't help smiling. She immediately liked her, wanted to be her.

Jenny looked around the restaurant, noticing the long bar filled with younger people, who were socializing and laughing, looking like they'd just left work. A tall back bar needed a library ladder to reach the top shelves. The original exposed-brick walls reached up to a patterned tin ceiling with old-looking fans, groups of which were run with belts from a single motor. Old black-and-white pictures hung scattered about on the walls.

"This is a really cool place. I love the funky decor," she remarked,

William nodded. "This was originally a bar back in Durango's early days. There was a shooting right outside in the street. Apparently the sheriff and town marshal got into an argument over the gambling going on in here, the sheriff against, and the marshal for. It escalated into a shootout and the town marshal was killed. The owners wanted to recreate that ambiance of the time. Wait until you check out the restrooms."

"So a real wild-west shootout. Sort of gives me the creeps."

A waiter offering menus and ready to take orders for drinks interrupted them. After their drinks arrived, the conversation drifted to literature, people, and so on. Jenny felt included, her ideas and responses considered and accepted. She was being an adult, and she was enjoying it.

She already loved Helen, the first woman other than her grandmother that she'd felt that way toward. She'd avoided the few women at the Farm, except for Annie, who was a good friend. And she'd never been close to any of the woman professors from her college days.

During the conversation, Helen said, "It's wonderful the universe has brought you to us. I'm so pleased to have met you and that you'll be staying at Will's this winter. I hope we can be friends."

Helen asked Jenny about her yoga practice and training. Jenny replied that a woman at the Farm had taught her, but that was the extent of her training, adding that she did try to practice regularly.

Helen invited her to come to her studio for her beginning yoga class. Jenny smiled, thanked her and said she would think about it. The three of them chatted on during their appetizers and dinner. Helen and Jenny got in some girl talk when they made a restroom trip.

Jenny found the darkly lit restroom to be as funky as the main restaurant. She loved the faucets made out of plain copper pipe and industrial-like valves. She looked at all the vintage movie posters on the wall. The whole place was fun. The whole night was fun.

After dinner and dessert, an aperitif, the night was over, goodbyes and hugs exchanged, and then home. Jenny couldn't remember being so happy, so accepted. No pressure, no strings. Helen even said they could be friends.

But there was the writing thing constantly looming over her head. As soon as they returned home, a knot of pressure and insecurity formed in her gut, and all the happiness faded.

She closed her door and locked it, and she checked her windows, locking all her insecurities in with her. All her trust issues arose like fumes from a steaming cauldron of fear. Will and Helen seemed nice. *But why are they nice to me? They must be setting me up to take advantage of me.*

She went to her bed and to a night when sleep wouldn't come, only fear and anxiety about Will and Helen and some secret agenda they must have to hurt her.

Then her head went to crazy busyness, like swallows hunting at dusk. Who was she kidding? She wasn't a writer, just a nonproductive trust-fund kid. She depended on her grandparents' support and their belief that she would do something with her life. But she wasn't. She knew it was wrong to ignore them, but she was so ashamed of the life she'd been leading—a life of isolation, fear, and sadness—that she couldn't bear to see them. She wasn't a writer; she was nothing but a failure. Sometime in the morning hours, she finally fell into a restless sleep.

CHAPTER 8

Jenny woke up early and went for a short run. William was outside when she returned and waved at her, but she pretended not to see him, went into the bunkhouse, and disappeared. She began avoiding William, ashamed of herself, afraid and embarrassed to see him. After two weeks with no poems, stories, beginnings, or endings, she grew increasingly frustrated as well as more fearful. She didn't deserve his feigned kindness. She was living a lie and needed to just leave, take her fancy clothes to Goodwill and get far, far away.

She had mobility. She could grab some better gear at the secondhand store and go to the desert. She could hide away down south all winter and head up into the mountains after the snowmelt.

She wanted to get away from all the pain, the fear and self-doubt, get away from all her baggage, just get away from people and expectations she could never meet. She did like Will, but her mistrust of his imagined ulterior motives grew with every passing day. He reminded her of her grandfather, but she couldn't bring herself to trust that he wouldn't want something more. All men want something more. And then there was Helen. What did she want? *Why would she want to be my friend? Why would anyone want to be my friend?*

She grew increasingly afraid and more vulnerable to all the forces unfolding all too quickly. All of it confused her. She didn't think she would ever revive, ever flourish.

She packed up her boxes of books and some clothes and necessities to take back to storage. Then reluctantly she went to say goodbye to William. Scared, with her heart racing, she knocked on his door.

He answered, and she just stood there for a few moments, looking down at the floor. Finally she was able to say, "I'm moving out!"

He looked at her incredulously. "What! Why? I don't understand."

"You don't need to understand," she said with venom in her voice.

"Did I do something? I thought you were happy here. I try not to bother you."

She looked up at him with all the fear, resentment, and anger that had festered the last few weeks and said, "I don't trust you and why you're trying to be so nice. Nobody's ever been nice to me. What's your real agenda? You're planning something that'll somehow end up hurting me. I'm out of here."

She turned and started to walk away but Will grabbed her arm and turned her to face him. "What are you talking about? I have no hidden agenda to try to hurt you. I promise that with all my heart. Please believe me when I say that. I do not ever want to hurt you or see you hurt. Ever! You have to believe that. I'm fond of you, like a daughter I never had. And there is no way I'd ever abuse my own daughter. Please trust me on this."

She looked up at him and realized how badly she was shaking. All the negative emotions and self-doubts of the last two weeks surfaced, and then the tears came.

Will very gently put his arms around her and held her gently, like a small wounded bird.

They stood like that for a long time until her sobs slowed and turned into whimpers. William led her to the sofa and got her a box of tissues and a blanket, and said he was going to make them some tea. "I think we need to have a talk."

She curled up, still whimpering and sniffling.

He returned ten minutes later, bringing them tea. He sat across from her in an easy chair, crossed his legs, and sipped his tea, waiting. She blew her nose and stared into space, unable to meet his gaze.

They were silent for some time, both sipping their tea. Finally Jenny started talking. "I'm sorry, Will, but I don't feel I can trust anyone. You, Helen, no one. I'm a complete failure in everything I do, especially writing. I've failed you and everybody." Once she'd started, she couldn't stop and went on to tell him about Old George, her uncaring father, his slutty partner, her subsequent wariness of people, her decision to never get close to anyone. She told how she never felt good enough for anything and like a complete failure. She avoided the deeper issues she couldn't find the courage or words to verbalize.

William listened, not saying a word, just nodding every so often.

She talked for most of an hour, pausing every so often to cry softly. William made more tea and brought in some snacks for them.

Finally she was done. She sat still, staring into space, and said in a hollow, weak voice that she would be leaving now.

She thanked William for all his kindness and got up to leave.

William said, with some force, "Sit back down, Jenny! What the hell are you saying? I don't want you to leave, especially not like this. You're in no shape to go anywhere right now. Also, as long as you are here, I want you to know that you're safe, that no son of a bitch will ever harm you under my watch. I may not have been the best of fathers, but one thing I did was protect my children, supported them, and nurtured them. I like you and enjoy having you here. Please believe that. Helen adores you. We're both happy you're here.

"I couldn't understand why you were avoiding me. I just thought you might be working and didn't want to be bothered, which I could well understand, and I wanted to give you your space. But hearing all this, it just makes me sad.

"I don't know what else to say," he continued. "I cannot believe what you just told me about your life, your abuse, and your rejection by those who should've loved and protected you. How did your brother survive?"

Her hollowness was reflected in her voice. "Number one, he was a boy, not a girl who was born just to please men. But he grew up in the same atmosphere. Maybe he was able to tune it all out. I'm not sure what kind of shape he's in. Maybe he's been able to lose himself in medical school, maybe he's just put it all aside. I saw stuff that went on with him too. I know he wasn't spared. I suppose that someday, he might have to deal with his own stuff. We've never talked about any of this with each other. I haven't ever mentioned any of this to anyone until now. I feel so ashamed, like such a fool, like my whole crazy life is my fault. I'm so sorry to dump all this on you. You're such a wonderful guy. You didn't need all this shit. I'm sorry. It's all so confusing and frightening to me. I'm scared." She choked back a sob and blew her nose.

William said, "Trust me, Jenny, there's nothing to be scared of. You are safe here. None of this is your fault. There's nothing for you to be ashamed of or sorry for. You were abused and essentially abandoned by your parents and community. I feel honored that you felt you could share this with me."

He gave her a reassuring smile and continued. "I see that we have some rebuilding in store, getting you some self-confidence. I have a friend in town who is associated with the women's shelter. She's a good counselor. I hope you might consider checking her out. I'll support you, and I know for certain that Helen will also. Please, please, consider my help."

She smiled weakly. "Thanks, Will. I'll consider your offer. I'm really tired. I think I need to rest. Thanks so much. I'm sorry for all of this." She got up and started toward the door.

"I could come and sit with you if you want. Maybe try to give you some support? So you can get some rest?"

She looked back at him. "No, I think I'm okay. Thanks. I just feel really drained." She turned away and left with her head drooping, and walked over to her house. She felt exhausted and emotionally empty. There was nothing left.

She skipped dinner and fell into bed. Her mind drifted to her brother, Michael, and she wondered how he was doing. His few letters seemed full of scattered ramblings. He seemed angry, even hostile in his writing. He seemed angry with her; why, she didn't know. She felt sad for a moment and then fell asleep.

She awoke to a knocking on her door; it was eight o'clock the next morning. She got up and went to the door to find William standing there. "Just checking in. Are you okay? I made us breakfast. Hungry?"

Jenny, still half asleep, tried to focus and think for a minute. "Ah, yeah, I'm starved. Let me wash my face and get dressed. I'll be over in a minute," she said with a weak smile.

"That sounds much better. Sounds more like you. See you in a minute. Don't let our food get cold."

Fifteen minutes later, she went into William's kitchen and found Helen who got up and hugged Jenny for a long time. Helen finally let her go, wiping her eyes. "Will called and shared some of your story with me last night. We talked for at least an hour. Oh, Jenny, I am so sorry. You are such a dear, sweet girl. I just cannot believe what Will told me. I'm in shock and didn't sleep at all last night thinking of you."

William said, "I'm sorry, Jenny. Please don't be angry with me for sharing with Helen, but I was really upset. I needed to talk to someone."

"It's okay, Will," she responded with a quiet, shaking voice. She couldn't cry again, she had no more tears. "I understand. I'm actually happy you did share with Helen. You both mean a lot to me. I want you to know that. I want to trust you, but it's hard. I appreciate everything. I really do. Thanks."

"Please, be assured, you can trust us. We're on your side," Helen said.

Food was ready, and they all sat and ate pancakes and bacon without much conversation. Helen and Jenny cleared the table and put the dishes in the dishwasher. They all moved with their coffee to the living area.

Helen broke the quiet, "I called my good friend, Joan, at the women's shelter last night and relayed a little of what Will told me, not mentioning your name or how I knew you. She and several women are counselors there and deal with this kind of thing all the time. They do both private and group sessions. She would love to meet and talk with you. Would you be up for something like that?"

"I'm not sure about counseling. I don't know what all

that entails. I'm feeling pretty raw and confused right now. I'm scared. I don't know what's happening to me. I'm trying to digest the fact that I dumped all this on Will. I don't know what got into me. I never shared any of this, ever … and now you, Helen, I'm sorry to be such a bother with all this shit. I really am."

"Oh, honey, there's nothing to be sorry about. You're certainly no bother. We want to help. Please let us do what we can to help. Please?"

Helen and Jenny talked on with more detail about Jenny's story, and William excused himself, leaving the two women to continue without him. Helen and Jenny talked on into late morning, then Helen left to go back home but not until Jenny had made arrangements to see Joan at the center tomorrow at ten. They would meet at the yoga studio, and Helen would go with her.

Jenny left also and went for a long run. She reflected on the events of the past two days: her despair, her sadness, and two people with whom she'd shared some of her deepest secrets.

She felt lighter, having shared some of the ugliness of her life. Neither Helen nor William truly seemed anything but caring and understanding. As hard as it was, it felt good to unload. She felt blessed to have stumbled onto these two people. She remembered what Helen had said, "It's so wonderful the universe has brought you to us. I hope we can be friends."

Jenny slept with dreams of green grasses growing all around her in a beautiful meadow with birds and wildflowers just below groves of lush aspen trees.

CHAPTER 9

Jenny awoke at seven o'clock to Cat's purring. How did she sneak in this time? It was becoming a habit.

After putting the cat outside, Jenny did a quick workout, ate a light breakfast, and was at Helen's studio at 9:45, anxious and scared to death, but determined to see this though. After talking with Helen at length yesterday, she felt some assurance that she might really have found someone who understood, someone she could trust, but she still felt wary and scared.

They walked the few blocks to the shelter. Joan was there to greet them as they walked in. Joan was a forty-something, pleasant-looking woman with hazel eyes and long auburn hair pulled into a ponytail. She wore casual clothes—jeans, a pullover top, and running shoes—and she looked fit.

Everybody in Durango seems to be fit.

They went into her office and closed the door. Joan began by explaining to Jenny what the center did. They had residential women who could be in danger from husbands or boyfriends along with others who were nonresidence. There were private counseling and group sessions. All situations were different, but the outcome of abuse was usually the same: fear, shame, guilt, lack of trust, lack of self-confidence, wariness, and social isolation.

Jenny sat very quiet and listened. She tried to relax but was too frightened, wondering what this counseling thing would have in store for her.

Joan asked Helen to leave, wanting to talk privately with Jenny. Helen got up and said she'd wait outside for Jenny so they could have lunch together.

Joan and Jenny talked until 11:45. They came out with Joan looking pleased, but fear lurked in Jenny's eyes. They all exchanged hugs, and Jenny and Helen went off to lunch.

It was a beautiful, warm, late-autumn day, and they went to a restaurant with a patio so they could sit outside to enjoy the day.

"So," Helen started out, "how did it go with Joan? What do you think?"

Jenny looked out toward the mountains for a long moment, then turned back to Helen. "I think I like her, maybe what she has to offer. We discussed my major issues of fear and mistrust. I found out that I'm not so special and that even normal people may have the same issues but probably to a lesser degree. But on the other hand, mine are only the tip of a huge iceberg I'll need to come to terms with, given time and hard work, some possibly very uncomfortable work. But I think I'm willing. I feel so confused about everything. I thought my life was settled to being alone. Now there's Will, and you, and now Joan. I … I just don't know how to do all this. I didn't have anyone and now there's everyone.

"And I'm scared to death about it all, but I think I want to go ahead. She helped me realize that I've come to a turning point in my life. I can either choose to continue to ignore my past and stay stuck in my fear, mistrust, and continue to be isolated, or face it and deal with it. But I'm scared, Helen. There're some things I don't know if I can ever talk about." She ended with a choke in her voice, looked away again toward the mountain, and wiped away a tear. "My first counseling session is the day after tomorrow."

Helen said softly, "I can't fathom how difficult your life was, but now you have us and you have our full support. Will and I'll do whatever might be necessary to help you get through this. Please trust us. We're not going to hurt you."

CHAPTER 10

Helen stayed in close contact with Jenny after her meeting with Joan and urged her to check out her yoga classes.

Succumbing to Helen's urgings, Jenny arrived early for an eight o'clock class, nervous like it was her first day in junior college. Helen, who was in the front foyer, greeting people, punching passes, or taking payments, welcomed her with a smile and a hug.

"So how much is class?" Jenny asked.

"The first one's free, and we can discuss costs later. Go on in and find a spot for your mat. Then get out a blanket, a strap, and a block from the supply closet by the door."

Jenny looked around and saw there were several people already there. She picked a space in the back to be as unobtrusive as possible and unrolled her mat. She got a blanket, strap, and a block and checked the room out. It had a light-colored highly polished wooden floor, white walls and ceiling, and some pictures of colorful, strange-looking people decorating the walls. There was a large statue of someone on a pedestal behind where she thought the teacher would be.

Meanwhile, a number of other people arrived, some

chattering away, others quiet, looking as though they were entering another dimension. The group was mostly women, just two men. Some were around her age, some were older and several more fell somewhere between those age groups. No one paid much attention to her. A twenty-something woman walked over next to her, smiled at her, unrolled her mat, and sat, assuming an erect cross-legged position, which Jenny observed others doing and followed suit.

Helen came in, and the talkers fell silent. She walked to the front of the room, put her hands together, bowed, and greeted everyone. "Namaste."

Everyone responded, "Namaste."

This was all strange to Jenny, and she suddenly felt a little panic at what she perceived to be strange goings-on. Annie had shown her maybe about six to ten different poses, and they were all Jenny knew. There'd been no formalities, no "Namastes"—whatever that meant. She suddenly felt way in over her head, but she took a breath, held her resolve and reminded herself that she knew and trusted Helen.

The class was ninety minutes long. During the first seventy-five minutes, Helen led the class through a number of different poses, or asanas, calling out their names Jenny later found out were in Sanskrit, none of which had any meaning for her. Some of the poses were stretching, some required some strength, and some were difficult for Jenny, especially the balance poses. She felt clumsy. But Helen was constantly there, helping, correcting, and encouraging her as well as others. Then they did something at the end called Savasana, lying on her back and relaxing her body for about ten minutes. Jenny felt her body melting into the floor but was interrupted when everyone moved into the same sitting position as before class started, sitting erect with their hands on their thighs.

Helen said, 'Now for our meditation. This meditation will be on focusing on the out breath."

Jenny followed along and tried to focus on the out breath, but her mind raced with thoughts and apprehension about her counseling session tomorrow.

Jenny was grateful when time was up and all of them rose, rolled their mats, folded blankets, and proceeded toward the door, returning all the "props," as Helen called them. The woman who'd been next to her smiled again and said, "I haven't seen you here before. New to yoga?"

Jenny smiled back and replied with a weak laugh, "So it showed?"

The woman replied, returning the laugh, "We're all beginners. We're all still learning. It's a process. Isn't Helen wonderful? I love her classes. My name's Kelly, by the way."

Kelly was about Jenny's age and height with a mop of dark curls and big blue eyes. She looked to be in very good shape.

"I'm Jenny. Nice to meet you, Kelly. Yeah, I have some yoga experience but nothing like this. Wow, I thought I was in pretty good shape, but I'm feeling muscles I didn't know I even had. What is that meditation thing? I knew some people a while back who meditated, but I really know nothing about it."

"Hey, want to get a cup of coffee down at Raven's? We can chat."

Jenny's stomach knotted, and she froze. Her memory went back to college and Becky, a girl she'd liked and gotten along with during her sophomore year in college. She remembered her five roommates during her freshman year, all who'd moved out because they couldn't stand her aloofness, antisocial behavior, and sometimes cruel remarks. Then Becky came along, she gave Jenny the space she wanted and needed, and she became sort of a friend.

She remembered the night she was in bed just dozing off, when Becky quietly slid in alongside her, leaned over, and put her hand softly on Jenny's right breast and kissed her on the mouth, telling her she wanted to make love with her.

Jenny's response still echoed in her mind, "What the hell are you doing? No fucking way. Get the hell away from me! I don't want to make love to you. I don't want you touching me. I trusted you, and this is what I get. Get the fuck out of my bed."

Then, grabbing some clothes, she ran through the night to the union and slept curled up in a study cubicle. The next day, she cut classes, called a real estate rental agency, and found a furnished loft apartment about two blocks from campus. She moved all her stuff over to her new place, never seeing Becky again, and never letting anyone else get close to her again during the rest of her time in college. She became a true loner, trusting only in her self-imposed solitude.

"Jenny, are you okay?"

"Ah, yeah, I'm fine. Thanks for the offer, but I need to talk with Helen. Some other time."

"No problem. Maybe next time?"

"Yeah, maybe." She turned toward where Helen stood.

"So what do you think? I see you met Kelly. She's a regular. She's nice."

"Yeah, I guess. I just wanted to say thanks for your help and patience. I thought I knew a little but realize that I know nothing. I'll be back, but I'll have to first see how I recover from this session. And I've never had any instruction on meditation. I really wasn't too sure what to do. Can you teach me?"

"Love to. Can you come by the studio around one thirty? I'll meet you, and we can talk."

Jenny had some lunch and then browsed the bookstore to

kill time. She got back to the studio to meet with Helen who locked the front door. "I don't want us to be disturbed. Let's go into my office and have a seat."

Jenny liked Helen, but locking the door made her uncomfortable. She felt trapped but took a deep breath and sat down.

Helen asked whether she knew anything at all about meditation. Jenny replied that she'd known some folks at the Farm who did something like that, but she didn't really know anything about it.

Helen gave her some rudimentary instruction about what meditation is, simply sitting quietly, calming your mind through watching your breath, just being with yourself for a length of time. She talked about how busy our minds can be, always chattering and keeping us occupied and busy. Then when we sit and elect to do nothing, our minds tend to go into overdrive, shocked to find that we're just sitting quietly and doing nothing. The busy mind is what meditation helps us to let go of. It helps us to regain focus, quiet, peace, and equanimity. After a while, by simply sitting, watching our breathing, and simply letting thoughts come and go, our mental busyness starts to calm.

Then she went on to say that if Jenny was interested, there was a Buddhist group in town which offered regular introductory classes that would give her more insight into meditation practice. She thought it was maybe a six-week course. She found a slip of paper and wrote down the phone number of a contact person to call along with the address of the dharma center.

"Thanks, Helen. I'm not sure about doing that right now. I gotta see how this counseling goes. I feel that I've got a lot on my plate but thanks again. This helps. At least I won't feel so lost next time. Maybe I'll see if there's a class this winter, maybe after the new year."

They said their goodbyes and shared a hug. Jenny left and went home, spending the rest of the day at William's place, browsing through his library. She came across the section with his books. She looked through several more and selected one that seemed interesting, deciding to try it.

CHAPTER 11

Jenny's first counseling session with Joan was at ten the next morning, the beginning of two sessions per week on Tuesdays and Thursdays. She got into town early and hit another of the local independent bookstores. She looked through the literary section, looking for some early twentieth-century women writers, and found a book by Renée Vivien, *The Woman of the Wolf.* She remembered William mentioning her name. She read the first few pages and decided to buy it.

The woman at the cash register looked at the book, then at Jenny, and asked, "Are you familiar with this writer?"

"No, not really, a friend mentioned her to me."

"Well, you're lucky. We've had this copy for a long time. It's out of print now, I think. The owner kept wanting to donate it to the library book sale, but I convinced her someone would find it. Apparently, that is you."

"Good to know. Thanks." Jenny paid for the book and left.

She arrived early for her appointment with Joan and began reading Vivien's book in the waiting room. Joan was running late, but Jenny really didn't care since she'd become absorbed in her reading. She loved Vivien's writing and stories. There was a beautiful, sensitive female approach to how she wrote. It was soft, loving, sweet, and passionate. She wanted to go into this book and never come back out, just stay hidden inside it forever.

Joan came out and apologized for keeping her waiting, Jenny replied with a smile and said that she didn't mind. She took a deep breath and got up, following Joan into her office. She took a seat in one of two comfortable chairs and watched with dread as Joan closed the door. Even though Jenny knew Joan was there to help her, she still felt like the door was being closed on her tomb.

So now it begins, Jenny thought.

The first session laid some groundwork, and Joan spent time asking for more information about Jenny's background. She asked lots of questions without getting much, if any, response. During the second session on Thursday, Joan started doing some deeper probing with mixed results. She asked Jenny about her relationship with her father and his partner, asking how she felt about them and about why she felt that way. Jenny, not so skillfully, danced around the questions, glossing over things and avoiding going any deeper than superficial answers. Even by the third session, Jenny still treated questions superficially by avoidance or denial.

Halfway through this session, an exasperated Joan finally said, "Jenny, we need openness and honesty here if this is going to work and you aren't being totally honest or forthright with me."

Jenny dropped her eyes from Joan's gaze, head dropping, staring at the floor.

Joan continued, "Jenny, your injuries caused bruising, not only bruising on your mind, but bruising on your soul as well. We can heal the mind and body, but that will be only a superficial band-aid until we go deeper and salve the soul. To do that, you have to dig deep, get it all out, and then you can begin to heal. The only way is to talk about it, write about it, bring it into the open air, make it real, face it head-on, stare it down.

"You're at a point right now where you can either elect to help yourself or stay stuck. I can't make it happen for you. I can facilitate, but if you want me to be able to help you, I need you to cooperate by being honest with me and yourself."

Jenny remained silent, staring downward, her breathing becoming nervous.

"You say you like to write," Joan said. "Have you ever kept a personal journal? Have you written anything at all about your father and his woman partner, about your alleged abuse, about how you feel?"

Jenny looked up at her with her eyes but with her head still down, like a child being scolded. She just shook her head, saying quietly, "Yeah, I write stuff in a journal. And the abuse isn't alleged. It was real, dammit. It was damned real!"

Joan continued, "It was real? You haven't said one thing to me that would give me any idea any abuse ever even happened. You'll have to let go at some point if you ever want to get rid of all the stuff you're carrying with you. You'll have to address it, talk about it. Have you written anything about your life, about your father?"

"No. I hate him."

"Okay. Your homework from now on is to keep a journal of your thoughts, fears, worries, your childhood and your father. I want you to address anything from the past you're hiding from yourself and from me. Think you can do that?"

Jenny nodded, still staring at the floor, wanting to melt into it and disappear. She knew Joan was right. She knew she had to get it out. She thought she might throw up. It was time to go.

Jenny walked out of the shelter, her arms wrapped around herself, crying softly. She was so scared to talk about what needed to come out, hidden so deep for so long, things she wanted forgotten, things that couldn't be forgotten. It was all so unspeakable, so shameful, so ugly. Now that it had been prodded, she felt it growing like a cancer, a huge, insidious tumor.

She went back to the bookstore and bought a new notebook specifically for her personal journaling. She went to the coffee shop and wrote about her childhood for two hours, downing two cups of coffee in the process. She did as Joan had instructed and wrote about her abuse, wrote about things she'd never allowed herself to ever think about, things she'd rather keep hidden. She wrote about Dory and what she'd done to her, what Dory had made her do, about her father who was always stoned, drunk, or both, about things that went on in the yurt when she was supposed to be asleep, about seeing her brother fucking Dory when he was only fourteen years old. She'd wisely chosen a place to sit in a corner, away from anyone who might see her crying.

So, okay, she'd written out all the ugly crap hiding deep within her soul. Now, deep down, she knew the next thing would be to talk about it. Joan was right, the journal was her vehicle to address these repulsive, shameful things. Writing them down made them real, made them concrete. When she saw the words she'd written, anger rose within her, something she hadn't felt before. She realized she wasn't a helpless child; she was a grown woman carrying childhood abuse and guilt with her. She realized what a great weight it was.

CHAPTER 12

On Thursday morning Cat woke her up yet again with loud purring. Jenny was getting used to the feline sneaking in and had begun to like her company. She petted her and put her outside, then did some yoga, tried meditating like Helen had directed her, and went for a long run to try to steady her nerves and gain some courage so she could say what she knew had to be said. But she couldn't calm her racing mind. She quickly showered but was too nervous and almost sick to her stomach to eat any breakfast. She hurried off to her session.

With apprehension, she walked into Joan's office, removed her jacket, took a seat, and sucked in several deep breaths trying to stop her mouth from quivering. "Okay, I think I'm … oh, shit. Here we go, Joan. Are you ready?" she said in a barely audible whisper.

"Go ahead, Jenny. I'm here for you."

"I thought Dory was my mommy, but she wasn't," she said, speaking slowly and in a tiny, childlike voice. She drew her knees up to her chest, assuming a sitting fetal position, arms wrapped around them, and looked at the wall with blank eyes, gazing somewhere way beyond Joan and into her past.

"She touched me in my naughty place. She made me touch her in her naughty place. And she did the same with my brother. She told us to never, never tell anybody. Not anybody. It was like the naughty things I saw them do at night when they thought I was asleep. She made me do it a lot. I didn't like it, but she wouldn't stop. I couldn't tell Daddy or anyone because it was a secret. I shouldn't be telling you. It's a secret. It's a secret that Dory told me to never, never tell anybody. She would be mad at me for telling you. Please don't tell her I told you. Please! I saw her doing things like that with my brother too, even when he was older. I hated her!"

Joan sat quietly for a few minutes, to let things settle, then said softly, "Thank you for sharing your secret with me, Jenny. That had to be unimaginably hard for you as a child and to share it with me. I promise I'll never tell anyone your secret. I promise. I'd like to help you feel better about this naughty thing you think you've done. Please believe when I say that this wasn't your fault. There is nothing for you to be ashamed about. How old were you when she stopped doing this to you?"

"Thirteen, after I threatened to kill her with my knife. But my brother kept on. I saw them doing things the adults did to each other, when he was fourteen, and fifteen, sixteen, seventeen. I got sick, ran outside, and threw up when I saw them doing that. I hated them!" She stopped for a second, coming back to the present, breathing hard, shallow breaths, like she'd finished a hard run.

"Okay, Jenny, just relax and take a few deep breaths for a moment." Joan offered water, but Jenny declined. They were quiet for a few minutes. Jenny's eyes regained focus, and her breathing finally slowed.

Joan broke the silence. "Is there anything more you want

to say about this?"

Jenny sat still for a long minute and then shook her head very rapidly. She uncurled herself, moving her feet to the floor, then sat erect in the chair, knees together, hands properly folded on her lap, her head and eyes downcast. She suddenly put her hands over her mouth and started retching. Joan grabbed the wastebasket for her, but it wasn't needed, there was nothing to come up since she hadn't eaten anything.

After calming down, she slowly raised her sad teary eyes, looked at Joan and said with a quivering voice, "Please don't hate me, Joan. I'm really a good girl. Please don't hate me. I didn't mean to do bad things. I really didn't. I never did those bad things again, ever. She made me. I thought she was my mother, my goddamned fucking mother. And then I found out she wasn't my fucking mother. My real mother had died. Nobody even ever fucking told me. I fucking wish they were all fucking dead!" She let out a long wail and broke into convulsive sobs.

Joan got a cool, wet washcloth and went to sit beside her, wiping her face, placing the cooling cloth on her forehead. "Oh, my dear young woman, I could never hate you, never. Please believe me. You're so very brave and strong for sharing this with me, for getting this secret out from your soul. By putting this out, you can begin to heal, begin to be the wonderful person that you really are. I am always here for you, even if we aren't scheduled. Just call me anytime if you need to talk, if you need anything. Promise me that."

Jenny nodded, and Joan sat holding her in silence for four or five minutes until Jenny had cried it all out.

Joan gave her some tissues. "This is hard business for sure, Jenny. That was a very big burden to be carrying around for so long. You're so very brave to get it out. Are you feeling okay?

Can I get you some water or tea? Or anything?"

Jenny started to smile. "Yeah, I'd like some water now, please. My mouth is really dry. Oh shit. I cannot believe I told you this, Joan. Cannot believe I finally told someone this fucking shit. Please keep helping me, Joan, seriously. And this isn't all the shit. Believe me, but it's the worst of it. What about my brother? He's got the same fucking shit, Joan, the same fucking shit and more." She broke into sobs again, choking out, "Sorry for the language. I'm just so fucking mad!"

"It's okay," Joan said, holding her until she finally got all the anger, fear, and shame washed out with her tears.

Jenny dried her eyes and said with a weak smile, "So where's my water, Joan?"

Joan responded with a big hug and produced a bottle of water from her fridge.

Jenny drained the bottle without stopping.

Joan called out to the front desk and said she would be running over. She and Jenny continued talking, continuing to sort through some other issues mainly centered around this woman, Dory, and her abusing Jenny. They talked about the incident with Old George after which Dory had dissed her when she'd told her about it. That was when Jenny told Dory to "Fuck off and never, ever come near me again, or I will kill you."

Then Jenny said with fire, "I hate that fucking bitch for what she did. I hope she rots in fucking hell! Actually, hell is too good for her. There is no fitting punishment for that bitch. I hate her." She hung her head, looking at the floor, fuming. "I should have killed her. I should have stuck my knife into her fucking heart! I should have cut it out and ate it, the fucking bitch!"

Joan held up her hand. "Jenny, whoa, whoa. Take a breath.

You can be angry, very angry. You've a right to be as livid as you are right now. You've just shared something very profound, and you need to process it, which will take time. It will take time to come to terms with your anger and your grief, and yes, grief over what you've lost for so many years of your life, grief over a childhood that you never had. And forgiveness may seem hard right now, but at some point, you'll have to forgive yourself for thinking you should've done something different. And yes, at some point, as farfetched as it may seem right now, you will be able to forgive Dory … and your father. I will always be here to help you as you move through this process. I promise."

Jenny looked up. "I guess I have a lot of work to do, don't I? And forgiveness? I'm not sure I can do it, Joan. Right now I am so pissed. I am so really pissed off. Bringing this shit up just makes me fucking crazy mad. I hate that fucking woman!"

"I know you do, Jenny. I know you do right now. This is only the first step, and it's a giant one. The rest will be easier now; I can assure you."

"I hope so. This really sucks. I'd like to go now."

But Joan kept her and talked with her a little longer until she felt she had calmed down enough to go.

Jenny thanked her, gave her a big, long hug and walked out into the Colorado sunlight. She took a deep breath of late-autumn air and suddenly felt a thousand pounds lighter. She couldn't stop smiling and wanted to skip down the street singing. Instead, she went straight to Helen's studio, hoping to find her there, which she was. Jenny went in. "Do you have time to talk?"

"Of course. You seem quite happy. What's going on?"

They went into Helen's office and sat. Jenny began telling Helen about her session and then continued with all the details. Helen sat there, listening intently.

"Oh my God!" was all she could say in response. "Jenny, I'm so sorry. You poor, dear child. Such a horrible burden for you to have been carrying for so long, such a horrible thing to do to children. I thought what I knew before was bad enough, but this! Oh, Jenny."

She got up, went over, and hugged her for a very long time. Jenny snuggled into the hug, feeling a secure warmth she hadn't felt before as Helen loved her like the mother she never felt she had.

"Please don't tell William. I'll tell him when I'm ready. Promise. I'm not ready to do it right now. But I needed to tell you. You and Joan are the only ones who know. Please don't tell him or anyone. Please?"

"I won't tell anybody, Jenny. That will be for you to do on your own schedule. I know he'll understand. He cares for you very much."

"Yeah, I know. Thanks, Helen. Thanks for being such a friend. I love you."

"I love you too, sweetheart."

"And please don't pity me or feel sorry for me. I don't want that. I don't need that. That's not why I shared this with you. I just wanted you to understand. Okay?"

"Yes, I understand. And thank you for sharing with me. I feel honored that you trust me enough to have done so."

Jenny got up to leave, and Helen said, "Hey, want to have an early dinner? It'd be fun. My treat."

"Sure, love to, but please, I want to pay. I think I need to celebrate something, don't ya think? Let's do it up big!" Jenny grabbed her hand and led her to one of the nicest restaurants on Main Street.

CHAPTER 13

Over their dinner, Jenny asked Helen how she had become a yoga teacher.

Helen said she'd grown up in Santa Monica, California, where there were any number of yoga studios around. She hadn't been much for high school activities, so she'd decided to try yoga. One of the studios was an Iyengar studio about two blocks from her house. She tried it and found she enjoyed the exercise and the serenity.

Helen went on to say that she went to UC-Berkeley and found a studio close by, so she continued yoga through her undergraduate studies and grad school where she'd earned a master's in physical training. Then she worked in a gym as a trainer in LA for about two years but wasn't happy.

She came upon an article in a yoga magazine about B. K. S. Iyengar's place in India where one could go to become a certified teacher. She decided she wanted to do it and begged her parents to subsidize her again. They agreed, and she was off to India for about eighteen months. She got her certification and returned to the States.

"Wow, India," Jenny said. "That sounds so exciting."

"Yes, it was intense, but exotic and exciting. I loved the people, the crowds, the dust, the shops, the food. It was an amazing experience."

She went on about how she wanted to get out of LA but had no idea where to go, so she loaded up her mini van and headed east, exploring towns along the way. When she hit Durango, she was out of gas and money. She got a job as a waitperson in this very restaurant and searched for work as a physical trainer for three months until finally landing a job at a local gym. The gym allowed her to start teaching a yoga class, which quickly filled up, and all of a sudden, she was teaching three classes, beginner through advanced.

"I saved every cent I could with the dream of having my own yoga studio someday. Then a year later, my parents were killed in an automobile accident, and being an only child, I received a sizable inheritance. My father made a lot of money in real estate development. I found the storefront, remodeled it, and opened my studio."

Jenny asked, "So what is it with you and Will? You seem so good together. I can tell that you both care a great deal for each other."

"I still care for Will very much. He's the best ever, but we're better apart than we are together. I was never married before, and I guess I wasn't prepared for what marriage entailed. I had my studio, and Will had his writing. He was already successful and wealthy. He wanted to take a hiatus, buy a motor home and travel around the country, maybe for a year or more. But I had my studio, and I loved what I was doing and wasn't going to give it up. I took a week for our honeymoon in Hawaii, but then I wanted to get back and settle in again with my new husband and get back to work.

"But Will was in a writing lull. Had too much time on

his hands and was restless, constantly coming by the studio and simply getting in the way. I tried to get him to start taking classes or help out or get involved some way, but he wasn't interested. He finally just became a little overbearing, bordering on being obsessive. I told him one day to just please get out and let me do my business. He got angry, and we had a big fight, the 'You love your work more than you love me' thing. I pushed him out and slammed the door in his face. I stayed in town that night with a friend. I couldn't sleep, wondering what I had gotten myself into.

"Was I being selfish like he said? Had I made a big mistake in getting married? Did I really love him? I was confused. It had all seemed so right when we met and spent a year enjoying each other, and marrying him seemed so right. I finally cried myself to sleep about an hour before I had to get up to start my day."

Jenny frowned. "That seems so unlike the Will I know. He's so kind and sweet."

"Yes, he is. He wasn't like that back then. The next morning he called me at the studio furious. I had no clue how to deal with this sort of thing. I told him that I needed my space and my life, that I was forty-five years old and had no experience with marriage, that he'd been married twice before, that maybe his being so overbearing was his problem. He hung up on me.

"I was scared and called Joan. We had a long talk, and she asked me if I wanted to make this work, which I did. I loved him, and we had such wonderful times together, but as soon as I said 'I do,' he took possession. Joan suggested couples and single counseling, which I suggested to him. He reluctantly agreed, and we went for about three months, but he gave up. He couldn't deal with it. I continued doing counseling myself for about a year. In the meantime, we separated. I had rented my condo, and coincidentally the lease was up about that time, so I moved back in. Two weeks later, I filed for divorce.

"We didn't see each other for a long time. Then one day he called me and asked if I would have dinner with him. I'd been seeing this other man, Mark, for a few months but agreed, and we met here. We had a nice, leisurely dinner and a good, long talk. He told me he'd been clinically depressed after we separated. His doctor had him on medication for depression and urged him to get professional counseling, which he did and began to see patterns he had in all of his previous marriages that essentially caused them to fail. He apologized and asked if we might be friends. While we were no longer married, he considered me his best friend, and he still loved me.

"And that's the story. I've probably bored you to death with all this."

"No, not at all. I did ask. Thanks for sharing with me. I can understand better now. I'm never falling in love, much less ever getting hitched. No way. It'll just never happen. There's no guy that I'd ever trust to get that close to."

"Oh, now, don't be so sure about that. You're a very attractive young woman. Some really nice young man will sweep you off your feet someday."

"Bullshit!" Jenny replied adamantly. "I'll never let any guy get that close. Never, no way, no how!"

Two hours later, Jenny paid the bill and got up, a bit tipsy. Helen noticed and insisted that Jenny stay the night with her, that she wasn't in any condition to drive up the north valley. Jenny agreed with a goofy grin. They walked hand in hand to Helen's condo.

Helen called William to let him know so he wouldn't worry. She and Jenny chatted for a few moments and went to bed.

Jenny lay awake, thinking about Helen's experiences of a life that seemed so normal; she'd also had sad experiences, even tragic ones like the death of her parents. She was realizing that maybe all people had sadness and suffering in his or her life, that everyone had his or her own struggles.

CHAPTER 14

Jenny tried to get to the morning yoga class at least three times a week. She learned a lot and felt that somehow yoga and meditation helped her feel not only stronger physically but also stronger emotionally.

She saw Kelly at most every yoga class, and they chatted briefly afterward. Once in a while, Kelly asked Jenny to go for coffee, and one day Jenny decided to go with her.

They walked down Main Street a few blocks to Raven's Coffee Shop, where they sat and talked for over an hour. Jenny realized she was letting down her defenses but enjoyed talking with Kelly. She was a physical therapist and worked with two other PT people, a physical trainer, and two chiropractors. It sounded like interesting work. She'd been in town for two years, having moved here from Illinois, primarily for all the outdoor activities and to get away from a domineering father. She was a runner as well as a cyclist and a downhill and cross-country skier. She liked hiking and camping in the high country.

Jenny selectively shared a small part of her background, saying she was from Northern California, she'd gone to college at CU, and had moved here a while back. She wanted to be a writer and was presently unemployed. Also she liked running, hiking, and camping.

Kelly went on to talk about her father, who was always trying to run her life. He wanted her to be a doctor and had gotten her into the prestigious Princeton Medical School from which he'd earned his medical degree. But, fed up with doing everything her father demanded, she went to Princeton and opted to study physical therapy and sports medicine, a decision which infuriated her father. It was another reason she'd moved out to Colorado, to be away from his domineering attitude. She liked being on her own, making her own way. But her parents couldn't imagine that she could support herself and sent a monthly allowance, which she just put into a savings account. She didn't want to be known as a rich, spoiled, trust-fund kid. She had a hard enough time making friends as it was.

The talk moved to running, and Kelly invited Jenny to try trail running with her in the spring. She mentioned a running club that had Wednesday-night and Saturday-morning fun runs, usually with beers or coffee and good camaraderie afterward. Would she be interested?

As the conversation wore on, Jenny began to feel nervous; her heart started racing, and her chest tightened. Kelly was a little overwhelming for her. She was nice but talked a lot. Jenny's panic grew. She was getting too involved with this woman and needed to leave.

She jumped up from her chair. "I appreciate the offer about running, and I'll see you at yoga, but I have to get going for a meeting." With that, Jenny turned and left the coffee shop in a hurry to get away from a situation she wasn't sure she could handle. She could hardly breathe. She'd liked talking with another woman her age, but why should she trust her?

She might be just like everyone else.

At her next session with Joan, she talked about what had happened.

Joan nodded as if it wasn't surprising to her. "Abuse victims suffer with trusting others and thus choose to isolate themselves, as you did for your college years and two years after. It's hard to adjust to being around people, becoming close is even harder.

"You seem to be okay with Helen and Will. And the fact that you were able to have coffee with Kelly shows some progress. Give her time. Go for coffee again. This time, cut it shorter. Make it on your terms. Have an exit plan. And enjoy her company. You could use a friend your own age, and Kelly appears to like you."

"Thanks, Joan. It all makes sense, what you're saying."

She did follow Joan's advice and made it a point to connect more with Kelly after yoga. They went for coffee and Jenny found she enjoyed her company and girl chat. She started trusting that the relationship was platonic and that Kelly liked guys, not girls. Jenny thought she may have found a friend.

The Friday before Thanksgiving, Kelly asked her to go to this great outdoor gear sale held a few times every year at the fairgrounds exhibit hall. She told Jenny that, living in Durango, she needed gear. Right after yoga, they jumped into Jenny's Jeep and went to the sale.

Jenny, under Kelly's tutoring, bought some new clothes rather than the thrift store items she'd been getting for years. She got a down parka, a down vest, a pair of trail running shoes, fleece leggings, a pair of waterproof pants, some warm socks, long underwear, a fleece top, and, in one of her weaker moments at Kelly's prodding, snowshoes. Then, of course, she needed winter boots to wear. And there were gloves. And extendable hiking poles with big baskets to use with her snowshoes. And then a day pack with a hydration bladder. Last, two wildly colored stocking hats.

After over two hours of selecting, trying on, and laughing, she proudly paid for her purchases with her brand-new bank card. They carried all her new stuff to the Jeep and went downtown to have coffee, laughing and being silly.

Will was having Thanksgiving dinner for some people, including Jenny. She was excited and actually looking forward to meeting some new people. She knew Helen would be there. Will's son, Peter, was coming down from Denver, plus also another couple around Will's age and two younger couples. She knew Kelly didn't have any plans for the day, so she asked Will whether she could invite her for dinner.

She went over to Will's on Wednesday afternoon, offering to help out. He had her check the silverware to make sure it was all polished, and then he wanted her to set the table. She had no idea how to set a table, so he showed her, and she proceeded, being very careful, and then feeling proud of her finished work.

Thanksgiving Day came, and Jenny went over to Will's early. Helen was already there with an apron on and a big hug for Jenny.

"So what can I do?" Jenny asked. "I've never had Thanksgiving before and have no idea about anything, but I want to help."

Helen put her to work with peeling potatoes, then cleaning and cutting carrots, and cutting green beans. Will had the turkey in the oven early which was due to be done and carved for dinner at five o'clock. He proved to be quite a chef, and Jenny had fun working with him and Helen. Everything was ready to go when guests started arriving around two thirty.

Both Jenny and Helen went to freshen up. Will put out appetizers and drinks ranging from wine, beer, iced tea, and whatever mixed drinks anyone might want.

When Jenny and Helen returned, Will was pouring wine and talking with people as they arrived. Will called Jenny over to introduce her to two young men, Mark and Gary, who were partners. She liked them, and knowing they were together made her feel more comfortable and unthreatened. The three of them were having a conversation when Kelly arrived. She took off her coat, and ran over, giving Jenny, Mark and Gary a big hug. She'd helped Mark recover from a mountain biking accident and was happy to see them. Jenny wasn't used to being around so many people but despite all her fear and mistrust, she found herself having a good time and feeling giddy.

The older couple, Christine and Tom, seemed nice. Then there was the younger couple, in their early thirties, Greg and Sara, both of whom she'd seen at yoga but had met only briefly before.

At about three thirty, Peter arrived and was introduced around. He was like a younger version of Will, tall, fit and handsome. He had a nice smile, a shock of dark hair, and dark, soft eyes. He was in law school and due to graduate in spring of the next year. He joined right into the festivities and brought even more liveliness to the group. Like Will, he seemed genuine and polished. Jenny decided he might be an okay guy, like his father.

By five, everyone was seated, Peter between Jenny and Kelly. The bird was carved, and everything was on the table, steaming hot. Wine was poured. Will asked everyone to hold hands and to give thanks for whatever he or she felt thankful for.

Jenny's turn came, and she hesitated for a moment. "I am thankful to be spending my first Thanksgiving celebration ever with all you wonderful people. Thank you for being here, and thank you, Will and Helen, for being such special and wonderful people. I love you both."

Everyone sat in silence for a moment. Jenny used her napkin to dry her eyes. So did Helen and Will.

Food was passed, and the merriment continued on until after the pumpkin pie topped with whipped cream, after-dinner drinks, and coffee. Festivities concluded around ten after everyone had helped to pick up dishes, clean up the kitchen, and put all the leftovers in the refrigerator. Goodbyes, hugs, and 'see you soon's were exchanged.

Jenny asked Kelly if she might want to spend the night since she was acting a little drunk. Kelly giggled and thought it might be a good idea. Peter was staying with Will, so the three of them sat and talked, enjoying the last of the open wine, finally saying good night around midnight.

Jenny started to feel a little hesitant about Kelly staying with her, an old fear rising, remembering Becky from college. Nevertheless, Jenny led her over to her house, and made up the couch for her. They sat and talked a while longer, and both went to bed. Jenny, however, closed her door and wedged a chair under the doorknob. She felt safe and slept a sound sleep with dreams of being surrounded by interesting people, enjoying herself, and not being afraid. She awoke with Cat meowing, wanting to be let out of the bedroom.

They both slept late. Kelly was off work that day, so she and Jenny had some breakfast and sat chatting about yesterday's events over their coffee. Kelly asked about Jenny's comment that this was her first Thanksgiving.

Jenny told her a little about her childhood at the Farm.

"No one ever celebrated holidays much. There were no traditional or religious folks there. Most were trying to escape from all that and their parents and all the middle-class stuff. There were some Wiccan people, and we had winter solstice bonfires as well as a summer solstice thing. It was weird. There were drums, whistles, flutes, all sorts of noise, and people dancing around naked and some things I really don't want to talk about."

Kelly's eyes widened. "Holy shit, Jenny. I had no idea. What did your parents do?"

"Oh, hell, they joined right in. In reality, I had no parents. They were just some adult children I lived with, but trust me, they made sure my brother and I knew we were nothing more than a burden to them and that they couldn't wait 'til we left and were out of their hair. If it weren't for my grandparents, my brother and I would probably have been homeless in LA or somewhere, living on the streets, begging or whoring for survival," she said, her voice quivering.

"Holy shit," Kelly repeated. "Jenny, I can't comprehend it. That is so way different from my childhood in upper-middle-class American suburbia north of Chicago with my domineering father. I can't imagine."

"Yeah," Jenny said, "and that's why I'm in counseling, to try to cope with my childhood."

"Counseling? I didn't know. Are you okay? Is it helping?"

"Yeah. I guess. It sucks."

Jenny's last revelation seemed to drain the room of energy, and they both sat in silence for a long time. Kelly finally broke the silence. "Hey, what do you think of Peter? He's really cute, and I think he likes you."

"Yeah, he's all right, I guess. I think he likes you too. He seems to talk a lot. Pretty much dominated the conversation last night, as I recall. Sort of a know-it-all."

Kelly laughed. "We were all a little smashed. Maybe he just talks a lot when he's drinking. Still think he likes you."

Jenny shrugged. "I really never had a guy who liked me. I was pretty reclusive in college and for the last few years since I graduated. I lived in the mountains in the summers and in an old cabin a few miles north of here in the winter, except it burned down, and I sort of ended up here at Will's. You're probably the first girl, or anyone, I might call a friend. I don't really know how to have or be a friend."

Kelly's eyes widened. "Really? Thanks for considering me your friend. You are one interesting girl, and I think you're doing a good job being one. I consider you my friend too."

"You know, I'm really not interested in Peter. I like this guy I've been doing physical therapy work with for his arm. He broke it in a bike crash; he's a really nice guy. His name is Matt. He's a mountain biker, competes nationally, wants to get on the USA Olympic team. He's really cute, and I love it when he comes in. I'm hoping he'll ask me out sometime, but he seems a little shy. He wants to go back to school in sports medicine. He seems really smart. Graduated on a bike scholarship from Fort Lewis College. Maybe you and Peter and Matt and I could go out sometime," she finished, smiling.

"Well, Peter lives in Denver and is going back on Sunday, and Matt hasn't asked you out, so, probably not going to happen anytime soon."

"Well, we can always dream."

"Yeah, we can always dream, but I've a lot of other things to dream about other than guys," Jenny replied.

"Yeah, I know. I'm sorry. I really am. But please trust me to be a friend. I can be a good listener and probably won't have much advice since you have so many different experiences than I ever could imagine."

"Thanks. I really don't need advice or pity, but sometimes it's nice just having someone to hang out with, someone who isn't associated with my drama. Someone to talk to. This whole thing seems to involve a lot of crying; I'm really tired of it."

"I have big, strong, welcoming shoulders that'll always be available."

"Thanks, Kelly, you're great, and I appreciate you. You're very special."

"Hey," Kelly said, "why don't you come into town tomorrow night? There's a new indie film I want to see. We could go and have some wine and popcorn, maybe come in early, and we could catch a light dinner before."

"Sounds fun. Mind if I ask Peter to come? Might be nice for him to get out."

"Sure, ask him. It'd be fun. And you could get to know him better, hmmmm?"

"Oh stop. Just thought it might be nice for him."

"Yeah, right." She gave a coy smile. "Hey, gotta run. Lots of errands to do. Thanks for keeping me off the road last night. I was pretty goofy. And thanks for sharing. That's what friends are for. I like you, Jenny. Thanks for being my friend." She gave Jenny a quick hug and said, "Come by my place around four thirty tomorrow, and we'll get dinner and catch the movie. See ya." She headed to the door.

"See ya," Jenny said, as the door shut.

She spent the next few hours writing in her journal about friendship and yesterday.

CHAPTER 15

Jenny had been thinking a lot about her brother and her grandparents. She felt ashamed of herself for being out of touch for such a long time. She reread a letter she'd recently received from Michael. His writing was ragged and barely understandable, his thoughts random, disconnected, and hard to follow.

Dear Jenny,
I haven't heard from you forever. Where are you? I'm doing okay. What are you doing? I see our grandparents. Are you hiding somewhere? Why are you not here where you should be with your brother? They are fine. School sucks. It's all about the girls, and they always get better grades and hate me. These stupid teachers like all the girls. Especially the girl teachers. The girl teachers always give me bad grades. Grandma and Grandpa like me. Do you like me? The teachers do not like me. They do not respect me. I tell them stuff I do not like. Then they say I'm a bigot. They tell me maybe

*I should not be here. It's them that should not be
here. Girls are not smart enough to be doctors like
I am. Why are you not around here where you
should be? I am your brother, and you should not
be away from me. Where are you? Your post office
box is Durango. Are you there? Why are you there?
No body respects me. Maybe they need to be taught
a lesson that they should respect me. Maybe you do
not respect me like you should. I don't know.*
Michael

The letter disturbed Jenny, especially the way he started
out. It seemed almost hostile toward her for not letting him
know where she was, and then he wanted to know whether
she was deliberately hiding from him. Other parts of it she
found frightening, like him thinking he needed to teach these
girls a lesson. What was he thinking? He sounded so angry.

While at the university, she'd never had any professor
single her or anyone else out for any reason. If you worked
and studied hard, you were rewarded with good grades. For
him to feel so victimized didn't make sense to her, especially
the part about him thinking there was favoritism shown
toward female students. If anything, from her experience, it
was usually the opposite.

And his writing was so scattered and cryptic, like at an
elementary school level. It certainly didn't seem to be written
by someone in college. How had he ever been admitted to
college if this was the best he could write? She wondered
whether he was even in college and in a pre-med program.
Maybe he wrote it when he was drunk or stoned? Puzzled and
upset, she put the letter away. She wanted to respond to it to
let him know, if for nothing else, that she was okay, but she

let it slide because she didn't know what to say.

She walked over to William's place and asked if she could use his cell phone to call her brother.

"Sure." He retrieved his phone from the kitchen counter and added gently, "Maybe it's time for you to get your own phone."

She blushed. "Ah, yeah, I probably should. Thanks. I'll only be a minute."

She had Michael's cell number, which he'd sent her in one of his last letters, and she punched in his number. He answered almost immediately.

"Hi, Michael, it's Jenny."

"Jenny, where the hell are you? What the hell's going on? Are you okay? I haven't heard from you in over a year, dammit! I worry about you. Is everything okay? Are you all right? Why aren't you here? You should be here with me."

"I'm fine, Michael. Better than ever, really. Better than I could've imagined last year this time. I'm sorry for being out of touch. I don't really have time to talk since I'm borrowing a phone, but I'm thinking about coming to Denver to see you and Grandma and Grandpa in the next few weeks. Could you come up from the Springs? Would that be okay?"

"Okay? That would be so great! I haven't seen you or talked to you in forever. Grandma and Grandpa would be so happy; it would just make them so happy. I see them a lot, and their first question is, 'Have you heard from Jenny?'"

"Okay, gotta go. I'll try to call you again tomorrow or Sunday. Love you."

"Ah, yeah? Yeah, sure, whatever," he ended with what sounded like a sigh and a little laugh.

She clicked off, thinking there wasn't much difference between talking to him and the way his letter read. She didn't feel very good about Michael's closing remark either; it seemed dismissive. *What's with him wanting me to be there with him?*

"Thanks, Will, and you're right. I really need to get my own phone. Any suggestions?"

Peter overheard her, having just walked in. "Why don't I go with you? he said. "I could help if you want. I could give you some pointers."

Jenny thought about her and Kelly's date, and responded, "Sure, I'd love any help I can get, like, all the help I can get. I've no idea about technology, what to even begin to look for. Kelly and I are going to have dinner and see a movie tomorrow night. We could go into the phone store, then meet her and go out. Would that be okay with you, Will? If you want to, Peter?"

Will smiled. "Sure, go ahead, Peter. We've spent all day catching up, and we have tomorrow morning as well, so go on. Have a night out."

Peter grinned. "Then I'd love to. What time? The phone store will be at least an hour, especially since this is your first phone."

"How about two thirty or so? That should give us plenty of time to meet up with Kelly at four thirty."

"I'll be ready at two thirty, and we'll go phone shopping. See ya then."

She thanked William again and headed back to her house, considering what she'd just done. Was she getting too trusting? But it was Will's son, and he seemed genuinely nice and trustworthy. She didn't quite know how to process the possibility of trusting a guy other than Will and her grandfather. But the more she thought about it, the more she felt okay about being with Peter. She realized she was trusting herself to make this decision and felt it was a good one. She smiled, sat down with her journal, and wrote it all down. She went to bed early, still recovering from her late night, feeling sleepy and at ease.

Cat had sneaked in again and was purring with contentment as Jenny awoke. She wondered how cats could be so devious and sneaky. She'd have to talk to William about her.

She went for a ten-mile run, came home and showered, had a bite to eat, read her latest book for a while, and wrote in her journal. Then it was time to go. She went over and got Peter and they headed to the phone store. Peter suggested a wireless carrier both he and William used. It was reliable and had good coverage, none of which made much sense to her technologically deprived mind. She'd never had a phone, not even in college. She had basic knowledge on how to use a computer, but that was it.

They got to the store, and she saw an array of different phones in different sizes; some did this, some did that, and some did something else. Peter was partial to the Apple iPhone like the one he had and was explaining a little about it when a saleswoman came to help. She went over the features with Jenny, who understood about half of what the woman told her, but she realized it was a lot like, as well as compatible with, her Apple laptop, so the deal was done.

Jenny listened as the saleswoman went over various plans, and with Peter's help, she decided on one, and then it was a matter of paper work and getting everything connected and running. The saleswoman went over all the basics, including where and how to get online help, and assured her she could come by the store anytime for any help she might need. All of this, surprisingly to Jenny, consumed well over an hour. Jenny bought a few accessories Peter recommended, such as a protective case, a screen protector, and a car charger. She paid her bill and walked out, now connected to the world.

Jenny asked Peter to drive so she could play with her new toy. They still had some time to kill, so they went to have some coffee. She loved her new toy and only reluctantly put it away so she wouldn't be rude, but only after first entering Peter's number—her first.

Jenny asked Peter about law school and his plans afterward.

"I'd like to come to Durango after graduation and hopefully get an internship at a local law office and then study for the bar exam. I'm already beginning a search of various law firms. Dad knows a local lawyer pretty well, and together they're trying to help from this end. I'm feeling pretty confident. Dad is supportive and doing as much as he can to facilitate my getting to Durango."

He continued to go on and on about law school until she finally interrupted him to get him off the law-school thing by asking him about some technical aspect of her new phone.

After answering her question, he asked, "So how did you end up in Durango?"

"Well, interestingly, I had no plans after I graduated from CU, so I went down to the 'ride board' at the union the day before graduation and saw a request for a passenger to ride to Durango and share gas. This guy had a pickup, so I could take all of what little stuff I had; it wasn't much. I gave most of it away except for some clothes and my books. Got ahold of the guy, and he agreed to pick me up Sunday morning, and we drove down here to Durango.

"I stayed in town for a few days, got a storage locker for my stuff, went to a thrift store and bought some backpacking gear, supplemented what I couldn't get there at a local outdoor store. Spent the summer backpacking in the San Juans." She continued with the rest of her years to the present. "Not much to show, is it?"

"God, I couldn't do that, couldn't stand all that solitude. I'd be too lonesome. I need action, stuff to do. That's why I like law school. I like the challenge. What did you do all day by yourself? Weren't you bored?"

"Hiked and read sometimes. It was okay. And I had a few challenges too," she finished, trying not to be sarcastic.

"Yeah, but how much solitude does anyone really need? Didn't you miss people? Being around? Talking? Hanging with coffee and friends?"

She shrugged. "Ah, it was okay. I went into a town whenever to get supplies. It was okay."

He frowned. "Interesting, but I don't understand it. So do you think you're going into seclusion again? Like you're a nun or something, like in a monastery?"

Jenny was tired of listening to him go on about her and directed him back to being a lawyer and his idealistic expectations about helping people. He said he was interested in law as it pertained to the Native American people. He'd spent some time studying tribal law, especially the Southern Utes, whose governmental center was in Ignacio, twenty miles southeast of Durango, thus his desire to locate in the area.

Jenny realized all she could offer was her dream about being a writer. Other than her journaling, she hadn't written anything for weeks, months, even.

She was ready to leave and said, "Time to go and meet Kelly."

They met Kelly, had a light dinner, and enjoyed the movie with a few glasses of wine and popcorn. They said good night. Kelly headed to her place, and Jenny and Peter headed up to the north valley.

On the way home, Jenny mentioned she was planning to

go to Denver to see her brother before Christmas.

"That would be great. We could maybe get together when you're there. I could meet your brother. Maybe we could go out for some drinks and dinner. I've an idea. I'm coming back down to Durango in a few weeks to spend Christmas break with Dad. Normally I'd be with my mother, but she's going to be in London with her new boyfriend. So why don't you fly to Denver? I could pick you up at DIA and take you to your grandparents' place. You could spend your time there, and we could drive back here together. It'd be fun to have some company during the eight-hour drive."

"Ah, yeah, let me think it over. I haven't made any arrangements with anyone yet. I'm going to try to talk with Michael tomorrow and set something up. He actually lives in Colorado Springs for college. I'll call you and let you know one way or the other."

Peter walked Jenny to the door. "I had a nice time, Jenny. Thanks for asking me to come." He kissed her on the cheek, smiled, and walked back over to William's.

She went inside, her cheek burning where he'd kissed her. She stood inside her door for a few minutes, considering what had just happened, not knowing whether she liked it or not. It was a nice feeling, warm, like a luxurious bath. But it was also a bit unnerving and confusing to her; a guy kissed her, nicely, sweetly, respectfully. What to make of it? She didn't know. She went to bed, puzzled, but feeling warm and happy. She found her new best friend, Cat, snuggled in, waiting for her. Apparently Cat waited for her door to open and then sneaked in. Jenny made a mental note to watch for her.

Peter left at noon on Sunday but not without coming over to bid Jenny goodbye and asking her again to consider his offer about coming to Denver. She said she'd be in touch.

Peter commented again on having a nice time last night. She blushed, replying that she'd had a good time also, and thanked him again for his help in getting her new cell phone. They each said goodbye, and he was gone.

She thought about Peter's offer and didn't feel real excited about being a captive audience for seven hours in a car with him. Especially since he talked so much. She hadn't liked being confined in the pickup with that guy when she'd got out of college. She felt uncomfortable being alone with any man—other than Will, of course.

The rest of the day and the next, she spent writing in her journal about the last few days, trying to process her emotions, especially Peter's kiss. Had it been just a friend's kiss, or did he really like her? Was it a prelude to anything more? Deep down she wasn't really sure she liked the idea, or liked him that much. She'd had too many bad experiences with lies and unwanted sexual advances. She loved her grandfather, Dean, who was genuine and wonderful with all his support. But she didn't know whether she could ever trust any other man enough for a relationship.

CHAPTER 16

Jenny's first group counseling session was the Tuesday night after Thanksgiving. On Sunday she started to get nervous, her fears starting again: fear of people, fear of being bullied again, fear of the shame. She again started questioning her trust in herself and the people she'd become close to. She was getting close to more and more people, and it made her feel vulnerable.

Why would she think anybody would ever be different from those who had abused or frightened her? Why did she think she could trust Will, Helen, Joan, or Kelly? Or any of this counseling? Or this group session? In the last six weeks, she knew there'd been change. She knew it and felt it. But all this sudden change in her life was unnerving. She felt uneasy about everything and wasn't completely comfortable with it, but in many ways, cherished it.

She was also discovering something new about herself: resolve. She felt stronger in her belief in herself. She could still do as she had before, run and disappear. Or she could stay, keep going, move forward and see where it would all lead. She realized she had to save herself from herself, that she was her own worst enemy in many ways.

To move forward into a life she was now enjoying, she'd have to strengthen that resolve. She would have to take chances and would most likely get hurt again sometime. But Will had had three wives, and Kelly told her about a failed serious relationship. Helen, while married to Will for a short time, still loved him. And they seemed happy even though they'd been hurt. Everyone apparently had some hurt, some baggage, but had dealt with it or were dealing with it and weren't hiding away in the mountains. They'd gotten over it and were moving on with their lives.

She sat down Tuesday morning and began channeling these thoughts into her journal, which always seemed to help her better sort things through. She spent three hours writing, thinking, chastising, feeling scared, sorting through her emotions, fears, and desires. Jenny questioned everything, including all these new people in her life, especially Peter. She questioned her therapy and the childhood of abuse she had to face.

Could she ever be normal? What was truly normal? Was anything ever truly normal? She put her pencil down, closed the journal, pulled the elastic band around it, and looked out the window at the beautiful autumn day.

"I'm a big girl. It's time to get on with it."

She put on her running clothes and went for a ten-mile run.

When she got home and cleaned up, she sat down with Will's book, the one she'd selected a few weeks ago. She read the first five chapters. It was like what she'd seen in the other book she'd skimmed back when she first met him. The writing was geared toward, what she considered to be, the lowest common denominator. The characters and plot were predictable, and she could see no redeeming value in spending any more time with it.

By the time she needed to leave for group at six o'clock, she'd worked herself into a terrified frenzy. All she wanted to do was to get into her Jeep and drive as far away as fast as she could. But she made herself go and get to the shelter precisely at six thirty. She was happy she hadn't eaten since breakfast since she felt sick to her stomach.

She went into the shelter and the group session room. There were seven chairs placed in a circle. Two other women were there along with Joan. One looked up and smiled; the other just kept staring at the floor. Joan motioned for her to come in and sit down. Jenny could hardly breathe, but was able to give a weak smile and take a chair. She sat upright with her hands on her lap and stared straight ahead, making no eye contact. Four others arrived soon after, and the session began.

Joan smiled, welcomed everyone, and asked them all to introduce themselves, starting clockwise from her left. First was Shelly, then Ann. Jenny was next, but her mouth was so dry she could barely utter her name, which came out as a whisper. Joan came to her rescue and introduced her, and everyone said, "Hi, Jenny, welcome."

Jenny smiled, nodded, and whispered, "Thank you."

Introductions continued around the circle and finished with Mary, Barbara, and Juanita. Then Joan asked whether anyone had anything to share. Juanita started some observations from her week. She was discovering more about who she was, about how her past was affecting her less and less. She was feeling stronger. Everyone nodded in approval and thanked her for sharing. All the rest shared recent incidents, observations, and stories. Jenny listened intently to these women as they shared their stories of abuse, their anger, pain, triumphs, failures, and fears. Everyone had shared, and it was Jenny's turn.

Jenny wanted to get up and run. All she could mutter was, "A boy kissed me on the cheek."

Joan looked at her, nodded, and said gently, "Thanks, Jenny. Anything else you want to share about that? How did it make you feel?"

"I am confused about how I feel about it. I've never been kissed by a boy before. I've tried to understand and make some sense of it."

Juanita said, "Your first kiss, Jenny, on the cheek? That sounds sweet and innocent. Do you like him?"

"I don't know. I guess so. I just met him at Thanksgiving. We hung out together Saturday and went to a movie with a friend. He seems nice, but I just don't trust men, only my grandfather and my father."

Jenny noticed that Joan quickly wrote something on her pad after that last remark.

"All relationships seem to start too fast," Mary said. "It's best to take your time. Go slowly and let it unfold easily rather than too rushed. Discovering another person you like can be wonderful, or sometimes not so much."

Joan interrupted, "Thanks, everyone. It's eight and time to call it a night. Thanks, Jenny, for joining us and sharing. I hope to see you all next week as well as see you all throughout the week. Peace and be safe."

Everyone got up and hugged each other, chattering away about unrelated topics. Jenny felt like such an outsider and was starting to leave when Juanita and Ann came over, grabbed her, and gave her a quick hug. They told her how happy they were that she was there, that it took time, that this was the beginning of a process, and that it would just get better. They looked forward to seeing her again next week. Then the others paraded over with hugs and similar encouragement.

Tears filled Jenny's eyes, and she could only smile weakly.

Juanita, Shelly, and Barbara were going out for coffee and asked Jenny whether she would like to join them. Jenny realized she was starving.

"I'd love to as long as there's some food. I'm starved."

They walked down to a little Asian restaurant. Jenny and Shelly ordered food, and they all ordered tea. Jenny enjoyed herself with everyone asking her about her life and she about theirs. They talked about where they were from and what they did, but they avoided anything serious.

Home after ten thirty, fed, happy, and emotionally drained, she fell into bed, absent Cat, and instantly fell asleep with dreams that she and all these women were hiking together happily in the high country in bright sunshine and colorful wildflowers.

CHAPTER 17

On Wednesday morning, she got up and went to yoga class then she headed back to her place and went for a run. She spent the afternoon reading D. H. Lawrence's *Lady Chatterley's Lover*. She found it interesting but had a hard time understanding the sexual nature of the book and Lady Chatterley's emotions and feelings. She couldn't understand the idea of desiring a man, and she just couldn't fathom why she might ever desire a man. Why would she?

She easily avoided any writing once again except in her journal where she explored her dream. She decided she really liked the support of the group session and finding out she wasn't alone in her struggle; other abused women were struggling toward recovery the same as she. That comforted her.

On Thursday, she went for her session with Joan.

"So what did you think of group?" was Joan's first question.

"Ahhhh, all right, I guess. I was really scared and uncomfortable, but everyone seemed nice. I went out with Juanita, Barbara, and Shelly afterward for a late dinner. It was fun, and I liked them. They were really welcoming and made me feel better than I did at the session."

"I sensed your discomfort in the beginning, and I appreciated you sharing, as hard as it might have seemed."

"Yeah, it was hard. I hope I didn't sound hokey or stupid."

"Not at all. I found your comments interesting. First, the boy. Do you think you are ready for a boy in your life right now?"

"I don't know, Joan. It's all pretty strange to me with everything. I don't really have any idea about any of it. He seems nice. Will is his father. He lives in Denver. I'm going to try to go up to Denver to see my brother and grandparents before Christmas. He wants me to fly up. He'd meet me at the airport and then take me to my grandparents. Then he wants me to ride back with him when he comes back here for Christmas break. I don't know. I'd sort of like to, but there are all these red flags from my past that are popping up. I don't know whether I'm just being paranoid or what. It all seems so confusing.

"And then there'll be seven hours in a car with him, alone. And he talks an awful lot … might drive me crazy the way he rambles on."

Joan laughed. "Some people don't know when to shut up, believe me, I know. But my guess is, he may have been nervous and trying to avoid any empty space."

Jenny continued, "Maybe, but Joan, you know, sometimes I wish I'd never stumbled on Will's place that night, that the cabin was still there and I was just having a peaceful winter by myself. It would be so much easier. But, on the other hand, here I am. I'm feeling somewhat more social with people for the first time ever, and that feels good. What do you think?"

"Well, I'm not here to tell what or how to think. My job is to help you to be able to make your own decisions, hopefully good decisions, about what you want for your life, to help you get over your fears, your trust issues, and regain some self-confidence so you're able to deal with your past in a responsible, productive, and sane way, and move into your life that you deserve to be able to do.

"On the other hand, where would you be if you hadn't ended up at Will's that night? I think you're beginning to get your life in order and should continue to do so now that you've started on this journey. As I said early on, this process can be a tough business, but I think you're a pretty tough girl. So, I need to ask you, do you think this guy is worth the risk?"

"I don't know, Joan. He's Will's son, and I love and trust Will. He's been so good to me. I want to trust him; his name's Peter. He treats me nice, and he's really good looking. Yeah, I guess I like him. But I've never really known any guys except, well, you know. And how can I know if I like the first guy I meet?"

"Well, Jenny, you have to start somewhere with men. I wouldn't be too concerned right now if this is Mister Right. I would say, if you feel good about him in your gut, trust that feeling and take a chance."

"Ahhhh, well, yeah, maybe. I'll have to think about it. I am sort of leaning toward the Denver thing. But really, seven hours in a car with him? I don't know. Maybe it wouldn't be all bad?"

"Give it some thought. If you want to talk about it later, just call me or make an appointment, okay?"

"Yeah, sounds good. Thanks."

"So, Jenny, I want to ask you something else you mentioned in group, that the only men you trust were your grandfather and your father? Please explain. I thought you hated your father."

"Yeah, I know. That must have sounded weird, but I was

really thinking of Will when I mentioned my father. I just love him so much. I wish he was my father, not that piece of trash who's my real father. I know it's weird." Her voice was shaky, and tears formed. She put her hand to her forehead and turned away, sniffling.

Joan handed her a box of tissues and waited.

After a few minutes, she dried her eyes and blew her nose. "Sorry, it's just that I guess I really want a father, a good father. I guess I've sort of adopted Will in some weird way. Is that wrong? Do you think I am totally twisted, wanting Will for a father and then liking his son? Am I crazy? It all sounds so wrong."

She grabbed the tissues again and took a moment to dry her eyes and blow her nose.

"It's not weird or twisted," Joan replied. "I can understand you projecting your image of a father onto Will. He's a great guy. I've known him for years. Apparently he likes you and feels comfortable and happy that you consider him in such high regard. I don't know of any young woman who doesn't idolize her father, or in your case wants and needs a father to idolize. If Will fills that void in your life as a father figure, I see nothing wrong in your adopting him. It would be nice if you actually told him you were adopting him. He'd probably like it. And as far as you liking Peter, there is no blood relationship between any of you, so it's hardly incestuous, if that's what you're thinking. So you shouldn't feel weird in any way. Okay?"

"Okay, that makes me feel better … I think. But do you really think I should tell Will? What if he freaks out?"

"I don't think he'd freak out. I think he'd love it. I know he's very fond of you. He's told Helen and me as much."

"Thanks, Joan. Whoa, hey. Time's up. I gotta go. Meeting Kelly after she gets off work for a girl's dinner and chat. I want to tell her about Peter." She got up and put on her coat. "See ya." Then she was gone, leaving a grinning Joan behind.

Jenny met Kelly at a pizza place, where they got a seat and each ordered a glass of chardonnay.

Kelly asked, "So what happened with Peter?"

"He kissed me good night, on the cheek."

"Oh my God. He so likes you."

"He wants me to fly to Denver and then ride back with him when he comes back for Christmas break."

"Oh, holy shit. Ya gonna do it?"

"I don't know. What do you think I should do?"

"Oh, what the hell," Kelly said. "Do it. It'll be so fun."

"I don't know; it's really scary."

"But he likes you, and he's so cute."

"You really think I should?"

"Of course, you should, silly girl."

The server came. "Are you ready to order?"

"Ahhhhh, yeah," Kelly replied. "A medium vegetarian with ground beef. That okay?"

"Well, that's really not a vegetarian," the waiter said.

"No, but we want the veggies and some ground beef. Is that gonna be a problem?"

"No, not at all. Thanks. I'll get it right in. And two more chards?"

"Yes, please."

He left.

"So you gonna do it?" Kelly asked,

"I really need time to think. I've got so much to deal with right now. I just don't know if I need something like a relationship with a guy of any sort. Yeah, Peter's okay, but we just met. It's just that … it's just that I have so much shit to deal with."

"I'm sorry if I seemed too pushy. I can understand with all you've told me."

"Oh, Kelly, you really have no idea. What I've shared with you only scratches the surface, really only scratches the surface. Maybe someday I'll share more. Not right now, though, not right now." She trailed off, looking beyond Kelly into somewhere beyond both of them, into another world.

Kelly shook her head. "And I think I had it bad with my domineering father, who wanted me to do this, succeed at that. I'm still pissed that he considers me a failure because I didn't want to go to med school and be like him. He should have had a boy rather than me. But when all is said and done, he's my father, and I do love him."

Jenny wistfully asked, "Do all kids have issues with their parents?"

"I don't know Jenny. I haven't a clue."

They remained silent until their pizza arrived, then they dug in and ate with some small talk, paid their bill, and said goodbye with hugs.

Back home, Jenny wrote in her journal until past midnight, trying to digest her day and everything that had come down, especially Kelly's excitement over Peter and that Jenny should be excited about him, when, in truth, she really wasn't. He was nice, but she felt he might be a distraction in her life, especially right now. It might be too much.

Jenny spent her week waffling one way or the other. She didn't like feeling pressured. She decided to talk to Will and seek his advice. She went next door and knocked.

"Jenny, I haven't seen you all week. Are you avoiding me again?" he said with a smile.

"Sorry Will, no … no, I haven't been avoiding you at all, really. I've had just so much on my mind." She told him everything about Peter and about her meeting with Joan.

She looked away into space and hesitated before continuing, "Will, you've been so wonderful to me. Oh God, this is so hard, but I totally love you. I see you as the father I never had, and I … I want to adopt you to be my father. Please?" She said this very rapidly, turned away, and started to cry.

William remained silent for a minute while he fetched some tissues for her.

"I cherish the fact that you have asked me this," he said when she'd taken a tissue. "I'd be honored to be your adopted father, Jenny. You've come to mean a lot to me, and I'm grateful you've entered my life."

She looked up with a weak smile. "Thanks, Will. This healing and sharing and dealing with all my shit certainly use up a lot of tears and tissues, don't ya think?"

Will sat for a moment. "Yes, it does. Sadly. I found that out the hard way also. Trust me when I say I can understand. Believe it or not, I used up my share of tissues as well. It's hard, but it'll be worth it going through the pain and getting rid of it."

They both remained quiet for a long time.

Will finally broke the silence. "I'm more than proud and honored to be your adopted father. You've become like a daughter to me, and yes, Jenny, I love you too."

She jumped into his arms and hugged him so tightly he thought he might choke.

"Oh, Will, I love you so much. I promise I'll be a good daughter, I promise! Thank you so much. This means so much! You can't understand."

"I think I do," he said as he reached for the tissues.

They sat for a few moments, and Jenny said, "By the

way, Cat has been sneaking into the bunkhouse all the time lately. I like her and everything, but she's your cat. I feel like a cat napper."

William laughed. "Yeah, I know she's been visiting you. I think that she might have adopted you. I suggest you get a kitty box, some kitty litter, and some bowls for food and water for her. I can give you some food. Maybe she'll be a shared cat. Sound okay?"

Jenny laughed. "Sounds okay to me if it's okay with you. I was just concerned."

Will laughingly said, "I remember the first night you came here. You have come a long way, ah, with Cat, I mean."

Jenny picked up his double meaning and replied, "Yeah, Will, a long, long way."

CHAPTER 18

Jenny met with Joan again on Tuesday and started off by saying, "I think I'm going to take Peter up on his offer. I've thought a lot about it and it may be okay. I called my brother and my grandparents to let them know and got a flight to Denver tomorrow. They acted like they'd be excited to see me. I'm really anxious but excited as well.

"I'm still a bit reluctant to be riding alone with Peter on the way back. He seems nice and all, but there's something I need to tell you about an experience I had once with a guy when I was fourteen and was out walking through the Farm. This guy was about my age, and he started walking alongside me, and we began chatting about this and that, ending up walking into the forest.

"It was a really nice day, and I was enjoying being with this guy. He seemed friendly and interesting to talk to. We went to a small grassy clearing, sat, and continued talking. The next thing I knew, he grabbed me and threw me to the ground. He was on top of me, trying to kiss me. He had a hand between my legs, rubbing my crotch. I screamed at him to stop, but he didn't. He kept on saying, 'Come on, Jenny. I know you want it. Don't be a prude. Come on. I want to fuck you. You're so hot. You'll love it. You know you want to.'

"Somehow I managed to get away from under him and screamed at him, 'Go fuck yourself,' and ran away. He hollered, 'You fucking bitch, slut, cunt! You'll pay for this, you fucking bitch!'

"I never told anyone because I knew that no one would care. But I suffered the consequences anyway; that guy told everyone that I tried to seduce him, that I was a slut. After that I was constantly ridiculed, teased and bullied. I cut off what little association I had with any of the kids in the Farm, even my brother, along with most adults, except for Annie. And every time I was out, some of his friends, both girls and boys, said, 'Hi, slut' or 'How's the slut?' or 'Gettin' any fuckin' huh, bitch slut?'

"I stole some money from Dory, walked down to the mercantile store in the small town about two miles from the Farm, and bought a sheath knife with a six-inch-long blade. I wore it on my belt and was never without it.

"One day a guy started teasing me, then started shoving me, and I pulled out my knife and went for him, screaming, 'I'll cut your fucking heart out and eat it for lunch.'

"He threw up his arms and ran away. From then on I was known as Crazy Jenny. I loved it and tried to live up to my new name by acting crazy like threatening people that I'd kill them and eat their beating hearts. People started avoiding me, leaving me alone. Hell, I never had any friends anyway, so I was fine with being solo. They were the crazies, the idiots, the bullies. I lost myself in books and writing poetry and short stories about my fantasies.

"So, how's that, Joan? That was my fucking life. My earliest childhood memories of fights with my father beating on Dory, slamming her around, the bruises, the screaming, the crying, the fear, the attempted rape, the bullying. It seemed it was either fighting or sex, being filled with lies, abuse, and whatever else you might want to call it. It was a great fucking childhood."

Joan remained silent for a moment, considering all this. "How do you feel about all this now, Jenny?"

"How do I feel? You want to know how I feel? I'll tell you how I feel. I'm pissed off that I had such a shit childhood. I see other people my age that don't have all this shit, Joan. All this shit! I'm jealous of them and so pissed about the twenty-five years of me being so fucked up!"

"Jenny, I'm sorry about your childhood. Truly, I am. But I think you know that you're not alone. Others have suffered the same things, abuse and bullying along with the associated trauma. I also want you to know that you're not the worst case I've seen and counseled over the years. I'm sure that it doesn't make any of it any easier. You'll get over your anger someday and you will survive. It's work, but you will survive."

Jenny hung her head. "Yeah, I know. It just all makes me so mad that I want to scream sometimes. I'm tired of crying."

Joan reached over and took her hand, saying softly, "I know you are, Honey. It will get better. Just hang with me. We'll get through it. We will. I promise. One more thing I want to talk about before you go is about your grandparents. How long has it been since you've seen them, your grandparents and brother?"

"It's been over two years, the years I've been hiding away from everything."

"I think it'll be good for you to see them."

"Yeah, I know. It's way past time. They did so much for me, getting me away from the Farm, supporting me through college, and there's their ongoing support. It's been so long. I think they'll be mad at me for seeming so ungrateful. I'm ashamed and pretty nervous to see them.

"I guess I got so wrapped up in escaping from everything after college that I just cut off all communication with them along with everyone else. Then, as time went on, I became ashamed and afraid to contact them. I was ashamed that I wasn't doing anything with my life. What could I tell them? Hi, Dean and Susan. Thanks for helping me become a reclusive, homeless bum. All your support and caring really worked."

"I doubt that they'll be mad at you, Jenny. My guess is that they will welcome you with open arms and a lot of love. Trust that. I'll be waiting to see how it all goes. Anything else?"

"I think I covered enough, and more. Thanks, Joan. You're the best. I'll keep you posted."

CHAPTER 19

William took Jenny to her ten o'clock flight the next day. She relaxed into her short flight to Denver and began thinking about her grandparents, about how they had saved her. She remembered that it was about a week before her eighteenth birthday. She'd been walking across the compound and ran into the mail sorter, who said there was a big envelope in the mail for her.

She was surprised, since she'd never gotten any mail in her whole life, and ran to the mail room and, out of breath, got her envelope. She sneaked outside the compound where she could be alone and carefully opened it. Inside were birthday greetings from her grandparents, including ten new $100 bills and a note urging her to come to Denver and see them. They wanted to help her and they would help her get into college if she wanted. It was her ticket to escape.

That night she stealthily put a few things in an old bag. She didn't sleep at all but lay awake, waiting in anticipation until right before dawn, then she sneaked out of the place that had been her home for eighteen years. She'd hitchhiked before from the Farm to a little town about two miles away, so she knew how to get a ride. She made a sign that read "Sacramento" and caught rides in a few old farm trucks, with a woman salesperson, and last two young women about her age. She was in Sacramento shortly after noon.

She'd asked the last two women for the best way to get to Denver. Their suggestions were to hitchhike or take an airplane, bus, or Amtrak. She found the Amtrak station and bought a ticket to Denver, the next train scheduled to leave the next morning.

She found a room in a nearby hotel, flopped down on the bed, and wrapped her arms around herself in a self-hug and giggled. She was free; she was giddy; she was happy; she was scared to death.

It was mid-afternoon, so she went out and wandered the streets of Sacramento. Finding a sports store, she bought a few new clothes, a day pack, and a water bottle. Then she found a bookstore and bought two brand-new books. She'd never had a brand-new book before. To her it was like finding a treasure.

After checking out of the hotel early in the morning, she had a big breakfast at a diner and then strolled to the station, enjoying the new day, her second day of freedom.

She got to the train station, found out where she needed to wait, filled her new water bottle, and sat, reading one of the new books.

The train arrived at ten thirty. She boarded and found her seat, barely containing herself with excitement and nervous fear. The train left at 11:09. She would get to Denver thirty hours and twenty-nine minutes later, early evening the next day.

The train pulled out, and she went back to her book but soon became mesmerized by the passing scenery through the Sierra Mountains, Truckee, Reno, then into the Nevada desert.

Nighttime came with a restless sleep, and in the morning, Salt Lake, the Rocky Mountains, Denver. It was all over too soon. She wanted to do it all over again. She could never have imagined so much land, such big cities, such freedom.

She got off with her pack, found a phone booth, and called the number her grandparents had included in their note.

A short time later, a black Mercedes pulled up into the loading zone, and a handsome older couple got out, anxiously looking around.

She didn't remember what they even looked like, not having seen them since she was three years old, over fifteen years ago, but she knew it was them. Her grandmother, Susan, was about Jenny's height, with bobbed gray hair, appearing slim and healthy. Her grandfather, Dean, was probably a little over six feet with a full mop of gray hair, cut long so he could comb it back to hang over his shirt collar. He too appeared to be very healthy. She remembered how they'd almost smothered her with hugs, kisses, and tears of happiness.

They drove to a high-rise condo building, went into the secure parking garage, parked, then took the elevator to the penthouse. Jenny stepped into what she perceived to be such opulence that she never could have imagined it in her wildest dreams. She was used to simple communal living with only the basic necessities of life: a communal shower, a communal outhouse, and small cabins and, in her case, a small yurt. But her grandparents' place had art, fine furniture, views of the city; it was amazing. She walked around, just looking.

She remembered them telling her about the private investigator from San Francisco they had hired about a year before. It had taken him about six months to find her and Michael.

Jenny then remembered them telling her about how her

mother had died at childbirth, devastating her father. She'd never known what had happened to her mother.

Then she thought about how they'd supported her, helping her to get her life going.

The plane beginning its descent into Denver snapped her out of her memories. She was out of security at eleven thirty and met Peter at the baggage pickup. She got her bag, and they headed into the city. Peter took her to her grandparents' high-rise, and she made him come up with her so he could meet them. They took the elevator to the penthouse and got out to find Dean and Susan waiting expectantly. They ran to her and both hugged her, almost squeezing the breath out of her.

"And who is this?" Susan asked, going over to Peter.

"This is my friend Peter. The man whose house I'm renting is his father. Peter's a last-year law student here in Denver. We met over Thanksgiving. He picked me up at the airport, and I'm riding back to Durango with him when I plan on leaving in a few weeks. I hope it's okay if I stay that long."

"Of course it'll be okay. We were really hoping you'd stay with us through Christmas and New Year's," Susan said wistfully.

Dean chuckled. "Come on, Susan, Jenny has her life. Let's enjoy her company while she's here and not pressure her."

Jenny threw her grandfather a grateful smile and said, "Peter has to run; I wanted him to meet you."

Peter nodded. "Great to meet you both. Have a great time together, and I'll pick you up on the morning of the twentieth."

"Yeah, let's be in touch if anything changes. Call me to give me the time you want to leave, and I'll be ready."

With that Peter said his goodbyes and disappeared into the elevator.

"Let's have some lunch," Susan said. "We hope you're okay

with some cold cuts and baguettes. We have iced tea, water, or coffee if you want."

"Sounds great, and iced tea will be fine."

Susan brought out the cold cuts and the baguettes, along with lettuce, sliced tomatoes, and some chips and fruit.

"I'm so sorry and ashamed to have neglected you for so long," Jenny said. "You've done so much for me, shown me so much love. I'm sorry. Please forgive me."

Dean looked at her kindly. "We figured you had your reasons, Jenny. Yes, we worried about you. But Michael shared your few letters with us, so we knew you were okay."

"I'm sorry. It was wrong of me."

"Let's just write it off to experience."

She raised her eyes, reached out, and held Dean's and Susan's hands. "Okay, but, still, it was very thoughtless of me. Thank you. I love you both so much. It won't happen again. I promise."

"Then let's eat," Susan said and then went on to ask, "So … is Peter a boyfriend?"

"Not really, just a friend. He's a nice guy and great to hang out with. It's really no big deal."

"He seems nice, and a nice-looking boy," Susan added.

"Have you seen Michael lately? How's he doing?" Jenny asked, hopefully changing the subject.

Dean nodded slowly. "Ah, yes, Michael. I'd have to say we are a little concerned; actually, we're very worried about him. He stopped by about a month ago. He seemed strange, unfocused; it was hard to talk to him. He said he was having a hard time in school, then kept saying it wasn't his fault, that everyone was against him."

Susan joined in. "And he didn't look good. He was very thin and had dark circles under his eyes, like he'd been studying too hard and maybe not getting enough rest. We kept asking him if he was okay and if we could help."

"And then he started to be a little hostile toward us," Dean said. "He told us it was none of our business and left abruptly in a little huff. We haven't seen or heard from him since."

Jenny thought of his last letter to her, of how disjointed it had seemed. "I've talked with him about me being here. He's coming up from the Springs and we're planning on going to dinner tonight. I'm excited to see him again. Will you come with us?"

Dean shook his head. "Thanks, but we think it will be nice for you two to have some time to yourselves. We'll have time with you the next while. How about you, Jenny? Tell us what you've been up to. Are you working?"

Jenny was about to start telling them about everything she was dealing with but thought better about it. They were already worried about Michael and didn't need to be also worried about her.

"To be honest, I've spent a lot of time and effort in trying to be a writer, but so far, that hasn't worked out very well. I'm renting my little house from a nice man who is a published author, and he's helping me. I've been wanting to get myself gainfully employed. I have time, time that I'd like to be working, doing something. I just haven't a clue what. I need to take a break from trying to write and want to start exploring after the first of the year to see what's out there that I might be able to do. I really like living in Durango. I've met some nice people. I'll keep you posted."

She watched her grandparents as they nodded, as if in some sort of quiet agreement, or, she thought, maybe it was in despair at having an unproductive granddaughter.

The conversation had come to a lull. Susan got up to clean

away the dishes, and Jenny got up to help. The conversation drifted around from this to that for the rest of the afternoon.

It was getting late, and Jenny excused herself to freshen up and get ready before Michael arrived. She finished right before he arrived.

CHAPTER 20

When Michael got off the elevator, Jenny was struck by how pale and gaunt he appeared. Like her grandparents, she also thought he looked very unhealthy.

"Jenny, you look great."

She had her arms outstretched, expecting a hug, but he just stood at arm's length and smiled sullenly at her.

"It's so great to see you, Michael, just great." But she received no response, just a blank look.

They sat, and she tried to talk to him for about half an hour, but it was a one-sided conversation on Jenny's part, getting little response from him. While she was in mid-sentence, Michael got up and said, "We have reservations in about ten minutes. The place is close by. We can walk, but we should go now."

His lack of much participation in the conversation made Jenny uncomfortable, and she again asked her grandparents to join them, really wanting their company, but they again declined.

Michael and Jenny walked about a block to the restaurant. On the way, Jenny asked Michael about his life but received little information in return. After being seated at the restaurant they both ordered drinks.

"So why did you stay at the Farm so long when you could have left?" Jenny asked.

He snorted. "And why did you leave so quickly without a goodbye or anything? You just all of a sudden were gone, disappeared. Nobody knew what happened to you. Personally I liked it there. I stayed for two years after you left. Then I decided I wanted to go to college and came to Colorado. At least I said goodbye to Mom and Dad. That's more than you did!" he ended with a note of sarcasm.

"I left because if I stayed there one more day, I would have died. And as for 'Mom and Dad,' Julian was a drunk and a druggy and Dory wasn't my mother but a complete bitch."

"Oh, get over yourself! Mom and Dad were great. I loved Dory. But you were always a prude, always by yourself. No wonder everyone called you a 'slut,'" he said with a laugh.

She felt an old chill run down her spine, not liking where this all seemed to be going. Red flags went up with his remark, and she became wary. She hated that term, hated everything connected to it, and her brother seemed to think it was a big joke.

Not about to back off, she went on, "Yeah, I was a loner because of all that bullying bullshit I had to put up with. That's why I'm now in therapy, trying to get my life back after all the fucking sexual abuse from that bitch, Dory. I so hated her for what she did to us. So don't act like it was all a big joke. It wasn't! You might have thought it was funny, but I sure as hell didn't."

"What the hell are you talking about? Dory was great to us. Sexual abuse! What the hell are you talking about?" he said, laughing.

"Dammit, Michael, how can you even say that? You were there! You saw what she did to me. I saw what she did to you. What don't you get? Did you like fucking her, like her playing with your dick, making you have sex with her when you were, like what, thirteen? I saw it, Michael. I was there. I was part of it all! Remember?"

"Awe, Jenny, Dory was good to us. I don't know what the hell you're talking about. And therapy. What's up with that? You were always such a drama queen. God, just get over yourself. I should probably take you and knock some sense into you." His voice rose.

Her blood turned to ice. "Oh, fucking knock me around like Julian did to Dory? Beat her or fuck her along with all the other sex shit that went on. You want to knock me around, you skinny-ass piece of shit? You are just fucking like them. Do you beat up your women too? Is that what gets you off? I'm out of here! You're so in denial. You are sick, Michael. You are a sick fuck, just like the rest of them were." She started to get up.

But Michael leaped to his feet, knocking over his chair, and kicked the table, their drinks falling onto the floor, and screamed, "Fuck you, you bitch slut! Just fuck you, little cunt! You go to hell! I'll kick the shit out of you. Teach you a lesson, you stupid fucking bitch. All fucking women are nothing but stupid whores." He grabbed his jacket and stormed out the door.

The server rushed over. "Are you okay, hon? Do you want me to call someone?"

Jenny shook with anger and was bordering on tears. "Thanks. I'm okay. I'm so sorry for all that. Here, this should cover everything." She handed her a wad of bills. "I need to leave. I'm really so sorry for all that, really. I apologize to everyone for my brother. It's just a little sibling problem."

"Shouldn't you call someone? Are you sure you'll be okay?"

"I'm good. Thanks, I'll be fine. I'm only a block from where I'm staying with my grandparents. I should be fine. Thanks. I appreciate your concern, and I'm really sorry."

She got her coat, walked outside, and heard Michael from the shadows. "Okay, you bitch slut! I'm going to teach you a lesson right fucking now, you fucking bitch! You can't run or hide. I'll find you, bitch!"

Jenny saw him starting to come toward her and quickly ducked back inside the restaurant before he got to her. As soon as she got back inside, he stopped, waved a fist at her, and shouted something she didn't quite hear. He disappeared into an alley.

She got out her cell and called 911.

"Nine one one, what is your emergency?"

"It's my brother! He just went crazy. He's threatened to beat me!"

"What's your name and location?"

"My name is Jennifer Morse. I'm hiding in the Bomber Café on the Mall, on Sixteenth. I'm really scared!"

"Help will be on the way. Stay where you are and do not confront him. I repeat, stay away from him! Is there anyone else around you?"

"Yes, I'm in the restaurant, and there are a lot of people in here. I'll stay in here. I should be okay. Thanks! I'll be here."

The same waitress saw her and rushed over. "What's going on? Are you okay?"

Jenny started to shake even more and dropped her phone. "I'm scared. He's just crazy! He threatened me, said he wants to beat me."

The waitress picked up her phone, handed it to her. "You

stay in here. You'll be safe."

Two men standing close by overheard. One said, "Trust me. We're here for you. You're safe. He won't dare touch you."

Others from the restaurant gathered around.

Within minutes two police cars arrived, light bars flashing. Two uniformed officers came in, and Jenny and the waiter went to meet them.

"Hi, officers, I'm Jennifer Morse. I made the call. It's my brother. We had an argument, and he just went nuts and threatened me. I'm scared, really scared. He … he just went nuts!" she said, still violently shaking.

The waitress added, "I saw and heard a lot of what went on. He was really being crazy. He threatened her and got up and stormed out. She paid the bill and left but then rushed back in, calling 911. Apparently he was waiting for her outside."

"Thanks, Miss. Jennifer, can you describe him?"

"He's about six foot, thin, wearing a brown leather jacket and jeans, no hat, dark-blond hair. He's my twin."

The officer radioed the information to two other uniforms in the street, who dispersed to look for Michael.

"Let's go out and sit in the car where it's quiet and more private so I can ask you some more questions."

The other officer got the waiter's name and her statement, and a number of the patrons came up to give information as well.

"Jennifer. It's Jennifer, right?" he asked gently.

"Yes, but please call me Jenny." Her voice shook and tears threatend. The officer called for a female officer to get to the scene.

The female uniform arrived moments later and sat with Jenny, getting her statement and asking her more questions about Michael and their relationship, about where he lived and what had precipitated the event and some other details. Then she gave her a ride back to the high-rise.

It was only a little over an hour after she and Michael had left when she rang the security buzzer, was let in, and got off the elevator into the penthouse. Her grandparents were both reading. "Home so soon? Where's Michael?"

Jenny tried to respond but just fell into the sofa and started shaking again, crying with uncontrollable sobs.

Her grandmother came and sat beside her and tried to console her. "Jenny, dear child, what happened? What's wrong?"

After a few minutes, Jenny was finally able to get herself together and said, "I'm really sorry."

"Don't be sorry, darling. What happened? Was it Michael? Did you have a fight?"

"I don't know if I can tell you, if I want you to hear what happened. It was awful! Michael was just awful. I should never have come. I so wanted to see you and Michael. He hates women, thinks we are stupid and need to be hit and slapped because we're stupid." She started to cry again. "I'm not stupid, Grandma! I'm not stupid. Do you think I'm stupid, Grandma?" She moaned. "I never should have come, Grandma. I'm making you and Grandpa upset just by being here. I make everything so awful. It's all my fault."

Her grandmother held her, at a loss as to what to do or say. Finally, she said, "We're happy you came and are here. We wanted to see you. You are definitely not stupid. You're a very smart young woman. You cannot be responsible for Michael. We can't possibly imagine what your childhood was like. We really had no idea but are starting to get a better picture as all this unfolds. We both love you so very much, more than you can imagine. We want you to feel safe, and you are safe here. You will always be safe with us. I promise you that."

Jenny sat up, looking at Susan. "Thanks, Grandma, I love you both, you're wonderful to me and have saved me in so many ways, ways you can't ever imagine."

Dean asked, "Jennifer, would you want something to eat, if you're able? I am guessing you didn't have dinner?"

"Thanks, Grandpa, I am starting to feel hungry, starved actually. Could I have a glass of wine first, please?"

"Of course you can. White or red?"

"White, please, and some of those cold cuts would be fine. Please, I don't want to trouble you. Please don't make a fuss."

She had two glasses of wine, a big sandwich, and some chips and felt better. Then she told them everything about her last two years and her therapy. She went into some of her childhood but didn't share anything about her sexual abuse, sparing them and herself from that. Dean and Susan were silent and visibly shocked.

Dean finally said, "Jennifer, we had no idea. And therapy? What can we do to help? Can we do anything? Can we help pay? Is this therapist any good? Do we—"

Jenny held up her hand to stop him. "Grandpa, I'm really doing okay. My therapist, Joan, is wonderful. I have support from some wonderful people I've met, some close and dear friends. And I can afford to pay from your generous support. Right now, it's Michael I'm worried about. I've learned a lot in the last few months. What I saw tonight—"

Dean interrupted. "We'll do whatever we can to help both of you. If you ever need our help for anything …"

"I'm really okay, Grandpa, really I am. I'm really tired right now. I know it's only eight thirty, but if I could be excused, I really need to rest."

She went to her room and took a long, hot bath, trying to wash Michael and his anger off her. It took a long time.

CHAPTER 21

Jenny got ready for bed, comfy in her sweats, and decided to call Joan. She needed to talk about the disaster with her brother. She made herself a cup of chamomile tea, curled up in her bed, and called. Joan answered the second ring.

"Hi, Joan, it's Jenny. Can you talk? I need to talk to you. I really do."

"Yeah, sure, Jenny. What's up?"

Jenny told her what had happened earlier, everything in detail. How frightened she was of her brother. How she just wanted to be back home.

Joan was quiet for a few moments. "Okay, here's what I think. First off, we need to get a restraining order against Michael. From what you've told me, he seems like a loose cannon, and you could possibly be in serious danger. With the report you've given the police and that many witnesses, it shouldn't be a problem to get one. I'll start on it first thing tomorrow morning. You can sign it when you get back here."

"But won't that just make him angrier?"

"Jenny, he's already angry from the sounds of it. This is abuse, Jenny. This is bullying, pure, plain, and simple. From what you said, he fits every profile of an abusive man. You could be in danger, serious danger. Jenny, I've dealt with abused women for over fifteen years. I know! You're sounding exactly like the abused woman you are in so many, many ways. Yeah, he'll be angry, maybe angrier being served with a restraint. So let him. Secondly, get back here as soon as you can. You'll be safer here, and we have a lot more work to do. Are you riding back with Peter?"

"Yeah, but not for over a week."

"Then try to get a flight out tomorrow. Have your grandparents take you to the airport. You need to be with someone at all times until you're through security. Please trust me on this. You could be in very serious danger. He will be most likely stalking you. You stood up to him, and that really pisses guys like him off. You made him feel powerless. He wants his power back, and he needs to beat you up, or worse, so he can feel strong again. Trust me! He's most assuredly very dangerous."

Jenny stiffened up, no longer relaxed. Her heart started to race, and her breathing quickened. Talking to Joan made her realize, to a greater degree, how much danger she could be in. She desperately wanted to be back home safe in her little house, with Will next door. She knew he would protect her.

"Okay, Joan. I'll see what I can do about getting home tomorrow. Thanks. You're the best. Love you."

"Please keep me posted. Love you too."

Jenny immediately called Peter, who answered groggily, "Yeah, hello?"

"Peter, it's me, Jenny. Did I wake you? Sorry, it's late, I guess. I wasn't paying attention to the time. It's been a crazy night. I need to let you know my plans have changed."

She gave him a short version of the night's drama. "I'm

going to try to catch a flight out to Durango tomorrow, Peter. I'll see you in Durango."

"Whoa, wait, wait! Wait a minute. Flight out? This guy is threatening you? No way! I'll pick you up tomorrow at eleven, and we'll head back. I can get everything done here that I need to in the morning, and we can be out of here. We'll be in Durango tomorrow night and have dinner together at The Tavern. No problem."

"Wait, Peter. I thought you had finals and stuff. I can't ask you to do this."

"Bullshit, Jenny! No argument! I can seriously get everything finished up and organized to be out of here in the morning. I'll be there at eleven. Be ready. I was really sort of killing time because I wanted you to have time with your family. I'm sorry all this happened. Really sorry."

"Thanks, Peter. Okay then, I'll be here and ready at eleven. See you then. And thanks so much, Peter. I owe you one."

She crawled under the covers and thought of Peter. She liked that he seemed concerned and protective of her. It made her feel secure, and her heart swelled, thinking about it. She really was starting to like this guy. Jenny slept well, dreaming of Peter and her having a candlelight dinner together when he told her something she couldn't understand.

Morning came, and she rose early. She missed Cat and her early morning purring. She meditated, packed her bag, then went out to the living room where she found her grandparents having coffee and reading the morning's Denver Post.

Susan greeted her. "Good morning, Jennifer. There's fresh coffee. Did you sleep okay?"

"Thanks. Yes, I did." She went to the kitchen, poured herself a cup, then went in and told them she was leaving at eleven and why. They were upset she was leaving so soon, but after she told them about her conversation with Joan and went on to try to explain all the implications of what was happening, including the danger and her fear, they understood.

"But, Jennifer, I can't believe Michael would ever hurt you."

"I know, Grandma, but it's not a chance I'm willing to take. I saw way too much violence between Daddy and Dora. I know what it can be like. I don't need it in my life. Please believe me. I've seen and talked to some of the battered women who live at the shelter. It's never pretty."

Dean said, "It's not easy for us to understand everything you went through as a child, but we trust your judgment. We hate to have you leave so soon. We thought we'd get to spend some time with you is all."

"I know, Grandpa. Me too. We'll be together soon. I promise. I'll be back. Why don't you come down to Durango? There's so much I'd like to show you. I want you to meet William and my friends. We could ride the train to Silverton when spring comes. It'd be so much fun."

"We'll plan on it, Jenny, in the spring."

"I want to, just to have you—" She stopped, her voice shaking, and she wiped a tear. "My real family. I love you both so much. I miss you so much already." She hugged them both like she would never let go.

CHAPTER 22

Peter rang the buzzer shortly before eleven o'clock. Dean buzzed him in. He came off the elevator and went immediately to Jenny. "Are you okay? I worried about you all night. This thing with your brother scared me. Are you sure you are all right? He didn't hurt you?"

"I'm fine, Peter, really. He didn't touch me. It was a real ugly scene, though, really ugly."

He turned to Susan and Dean. "I'm sorry. I didn't even say hello. I was just concerned about her. I was scared. She is a really special friend."

"No worries, Peter," Dean said. "It's good to see you so soon again, too soon. We were hoping to have more time, but we're understanding more and more about what's going on. Please stop by when you're back in town. You're always welcome here."

"Thanks, Dean. I appreciate it, and I'll make it a priority."

"That'd be nice. We could talk about the law. I was an attorney for all of my life, and it would be fun to talk."

"That'd be great. I'll look forward to it. We've to get on the road, Jenny. There's some weather coming in, and we need to get over Wolf Creek Pass before it hits. Time to rock 'n roll."

Goodbyes were said, and then they were in Peter's Subaru heading out of Denver west on 285. It was a beautiful day with bright sun on new snow as they drove through the foothills up to Kenosha Pass. They shared some idle talk about the end of Peter's semester, about Jenny's grandparents, and about Dean being an attorney. Neither spoke of the incident with Michael.

On coming up to Buena Vista, they decided to stop for a potty break and get some coffee and snacks. Jenny offered to drive, but Peter insisted that she just sit back and enjoy.

After they'd been quiet for a long time, Peter looked over at her and said, "Jenny, I like you. I really like you a lot, and I, well, I guess I want to see you, maybe like more than friends. I really feel clumsy right now, duh, but I really want … well, I …"

She reached over and put her hand on his. "I know, Peter. Thanks. You're a nice guy. Right now all I want to do is to get to know you better. Okay?"

"Yeah, exactly what I wanted to say. Ah, thanks. Let's see how it goes. No strings. Okay?"

"Yeah, let's see how it goes."

Jenny felt her heart open with a warmth that flowed down into her belly as an unknown, never-before-felt tingle. Was this what D. H. Lawrence was trying to describe about what Lady Chatterley felt?

They rode in silence, listening to music, until after Salida, when Jenny broke the meditation. "Peter, there's some things I need to tell you, things you need to be aware of right now. I hesitate to tell you, but—" She paused for a moment to drum up courage. "I have a boatload of baggage that I'm carrying with me, a big boatload, maybe several boatloads. I'm dealing with a lot of shit. I was sexually and emotionally abused as a child by the woman I thought was my mother. In case you don't know I'm in counseling and group therapy.

"Michael's my twin, and yeah, I now apparently have him to deal with. Looks like he's in way worse shape than I am. I could go on, but that is pretty much it in a nutshell, the short version. I just want you to know what you're getting into with me. I may not be everything you think I am. You are dealing with a very vulnerable and insecure girl … in many ways a damaged girl.

"I want you to know that you can bail right now. I'd rather have you say right now that I might be more than you think you can handle. We all have our limits. Please, think about this and give a lot of consideration to what I'm telling you. I'm not kidding! This is some serious shit I'm coping with. With my counseling, I hope someday I'll be better and be done with it, but, no guarantees."

Both of them were quiet for a long time, then she added, "Just don't lead me on and then break my heart. I don't think I could handle that. Seriously, I don't."

Again they remained silent for a long while. Jenny silently prayed that she hadn't frightened him away.

Finally, Peter spoke. "Wow. I knew there were some things from your past. My dad alluded to it but gave no details. I appreciate you telling me. And, to be honest, you've given me a lot to think about. I really like you and want to spend time with you, but, I … I don't want to hurt you either, especially after what you just told me. I don't know. You have so much to deal with. I'd like to be of help. I don't know if I could help or just be a hindrance.

"Let's enjoy our time while I'm here over the Christmas holidays. Let's, let's … oh, hell. I don't know, Jenny. I just don't know. It has to be scary for you. I can't imagine how hard it must be for you. What you told me is scary for me right now. I don't want to get in the way. Let's leave it to rest until tomorrow at least and talk again so I can think it over. Okay?"

"Okay, yeah, sure, tomorrow," she responded, then quietly mulled over his response. It wasn't what she'd hoped for; she realized he wasn't ready for her.

After a quick stop in South Fork, they started over the 11,000 foot Wolf Creek Pass just as it was starting to get dark. The pass was clear, but they ran into light snow west of Pagosa Springs, and it got heavier as they drove toward Durango.

Jenny said, "I think we should skip our planned dinner in Durango and just head up valley and get home. This isn't looking real promising. What do you think?"

"Yeah, it's just going to get worse. There're some protein bars and apples in a sack on the seat behind your seat. I'd like one of each, please, and please help yourself."

"Thanks. Yeah, I am getting hungry." She turned and grabbed the sack, and they ate their dinner in silence.

By the time they got to Durango, it was nearly a whiteout and slow going. It was almost ten by the time they got up to William's compound.

Peter walked Jenny to her door. He looked at her and gave her a little hug, kissing her on the cheek. "You're the best, Jenny. You're a strong woman. I'm really sorry for you, sorry for everything. See you tomorrow." He let go, turned, and walked to his father's house.

She went inside, closed the door, and stood there, leaning back against it. She let her bag drop to the floor and sighed, replaying the last two days in her mind, especially the ride home, what was said and what wasn't. It was what wasn't said that weighed so heavily on her. *He feels sorry for me? Gotta think it over? Screw him!*

Finally she walked into her bedroom, kicked off her shoes, undressed, and, emotionally drained, fell into bed.

She dreamed she was wandering around, lost in a terrible snowstorm; it was night, pitch black, very cold. She was freezing and knew she was going to die. She saw lights coming toward her, closer and closer. Then she saw it was her Jeep. It stopped, the passenger door opened, and she looked in and saw herself driving. "Get in, Jenny. I'll save you."

When she got in, it was warm and she knew she'd be okay. They drove off into the night sky toward the dawn breaking over the mountains. Jenny awoke with a start and peeked out her window at the dawn rising over the mountains.

She lay there, confused about where she was. Was her dream real, or was this real? Finally, her head started making sense out of where she was and that she'd been dreaming, but it was so real. Then everything about the past few days erupted slowly in her head, like a bad movie in slow motion.

CHAPTER 23

Jenny checked the time. Eight thirty. Late for her. It was Friday; she'd missed yoga. She wanted to see Helen and talk to her, and she desperately needed to see Joan. She jumped out of bed and found her phone, but it had a dead battery. "Damn!"

She hooked it up to the charger, undressed, and went into a long, hot shower, trying to wash everything away. When she'd finished, her phone was charged enough to call Joan.

"Hi, this is Jenny Morse. Would Joan have any time to see me today?" she asked. "I really need to talk with her. Please say that she does! Please?" She ended with more of a call for help than a request.

"Ah, let's see. Yes, she had a cancellation at eleven this morning. Will that work for you?"

"Yes, yes, thank you so much! Yes, thank you! I'll be there."

She got dressed and made some coffee and toast with peanut butter for her breakfast, forgetting how little she'd eaten yesterday. She was already too preoccupied with wanting to remember everything to tell Joan. She found her journal and wrote everything she could remember, bringing it all back to life. It made her very sad and frightened about her life, about her grandparents, about Peter, and about Michael— especially about Michael. By then, it was already ten thirty. She grabbed her jacket and phone, and raced out the door, almost knocking over Peter on her way out.

"Hey, good morning. How're you doing? Have time to talk about yesterday?"

"No time right now. Gotta go. See ya later."

She climbed into her Jeep and raced off, leaving a confused Peter standing on her porch with his mouth hanging open.

She took the main highway and pushed the speed limit all the way in, arriving for her appointment at 10:45. As it turned out, there hadn't been that much snow overnight, and roads were clear, melting dry under the Colorado sun at an elevation of sixty-five hundred feet.

She had so much she wanted to talk about. She needed to get some answers and help processing it all.

Joan popped out of her office about five minutes later. "Hi, Jenny, you made it back."

"Yeah, around ten last night, later than we planned with the snow. Oh, God, I'm so happy you have time. So much happened, so much to talk about. I don't know where to start."

"Whoa, slow down. I can skip my lunch hour if I need to. I was concerned after your phone call, so tell me what's going on."

Jenny went into greater detail about her brother and their ill-fated dinner date.

"That doesn't sound very good," Joan said. "It must've been very scary for you. I called our attorney this morning about a restraining order. He was going to call the Denver police and have them fax him a copy of the report. He hasn't gotten back to me yet. What else?"

Jenny talked in length about her grandparents and that they were happy to see her and might come and visit. She dreaded to talk about, or even think about, her conversation with Peter and his response, but she finally told Joan everything.

"It was very brave of you to tell him, and you did the right thing in informing him about your life. I can't imagine it was easy for you. And his response, as you describe it, doesn't surprise me at all. The beginning of any relationship is usually very heady and sometimes very disillusioning. I'm sure he had already put you up on a pedestal as being perfect in every way, flawless, pure, like the proverbial fresh flower. What you told him had to shatter any idealistic notion he was carrying around, that he came over when you were leaving could be a good sign."

"Or a very bad sign."

"Yeah, possibly. Let's hope not. From what you've told me about him, he seems grown up and mature. That's good. You should talk with him when you get home, to save yourself from worrying more than you already are."

"Yeah, I'll call him before I leave for home and see if he has time or even wants to after I shrugged him off this morning."

She was about to continue when Joan's phone rang. "It's our attorney." She picked up, listening intently for about five minutes. Then she thanked him. "Will you fax me a copy of that report? Good, I'll watch for it." She cut off and looked at Jenny for a moment. "I'm sorry to have to tell you this, but Michael has been arrested and is in jail, and it's worse than we thought.

"Apparently, your grandparents had just finished lunch and were about to go out for the afternoon when their buzzer rang. It was Michael. They let him in, and he charged out of the elevator, screaming at them, looking for you. I guess his language was ugly and profane. He was completely out of control.

"Your grandfather told him to leave, but Michael just continued on, going into bedrooms, looking in closets, screaming he was going to kill you for calling the police. Your grandmother phoned 911, and Michael started for her, but your grandfather grabbed him and put him on the floor with his knee on his back and holding his arms.

"Michael screamed profanities at both of them, until a few minutes later when two police officers entered and cuffed him. One of the officers dragged him to the elevator and was joined by two more officers. The four of them took him away, with Michael still screaming, totally out of control. The first officer asked your grandparents about what had happened. They explained everything, including last night and what happened to you. The officer said they were aware of that and had been keeping an eye out for him. He was being arrested and would be charged with assault and making serious threats of bodily harm.

"Your grandparents agreed to press charges against Michael. The officer said that they would be notified of what was going on and gave them his card, ending by saying Michael would be booked and held until court on Monday. They could call the station any time to check on his status."

"Oh shit! Are my grandparents okay? Are they all right?"

"Yes, somewhat shaken up, I suppose, but they weren't physically hurt or anything. They're fine. But it gets even worse. Hang on, this won't be easy for you, but there were five outstanding warrants for Michael down in the Springs. He apparently attacked and beat five women, two of them so severely they had to be hospitalized. There were four of his fellow students and one of his professors. The police had a

BOLO out for him. He was hiding out in Denver for the last few weeks, flying under the radar, until all this came down with you and your grandparents. He's not being a model prisoner at all. He can't seem to help himself by keeping his mouth shut. He keeps going on about how you and your grandmother are nothing but 'stupid bitches' that need some sense knocked into them, how those stupid girls in Colorado Springs were 'bitch whores' who didn't appreciate how great he was. They deserved to get slapped around. Didn't anyone realize that he was helping them to understand how to please their men?

"You were very lucky. We don't know what is going to happen to him, but I'd say he's definitely not well and needs a lot of help. He needs to be incarcerated and away from society. I'll add that he should be institutionalized rather than imprisoned. We'll have to wait and see. In any case, we should have no problem getting you a restraining order against him, which may be moot because he may be behind bars for a while, maybe quite a while."

Jenny looked through Joan, out into some far away place. Finally she refocused and asked, with panic in her voice, "If I hadn't gone up there, none of this would have happened. It's all my fault. I should have never gone. I need to help him. He's my brother! He needs my help! I need to go back up to Denver and see what I can do. Maybe if I could see him, talk to him."

"No, Jenny! No! There is nothing you can do for him. Nothing! I repeat, nothing! You need to stay here and get yourself grounded. You are in no shape to do anything but try to help yourself. I can understand you wanting to help him, but there's simply nothing you can do. Nothing! Understand?"

"But I could tell the police it was all a mistake, what happened with me, tell them I lied, tell them none of it really happened."

"Jenny, there were, how many witnesses? They all corroborated what happened at the restaurant. Then there was what happened with your grandparents, not to mention the warrants from Colorado Springs. Jenny, there is nothing you can do! Get that into your head! I'm sorry. I am truly sorry, but there is nothing. You. Can. Do! Are you hearing me? He's in trouble. But you have to think of yourself first. It is not your fault. None of this is your fault."

"Yeah, Joan, I know. I know. It's just … everything is so crazy. Everything's falling apart. Everything I'm trying so hard to make better just gets worse. I … I'm just so mixed up with everything: my life, Michael, Peter, everyone. I just want to run away. Everything was so much better when I just was with myself. I was able to keep the demons away. Now they are eating me alive." Tears ran down her cheeks.

Joan handed her some tissues. "This is hard, Jenny, very hard. No one planned on what Michael was like or what he was doing. It's a huge shock for you. I believe I said early on it might get worse before it gets better. It has definitely gotten worse. Those demons have had a long time to grow, fester, and get strong, but you are stronger, much stronger, and we're not going to let them run you out of Dodge. We will conquer those darn demons and get through this together. Please, please believe me when I say this, but we will. I promise. Okay?"

"Yeah, thanks, Joan. Yeah, I know what you're saying's true. I appreciate what faith you have in me." She smiled weakly. "I probably need to leave. I've taken up most of your lunch break."

"That's no problem, but I want to be sure you're okay. Don't do anything stupid on me now."

"I won't. I promise. My head's starting to feel more clear. I want to try to catch Helen. She's always good at grounding me."

"Okay, get out of here then. Please call me and let me know how you are and whether you talk to Peter. Promise. Either promise me, or I'll send the sheriff after you. He's a personal friend and will do what I ask," she finished, smiling.

"I'll call for sure then," she bantered back weakly.

"Great. I'll be anxious to hear how you're doing."

"Thanks, Joan. Thanks so very much for … for everything. Love you."

"Love you too, sweetheart. Love you too. Don't forget group session Tuesday night."

"See you Tuesday then." Jenny grabbed her coat and left.

Jenny hurried to Helen's studio, hoping she was there and not at lunch. When she got there, the door was open, so she poked her head in. "Helen, are you here?"

"Yes, I'm in the office. Come on in, Jenny. I thought you were in Denver until next week."

"Oh, Helen, so much has happened. I just spent since eleven talking to Joan about all the shit that happened. So much shit seems to be coming down on me I think I need an umbrella. Have you had lunch? I'm starved. I need to talk."

"I haven't eaten, and yes, I'm starved too. Let's go." She got up and grabbed her coat, and they walked out.

It was a beautiful sunny day, and so unseasonably warm after last night's snowstorm that people were walking around in shorts.

"Shorts in late November. A little excessive, don't you think?" Helen said.

"Yeah, but it's such a warm day. Maybe too warm?"

"Very dry. All we really had was that freak snowstorm in early October. Then last night which wasn't that much. Even the mountains don't have much. It will make for a dry summer unless we pick up some storms after the first of the year."

They got to The Tavern, their favorite lunch restaurant, and each ordered water and a glass of iced tea.

"So, Jenny, what's going on?"

Jenny leaned over and started to unload. It was easier the second time, more clear and more manageable. The server returned with their teas, and they ordered without even looking up. Then Jenny continued nonstop. Helen sat, listening intently with her eyes wide, amazed as the drama was unfolded to her.

Finally Jenny concluded, "And that's about it. Yeah, that's about it, I guess. Everything is all so messed up. What should I do, Helen, especially about Peter? I thought I might really like him, and it's probably over before anything even really started. Oh well, maybe it's for the best. A guy in my life is just another added thing to have to deal with. There's just so much right now."

"I know what you're saying, but one positive thing is that he was there to talk to you this morning, so he must not have totally given up on you."

"Yeah, I know. I really cut him short. I was in such a hurry to get to my meeting with Joan. Maybe I should call him. What do you think? I'll be back home in an hour. It'll wait, I guess."

Helen nodded. "You have so much on your plate. I think maybe if you look at it in pieces, if you can break it up: Michael, Peter, your grandparents. Maybe you could deal with one piece at a time. Just a thought."

"Yeah, good advice. Makes sense. I'll give it some thought. But to change the subject, I want to find a job, find something to do. I have too much time. All I seem to do is sit around, writing in my journal and worrying about everything. Do you have any suggestions? I don't really have any skills. A degree in rhetoric and literature, and camping for two years, doesn't say much."

"What would you want to do? What do you enjoy?"

"I don't know. I thought I wanted to be a writer, but my head is so messed up that when I sit to try to write something, all the uglies are there, banging around inside. I can't stay focused. Maybe something external would help me be on course."

Their food arrived, and they took a moment to start eating before continuing the conversation.

"How about trying to get something in a sports store? There are at least five or six in town. You're very active and athletic."

"I could try, but I'm not sure I can deal with people that well. I still feel uncomfortable around strangers. I still have so much to work out."

"Well, would you feel comfortable working for me, at the studio? Vicky is leaving after New Year's. She and her husband are moving to Denver. He landed a new and better job up there. I'll need a replacement."

"Wow, that would be great, but I can't teach yoga. I have no creds, and I don't want to leave here right now to go to India to study yoga. Good idea, though, and thanks for the offer."

"Now just wait. First of all, you don't have to go to India to study. There are several schools here in the West that you can go to study if you ever decide you want to get certified to teach. Plus there are any number of workshops you can go to for more advanced training and practice—that is if you really get serious about yoga. But we won't worry about that right now.

"What I was thinking is that you could do the beginner's classes. There are three a week. I'd move Sara to the intermediate level. She'd like that, and she's ready. You're a quick study; you're already at the intermediate level. I can teach you what you need to know if you're ready for some hard work and a quick learning curve. I'd need you to start in early January. The pay isn't spectacular, it's a percentage based on the number of students in your class. I have several good books I can lend on yoga, body structure, and musculature."

"Oh, let me think about it. Can I let you know, maybe tomorrow? It sounds great but I'm not too sure about teaching a group, though I guess everybody would be busy doing their yoga and I'd just be a facilitator. I don't know. Let me think on it tonight."

"Tomorrow will be fine."

They finished up, paid their bill and left, then said their goodbyes and went their separate ways.

Home at last, Jenny felt drained from today, from Denver, from Peter, from everything. She felt cranky, so she went for a run. Fifteen miles later, she'd returned. The run and a hot shower washed the day away and cleared her head.

She wanted to return some books to Will's library, but no one was home, so she went in and replaced the books on the shelves. She was on her way out when she noticed a sheaf of papers on the coffee table. It looked like an outline, so she snooped to see whether Will was starting on a new book. She started to read it, and thought her head was going to explode.

Fuck, this is about me, all about me, my life, stuff I told him! That fucking bastard! Stealing my life for one of his trash fucking books.

She tore the outline in half and scattered the pages, then ran back to her house, slammed the door, and fell on the floor, pounding her fists in anger and sobbing. After her wave of anger abated, she lay there for a long time, considering her options. What she should do? Who was she able to trust? Helen? No, she'd be in Will's camp. Joan? Probably. Kelly? Maybe. Peter? No way.

A knock sounded on her door. She ignored it, but the knocks continued. Finally, she said, "Go fucking away! I want to be fucking alone. I'm tired. Just please get the fuck away!" She heard who ever it was walk away, their footsteps crunching on the gravel drive.

That night she dreamed of being in the mountains, alone in her solitude from last summer, and the whole world disappeared and everyone in it. She was wonderfully alone, by herself, no one in her life.

She awoke late and shook herself awake. She'd just started to do some yoga when the knocking started. "Dammit, please just go away."

She heard Will say, "Jenny? What's going on? Did you tear up that outline? Why? It was —"

"Just get the fuck away from me, Will. I don't want to see you or talk to you. Just go away and leave me alone."

"Okay. Can we talk later?"

"Just get the fuck away from me!"

"Okay. We can talk later."

She heard him walk away. *Thank you.* After breakfast she curled up on her couch with her journal and started to put her thoughts down. Her first words were, *I'm feeling overwhelmed and feel like I'm suffocating. It seems that every time I start to trust someone, I get screwed.* She stopped and reflected on what she'd just written.

Then there was another knock on her door, and she heard Will say, "Jenny, are you okay? Do you want to talk?"

Jenny went ballistic. She flung open the door. "You fucking bastard! I saw your goddamned outline yesterday.

You're writing a book about me? You son of a bitch! How fucking dare you! You are a lying cheat just like every man I've ever come across! Get the fuck away from me!"

She started to slam the door in his face, but he caught it. "Jenny, let me explain. I was writing that outline for you. I thought maybe you could do your own story, like a memoir. It was just a thought to try to help you start writing. Truly!"

"Bullshit! I thought I could trust you, and you betray me like this. You could have told me, goddamn it! We could have talked about it. Please leave me the fuck alone! I have to think."

"But Jenny, please—"

"Get the fuck away from me!" she screamed. "Just get the fuck away! Leave me alone!" She turned away and started toward her bedroom, hearing the door close and footsteps walking away.

She sat, trying to calm herself down, and came to a decision. *I gotta get outa here.*

She got dressed, packed up some camping gear, grabbed the passport she'd gotten when she thought she might go to Europe after college, and wrote a note. "Out of town. Don't wait up. Fuck you all." She stuck it to her front door, threw her stuff into her Jeep, and headed south toward Arizona.

Fuck 'em all. I'm so outa here. Fuck William, fuck Peter, fuck Michael, and everyone else. She turned off her cell phone, found some vintage rock on the radio, and cranked it up.

Somewhat calmed down by the time she got to Durango, she decided to stop at Desert and Mountain Outfitters. She bought a water filter, some freeze-dried food, two water bottles, a new backpack stove and fuel, a large cooler, a few other necessities, and maps of Arizona and New Mexico.

"Heading out? Where to?" the cashier asked.

"South, the desert."

"Make sure you take an extra can of gas and water if you're heading out in the desert very far. And tell somebody where you're going and when you plan to return."

She considered this and asked where would be a good place to get some gas and water cans.

"I'd try the farm supply store south on Highway 3. You'll see it, it's on the left side."

"Thanks." She paid and started to leave.

"Safe travels and have fun. Wish I were going," he said with a chuckle.

Jenny gave a dismissive glance back at the remark and left. She threw her new gear into the back, skipped the farm supply store and headed toward the Four Corners and Arizona.

CHAPTER 24

The vast emptiness of the Diné (Navajo) Nation swallowed her up, helping to clear her mind, her anger, her frustrations. Needing gas and a potty stop, she stopped in a little town called Kayenta. Curious about the interesting rocks she saw behind a ridge to the north, she asked a person at the gas station. He told her it was Monument Valley, that it was beautiful and she should go up there. But, having gotten a late start, she wanted to keep going. In the late afternoon, she stopped in Flagstaff for a break. Flagstaff was too big and busy, so she continued south on Interstate 15 toward Sedona.

Arriving in Sedona an hour later, she found a hotel and had some dinner in a Mexican restaurant. Afterward, she walked around the town, but after a while she realized she was simply walking and not paying any attention to anything except feeling tired, angry, confused, and afraid. She went back to her room and wrote in her journal about where she was, where she was going, and why. She then read until ten and went to sleep, dreaming about being somewhere in a place of red stone and meeting a strange woman who took her to a magical place where she saw herself as a glowing, rainbow-colored orb that flew over a spectral desert sea.

After waking around seven, she did some yoga and went for breakfast. The day was already warm with a bright sun soaking into the red landscape that surrounded the town. She was in a funk, feeling alienated, listless, lacking of energy and motivation, and she'd lost interest in camping. She walked the main street, letting her anger fester. She'd walked this street last night, but now she looked around. Even though it was Sunday, the street was coming alive with some stores opening for business. It was very much a tourist town with T-shirt and souvenir shops everywhere and shops selling rocks.

She continued walking, looking in shop windows, checking out a bookstore, but was feeling too sad and depressed to browse. Finally, she went back to her room and fell asleep, awoke and read for a while. It grew dark and, not feeling like eating, she crawled back into bed and lay there awake with her racing mind, telling her over and over again what a fool she was for ever trusting anyone.

Lying there, feeling sad and lonesome, she remembered the nice times she'd recently had with everyone, how happy she thought she was then. She thought of how pissed she was at Will and her brother and began to panic. She remembered the sleeping pills and antidepressants Joan had wanted her to have. She had them in her toiletries. As much as she hated drugs, she reluctantly took the prescribed dosage and went back to bed. Her mind slowly stopped running wild. She calmed down and fell asleep into a dreamless night.

Her funk continued the next day. She went out for breakfast and was starved from not eating the night before. After having eaten, she walked down the main street again and stopped in front of a rock shop that a woman had just opened up. She went in.

The shop had all sorts of rocks, tapestries on the walls, several shelves of books, and a display rack of incense and holders. Statues filled one area, one she recognized as similar to the Buddha at the yoga studio. She wandered about, curious about it all.

A forty-something woman with long dark hair streaked with gray, wearing a long, flowing, purple-pink dress, appeared from the back. "Hi, how can I help you? Looking for anything in particular?" she asked with a warm smile.

"Not really. Just looking. I was interested in your place since I've never been in a rock store before."

"Well, we have stones," the woman corrected her. "Are you familiar with crystals and the energy some stones have to offer?"

"Really? Ah … no, ah, not at all … don't know anything about stones or energy."

"Come over here and let me show you some things."

The woman took Jenny's hand and led her to the rear of the store. She showed Jenny a clear stone, about six inches tall and maybe two inches across the base. It had six sides and was tapered to a point.

"It's beautiful!" Jenny exclaimed.

"This is a quartz crystal, a very nice one. Now let me show you this." She handed Jenny a much smaller version of the same stone with a five-inch very light chain attached to the base and a small rounded version of the clear stone on the other end. She told Jenny to hold the round stone with the tips of her fingers with the pointed one hanging down.

"This is called a pendulum. Now hold it over this one I just showed you. Hold it as still as you can, and let's see what happens."

Jenny thought this was weird but, interested nevertheless,

she did as directed. Slowly the crystal on the end of the chain began to wiggle and then it started moving in a clockwise direction around the larger crystal on the counter. It moved faster in an increasingly larger circular motion.

"Oh, hon, it likes you. You make it happy. Look how strong the pendulum is spinning. That is a huge circle of energy. Here, let's try it on this one."

Jenny tried it and got the same circular motion, but it wasn't nearly as strong. She tried yet another, and the pendulum started going counterclockwise. The woman snatched it away. "No, no, no, not this one for sure."

"So this is all very interesting, but, so, why would anyone want a crystal? What are they good for?"

"Well, they can be used for healing, for focus during meditation, for clarity and help in making decisions, and they can clear bad energy from a space, just to name a few things."

"Hmm. Interesting. Very interesting."

"I also do readings and energy healing. Interested? I see some things in your aura. Are you having any difficulties with things from your past … or present, maybe?" the woman asked warmly.

Jenny considered this. As weird as all this was, she found herself feeling comfortable with and drawn toward this woman.

"By the way, my name is Amanda."

"I'm Jenny. Nice to meet you, Amanda. So what does a 'reading' accomplish?"

"Well, I can see areas of negativity that may need clearing or healing or both for that matter. I can help clear away bad energy that any issues might be causing, energy that might be blocking you. I certainly see some dark spots in your aura."

Jenny had heard about auras, energy fields surrounding the body, but never knew or heard of anyone ever being able to see one.

"So want to give it a shot? We can see what happens."

"This isn't like fortune-telling hocus-pocus or anything, is it?"

"No, not at all. It's just about clearing away negative energy."

"How much money are we talking about?"

"I have a reduced rate for first timers, so a reading and clearing will be seventy-five dollars. Also, I want you to have that crystal. It likes you, so I'll give it to you as part of the deal. Does that sound okay?"

"I guess so. What do I have to do?"

"Let me put up my Closed sign, and we'll go into the back room."

Jenny began to feel nervous about this whole thing; she felt her heart rate start to increase. It seemed a little too strange. But a moment later, when Amanda led her into a quiet room in the back of the store and lit some candles, asking whether Jenny minded incense, she felt a nice quieting warmth come over her; her heart rate slowed and her body relaxed. Something about Amanda made her feel relaxed.

"Incense? Sure why not?"

"I like it," Amanda said. "It helps clear any bad energy in the space."

Jenny's breathing became more relaxed and her busy mind grew quiet.

Amanda asked her to lie down on a long, padded table, like a bed, except it was higher. She got Jenny comfortable with a pillow and some support under her knees.

"Now, Jenny, just relax and breathe normal. I won't be touching you, and this won't hurt, I promise."

Jenny, already feeling relaxed, closed her eyes and felt a nice warmth wash over her. All was quiet for a time. Jenny knew Amanda was moving about. She never felt any touching, but somehow she sensed Amanda's hands moving above her, as if caressing her with energy. She felt herself calming down to the point where she was completely relaxed, her breathing slow, mind calm, like sometimes when she meditated.

Amanda said very softly, "Okay, Jenny, I'm seeing some sort of terrible trauma in your past, like a dark cloud that you carry with you. Would you like me to release this negative energy from you?"

Jenny, feeling so relaxed she could barely talk, mumbled, "Yeah, sure."

By this time, Jenny's breathing was so slow and shallow that it was almost imperceptible. She felt a soft lightness come over her, almost like she might float off the table.

Some time later, maybe minutes, maybe hours, Jenny had no idea, Amanda said very quietly and softly, "Okay, Jenny, we're done. Take your time, get up slowly and come out front when you're ready. There's no rush. Please excuse me. I need to take a moment to go and cleanse myself now. Come out front when you're ready." Jenny felt Amanda leave the room.

She lay there for what seemed to be a long time, trying to get some movement into her body. It was like she was paralyzed, but she also relished the total peace she felt and didn't want to disturb it. Finally, she was able to sit up, turn, and get her feet down. She opened her eyes, taking a moment to try to get some focus, get some bearing. She didn't know if she could walk. Her whole body felt like rubber. She sat for a few more moments to regain her balance, and walked carefully into the main store.

"Oh Jenny, there you are. Are you okay?"

"Yeah, I think so. I still feel a little fuzzy."

"You'll be fine in a minute or so. I found a lot of trauma

from your past and some recent. I cleared away all that I could and I did the best I could, but there was a lot of dark stuff. I gave you healing energy to your body, mind, and spirit. Whatever has been bothering you should be hopefully mostly gone, but there was a lot and might well be more. You might want to come back. Here's a bottle of water. Make sure to drink plenty of water today and tonight. Lots of water. How are you feeling now?"

Jenny took the water, opened it, and drank half the bottle. "Thanks. That helps. So what the hell just happened in there? It was amazing. I've never felt so relaxed in my entire life."

"Jenny, please excuse me for saying this, but I have never seen as much stuff as what you were carrying around. It was so stuck, but I managed to move it and hopefully got rid of it for you, at least as much as I could. If I might ask, did you have a bad childhood? Don't answer if you don't want to."

"No, it's okay. Yeah, my childhood … it wasn't the best. Pretty much sucked, actually, but wow, I can barely stand up, much less walk very well. I feel lighter, more open. Whatever you did, it was amazing."

"Thanks. It's what I do," Amanda said. "Just take your time. Sit for a while. I need to open the store back up. Excuse me."

Amanda returned with Jenny's new crystal, wrapped in tissue paper and in a little box. She explained how to work with a crystal, how to cleanse it with saltwater or exposure to the full moon, how to charge it with intention, and how to use it for healing and meditation.

Jenny asked about the pendulum. Amanda explained how to use it to help make decisions and detect negative areas in your body or aura. She talked about how Jenny needed to check every so often on what direction a "yes" might be to make sure it was clockwise or counterclockwise. Sometimes it changed, but most generally, a yes was clockwise. She explained how to track energy patterns in the body if and where negative, or positive, patterns might be. Last, she recommended a book to Jenny that explained everything in greater detail.

"I'll buy those as well, and I'll pay you for the crystal. You don't have to give it to me. I want to make it right with you."

Amanda started to protest, and Jenny raised her hand. "No, just tell me how much this all comes to."

"You're a tough customer. Won't take freebies. Okay. Ah, total comes to, how does one hundred dollars even sound? Okay?"

"I still think you are shortchanging yourself, but okay. Thanks Amanda. That was a great experience," she said, handing over her bank card.

"So are you going to be around a while?"

"I was planning on going out and doing some camping and hiking, some exploring."

"This is a very high-energy area. Energy vortices abound. Come here a second." She dug under her counter and gave Jenny a little stone hanging from a waxed cord. "Wear this. It will protect you from any negativity out there. There is some nasty stuff as well as the good. This will help."

"What do I owe you?"

Amanda held up her hands. "Nothing. Come back and see me before you leave the area. I'd like to see how you're doing, maybe do another cleansing if you want. I'd like to make sure I got all the bad stuff out of you. Okay? Promise me."

"Yeah, I'll come back for sure, Amanda. Thanks. I'd really like to see you again."

She smiled. "Thanks." And with that, Jenny left, feeling like a new person, like she could float down the street.

The weather was pleasantly mild during the day, but she

knew the nights were fairly cold, getting down to the thirties. Even though the nighttime temperatures were chilly, she felt a new surge of energy for going camping for a few days. With an updated heavier winter weight sleeping bag, she thought she'd be comfortable. She found a tourist information kiosk and talked to the attendant, asking her about where to go, places to camp, and things to see.

The woman gave her a detailed map and showed possible places. She gave her several brochures and a guidebook that covered the joys and dangers of back-country travel.

Jenny left and checked out of her room, then found a place for lunch since it was already well past one o'clock. She found a quiet café with outdoor dining, wanting to be outside in the warm sun. She ordered a salad and iced tea, and began to look through her new information, planning where to go.

The server came with her order. Jenny stopped her and asked her about vortices.

The girl replied, "They're everywhere around here. Where are you planning to go?"

Jenny showed her several options she was considering.

The girl pointed to a spot. "I'd go there. I've camped there a few times, and it's amazing. I had the most incredible dreams there."

"Like what?"

"It's hard to explain. You'll have to just go and find out for yourself."

"Okay, this might be a silly question, but, so, really, what is a vortex? Everybody I talk to here talks about vortices."

She laughed. "They're apparently high-energy areas in the earth. Sensitive people can read them and tell you where they are. I heard they're caused by energy lines in the earth, or 'ley lines' as the locals call them. I'm not sure, but I know when

I'm out there I feel different energy things. It's sort of weird. I'm from Arkansas, I visited here three years ago and never left. I love it here for other reasons as well, just generally a lot of interesting people, a lot of new-age types. Know what I mean?"

Jenny nodded. "Yeah, think so. Yeah, thanks. Been good talking with you. Thanks." She hadn't a clue, having no experience with all this energy stuff.

The waitress replied, "Yeah, have fun and enjoy. Nice talking." She turned to leave.

Jenny stopped her and ordered six sandwiches and a quart of potato salad to go.

She ate her lunch, got her to-go food, paid her bill, and left.

CHAPTER 25

She stopped at a gas station, where she filled up and got some ice for her cooler. Then a grocery store, for fruit, three one gallon jugs of water, and two bottles of chilled wine. She turned on her cell phone for the first time since she'd left and saw six calls and three texts from Will, four calls from Helen, and four calls and four texts from Joan She looked at Joan's texts first. They all said the same thing: *Jenny, please call me. We're all worried about you. We must talk.*

Will's read: *Jenny, I'm sorry. Please call. Where are you? I'm worried about you.*

After considering all three of them and realizing that it was Tuesday and she would be missing her therapy session and group, she felt she needed to call Joan. Also, she felt Joan was the one person she might trust.

Joan answered immediately. "Jenny, my God, where are you? We're all worried. Are you all right? What's going on?"

Jenny told her everything: where she was, how overwhelmed she felt about Michael. Then she told her about seeing Will's story outline and about the betrayal, the anger and the sadness she was feeling.

Joan responded, "I can understand how you must feel, Jenny. I've talked with Will, and he's really upset. He thought his outline would be a great surprise, but now realizes he should have talked with you first. You need to talk with him, Jenny. Please call. He feels terrible about all this."

"I'll consider it, Joan. Right now, talking with you is all I can do. I need a break for a few days. Tell everyone I'm okay. I'm on my way out into the desert to camp for a few days. I'll be in touch when I get back. Thanks, Joan."

"Be careful and please call Will, okay?"

"Yeah, maybe when I get back."

"Now, Jenny!" Joan said more forcefully.

"Yeah, okay, I'll call. Thanks again. I'll call you again in a few days." She ended the call. She didn't want to talk to Will but gritted her teeth and punched his number.

"Jenny! Where are you? What's going on? I've been trying to call you! We've all been trying to get ahold of you, wondering what's happened to you."

"Will, I am still really pissed at you for that goddamn outline I saw. I really feel betrayed by someone I trusted to, I don't know, just someone I thought I could count on to be honest and caring. But, but, how could you do that, Will? How could you? My life is my own fucking story! Not yours. For you to assume to think you can write about it just really pisses me off."

When she finished, he just said, "I understand how you can feel this way. It was wrong of me. I should never have done that without talking with you first and getting approval. We could have worked together on it, or maybe not at all. It was a bad idea. I was wrong, and I am deeply sorry. Please don't hold it against me. You're very special to me. It breaks my heart that I made you so angry."

Jenny listened and felt a tinge of compassion rising inside her. "I'm sorry too, Will. Maybe I overreacted, but with my brother and that mess, and then seeing your outline, it just pushed me over the top. I was feeling too overwhelmed and just needed to breathe."

"I understand, Jenny. I apologize for everything. Where are you? When are you coming back?"

She told him where she was and what she was planning but gave no indication of when she might return, because she hadn't a clue. She would be back when she was back.

"Take your time and please come back safely. Tell someone where you're going. Please do that for me, okay? Hopefully you'll be back here for Christmas so we can all be together. I am planning on having a big dinner."

"Don't know about Christmas. So Christmas is like in, what, three weeks? Right now I can't guarantee anything. And yes, I'll tell someone before I venture out anywhere. I see I have calls from Helen. Please let her know I'm okay. See you. Bye."

"I love you, dear, sweet girl. Be careful."

She answered with a flat, "Yeah."

She took several deep breaths, let the phone conversations disappear, and returned to the lightness and happiness she was experiencing before.

Not knowing anyone to tell where she was going, she skipped that detail and headed west out of Sedona for about ten miles. She found the road she was looking for and turned off onto a rough road she had to navigate carefully and slowly, avoiding the huge holes that were everywhere. About thirty minutes later, she got to a place she thought was where she wanted to be.

Finding an area well off the road, she unloaded her tent, sleeping pad, sleeping bag, cooler, and cooking gear and set up camp. She sat down on her little camp chair, poured herself a glass of wine, and thought about everything that had happened, especially her experience with Amanda. It was all strange, very, very strange.

Then she thought back to Denver, back to Durango, back beyond Durango, beyond, beyond. She suddenly realized none of it mattered: Peter, Michael, William, Helen, Joan, her grandparents, Dory, her father, the abuse, her whole past. It was as if it all were a dream of some sort, like her past was only an illusion. There were no demons, there was only emptiness. She remembered everything, remembered all the people, but she felt free of it all, like it was all there, but it didn't matter in her present state of being. She felt a little awestruck. Then she went back to what happened at Amanda's store and what she'd said: "I have never seen as much stuff as you were carrying around. It was so stuck, but I managed to move it and hopefully got rid of it for you."

It still seemed to all be there but just didn't seem important. She got out her new crystal and looked at it, handling it. It felt wonderful, made her feel good to hold it. Then she rewrapped it, placed it carefully in its box in the Jeep's glove box and locked it.

It would be daylight for another hour or so, so she went for a short walk through the rocks, scrub oak, and piñon, feeling joy at being in this place. It was different; she felt different. Her life was becoming different. She felt new, like the last few months and everything, everyone, had actually maybe made a difference.

Jenny went back to her camp and found a guy standing there, ragged, long haired, unshaven, and as best as she could determine, he was about her age. Her red flags immediately went up and waved in a strong wind.

CHAPTER 26

"Hey, this your camp? My name's Chris. Would you mind if I camped over there?" He motioned with his head to a place by a huge rock. "Don't want to be a bother or be in your way. I'll move on if you want, but this is a favorite spot of mine. Sorry about the way I look. Been out camping for two weeks."

"Yeah, hello. Knock yourself out. It's a huge place. I was just leaving as soon as I break camp."

"You don't have to leave on my account."

"I was leaving anyway. No bother. I have to get back." She busied herself with quickly breaking her camp, avoiding looking at him. She loaded her Jeep and within ten minutes left with that guy watching and scratching his head.

It was too late to find another spot to camp, so, frustrated and angry, forty-five minutes later, she pulled into the hotel she'd stayed at over the last few nights.

Over coffee the next morning, she started looking over her maps for other locations she might try, especially looking for places more out of the way. She sat for a while, writing in her journal about yesterday and about how afraid she'd been when that guy showed up, how she'd wanted to escape rather than hold her own. It was now close to noon and she had some time to kill, so she decided to go by Amanda's shop again and say hi.

She walked in and came face-to-face with the same guy who'd been at her camp last night. He looked just as shaggy as the night before.

"You!" she said, staring at him.

"Oh, hi," he said. "I remember you from last night."

Amanda appeared. "Hi, Jenny, you're back so soon? I thought you were going to be out for several nights. Do you know each other?"

Jenny stammered, "He came into my camp last night. No, we don't know each other."

"Chris is a friend of mine. Chris Holdsworth, this is Jenny. I'm sorry. I forgot your last name."

Jenny felt her cheeks flush with both anger and embarrassment.

He looked at her. "I'm curious why you bailed last night. You looked pretty well set up to just pull stakes like that. I'm sorry if I scared you off. I'm pretty harmless. Just ask Amanda."

Jenny looked at Amanda, then at Chris, not knowing what to say. The best she could muster up was, "A girl can change her mind, can't she?" With that, she turned and started to leave. "Good seeing you. See you later. I'm going camping."

"Wait up a minute, Jenny," Chris said. "I'd like to apologize for last night. Why don't you let me buy you lunch to make up for it?"

Jenny turned, about to turn down his offer, when she saw Amanda smile and give her a you-should-definitely-accept-his-offer nod.

Jenny considered the invitation another moment and said, "Yeah, sure. Why not." She looked back at Amanda, who smiled and nodded her approval.

Jenny didn't feel at ease with this guy. Even though he appeared to be a friend of Amanda's; she didn't really know Amanda either. But she'd be at a restaurant and wouldn't be alone with him, so she felt somewhat okay. She would do the best she could to survive this lunch.

They bid Amanda goodbye, left, and walked down the street to a café Chris suggested. Once seated, Chris was first to speak. "So, Jenny, where're you from?"

"Up by Durango."

"Durango? Been there. Nice town. That's the place with the train?"

"Yup, that's the place."

"So what are you doing around here? Come for some new scenery and warmer weather? Or are you another energy freak like I am?" He laughed. "I've hung around Sedona for the last few years. Love this place. Work with a landscaping outfit to support myself so I can spend as much time as I can being out here in this amazing place. It's like my home out there."

"I guess it's interesting. That's what I keep hearing anyway. I got into town a few nights ago and have already met some interesting people, starting with Amanda, the server where I had lunch a few times, and now you."

"Amanda? She's the best. She's one of the first people I met, and a friend. Man, she so helped me unload a ton of stuff from my last job. I worked in the Silicon Valley and was burned out at twenty-three. I don't plan on being a desert rat forever. Right now is my time, and I'm enjoying the ride.

"So what's the real reason you left so quickly last night? I'm really sorry. I would have just kept on going if I knew I scared you. I was headed back myself. Caught a ride in early this morning."

"Let's just say I haven't been having the best few weeks, and my nerves are pretty raw and on edge. And yeah, you did freak me out when I saw you there. Something just told me to leave. And I was pissed off that you showed up, but hey, it's a free desert."

The server came and took their order.

Chris continued, "Well, I apologize again. I'll tell you what. Let me get home, clean up, and repack, and I'll go out with you. I know this place really well and can show you all sorts of cool places, my present to make up for ruining last night."

Jenny knew this was something she definitely shouldn't do. Her negative reaction must have showed, because Chris said, "If you're still worried about me, Amanda will give me a good reference. I'll head to my place after lunch, and you can go and talk with her. If you still don't want to, I'll understand. It's just that it's not every day that I get to invite a beautiful woman out into the desert."

"Don't try to bullshit me with flattery. I don't put up with bullshit. Thanks for the invite, but I don't think so."

Not dismayed, he said, "Here, let me give you my cell number in case you change your mind."

Jenny hesitated, then said, "Sure. Why not." She got his cell number but avoided sharing hers. The rest of the lunch was spent in small talk, which Jenny hated. He paid for the meal and headed home to his place. Jenny walked back to Amanda's.

Amanda was waiting on a customer, so Jenny looked around her store at all the stones and other things she had for sale.

After the customer left, Jenny said, "Okay, Amanda, what's going on here? You're giving me those signals. Are you trying to be a matchmaker?"

Amanda laughed. "No, just helping things unfold as maybe they should. I see you and Chris being friends, possibly more. I see you both would get along well together. That's all. What do you think of him?"

"Well, he seems okay, I guess. I've never been really tuned into guys. He talks a lot. He wants to take me out camping and show me around, but I'm not real comfortable around men and don't want to go out alone into the desert with a strange man I don't know, and even if I did, I'd still be nervous."

Amanda nodded. "That's understandable, but I've known him for almost four years. I can honestly say he's one of the most genuine, sensitive, and kind men I have ever met." She smiled dreamily. "I wish I were twenty years younger. He's explored this desert for as long as I've known him, and he does know quite a few interesting places out there. He's taken me to several. It's up to you, but I'd talk to him, see what he has in mind."

"You seem to think pretty highly of him. Maybe you'd like to go with us. It'd make me feel more comfortable."

"I wish I could, but I've got the store and a lot of online orders to get sent out. I just can't right now."

"Yeah, I understand. Maybe I'll just head out by myself."

"Just go out for a few hours with him. No camping. He's a good guy."

"I'll think about it. Thanks, Amanda. I'll let you know."

"Good luck and hope to see you soon."

Jenny left and called Chris as she walked toward her Jeep. He picked up quickly. "Hello?"

"Hi, Chris, it's me, Jenny. I'm willing to consider your offer but only for a day trip. No camping. Can I meet you somewhere?"

"That'd be great. I just got out of the shower. Why not come by here, if you want? It's close, and I'll be decent by the time you get here. Here's the directions—"

"No, I don't want to go to your place. Maybe meet at the convenience store on the west end?"

He chuckled. "Okay, have it your way. I'll be there in about fifteen minutes."

Jenny got to her Jeep and went to the convenience store, but she didn't see Chris there yet. She began to panic, turned around quickly, tore out of the parking lot, and headed back into Sedona with her head down so he maybe wouldn't see her if they met on the road.

Back at her motel, she called Joan, who was tied up for the next hour with an appointment. The receptionist would have her call as soon as she was finished. Jenny got her journal out and wrote about her experience with Amanda and Chris, trying to decipher her feelings. She continued on about where she was and whatever it was she thought she was doing here. Why not just leave and go somewhere else, farther south and into the desert as she'd originally planned?

Forty-five minutes later, her phone chirped. It was Joan.

"Hi, Jenny, what's up?"

Jenny explained everything that had happened with Amanda and Chris and told her how mixed up and frightened she felt.

"So, Jenny, do you think this guy is dangerous?"

"No, it's not that. Amanda seems nice, and they're friends, and I like her. I just don't know what to do. And I don't even know why I'm concerned about this or even considering this. God, Joan, I just get so confused sometimes."

"I understand. This has been a hard few days for you, especially with Michael and all, but tell me this. What does your gut say?"

"My gut? It wants to go. He seems nice. He has soft, kind eyes and a warm smile. When he talks to me, he looks into my eyes. He knows a lot about the desert here and wants to show me around some of the energy spots, or vortices, as the locals call them, but my head says, no, no, no."

"Okay, Jenny, here's what I think. Obviously I know and understand your trauma and understand your fear of men in general. I'm not saying do this, but I think it might do you some good to go on a hike with him. Give it a shot. Keep it short. Sometimes our gut tells us to do something, and our rational minds think otherwise. You're at a place now where I think you could start exploring outside your fears. It might be a good thing, as scary as it might be, to start to break out of the cocoon you've had wrapped around yourself for so long."

"But Joan, what if he turns out to be a bad guy? I have no experience with guys. I don't know how to evaluate them, trust if they might be good or bad. I wish there was someone else who could go too. I asked Amanda, but she's busy."

"It's hard to evaluate anyone, especially quickly. It can take time. Sometimes we all face our fears and have to take chances. I had a fear of heights when I moved to Durango some years ago. I met some women who convinced me to go out into the high country to hike with them. Some of the trails were pretty precarious, but I survived, after crying several times. I still respect heights, but I broke through that fear."

"I hear what you're saying. I'll think about it. I was supposed to meet him, but I bailed out, couldn't do it. Maybe he won't want to now," she replied, half hoping that would be her way out.

"Has he called you?"

"I didn't give him my number."

"So are there any places you could go to that might have others out hiking as well?"

"I could call his friend, Amanda, and ask. See what she thinks."

"Think it over, Jenny. At least call him back and talk with him about it. You might want to explain your fears, not in great detail of course. Or just let it go if you would feel better."

"Yeah, I'll think about it. I'll let you know."

"Call me anytime. I mean that. Don't ever hesitate to call. Okay?"

"Thanks, Joan. How was I so lucky to connect with you? You've helped me so much already. Thanks."

"That's what I try to do. Be careful and call."

Jenny lay back on the bed and considered all Joan had said, then punched in his number.

"Hi, Chris, this is Jenny. We were supposed to go hiking. I sort of missed our date. I'm sorry."

"Yeah, I waited for you for a while and finally went home. Are you okay? Everything all right?"

"Yeah, I'm okay. Thanks. Maybe tomorrow, if you're still up for it. Is there any place we could go where there'd be other people? Maybe someplace close to town? I'd feel more comfortable until I get to know you better. Would that be okay?"

"Perfectly understandable. I know a place like that. Usually some others are out there, even this time of year. Maybe at ten tomorrow morning. Bring some lunch and water."

"Okay, ten then. At the convenience store?"

"This place is on a different road out of town. Can I stop by where you're staying, and we can go from there?"

"Only if I can drive," she said. If she drove, she would have more control. She told him where she was staying and felt the reassurance of her knife on her belt.

"Absolutely. I'll see you then."

Jenny lay back on the bed, considering what she was doing. Her head said, "Are you crazy? What are you thinking?" But her gut and her heart looked forward to the next day. The whole situation was confusing and made her uncomfortable. She went down to the hot tub and pool for a soak, then went out for a quick dinner and headed back to write more about the day.

Jenny rose early. She meditated, did some yoga stretches, and went out for breakfast. She checked her water and packed her day pack with some trail mix and protein bars. Then she took a deep breath and waited for Chris to show, which he did at exactly ten.

CHAPTER 27

When he got out of his old Toyota pickup, she noticed he'd cleaned up and shaved off his beard. He was actually a decent looking guy. He had long, dark hair, now in a ponytail, and he looked to be nicely built. She immediately compared him to Peter. Peter was okay, but Chris was more than okay even though he also talked a lot. She felt a little something happen deep inside, a little surge of warmth. While it was a good feeling, she chose to dismiss it.

"Hi," she said. "Ready?"

"Sure. Let's go."

They got into the Jeep, and he gave her directions to a place just a little north and west of town, then he directed her into a parking area with several other vehicles already there. Seeing them there made her feel better, but she had butterflies, not knowing whether from fear, excitement, or maybe a bit of both. They hefted their day packs on and got ready to go.

"So lead the way," Jenny said. "Show me your desert."

"Walk alongside me so we can talk. The trail's wide enough here. Again, I apologize for upsetting you, which I know I did. I know I looked pretty ratty that afternoon when we first encountered one another. I probably smelled pretty rank too."

"It's okay. I just wasn't expecting to see anyone else out there. I'm used to being in the Colorado mountains, where I seem to be able to avoid anyone else. You just threw me off guard."

"Again, sorry. So tell me a little about yourself."

For a few breaths, she considered how much she should share, then said, "Well, I keep telling myself I want to be a writer, but writers write, and I'm not writing anything at the moment, so I guess I'm presently being a desert rat or, in my case, a mountain rat."

"A writer? Me too. I graduated from UCLA five years ago. A double major, journalism and creative writing. I landed a job right after graduating, up in Silicon Valley, for a tech outfit. I was pretty excited, but after I found out my days were eat, sleep, and work with never a free moment, my excitement quickly faded. I literally spent all my waking moments in meetings, writing copy, and grabbing a sandwich at my desk. Granted, there were a lot of perks—a gym, meditation room, game room—but I never had time to enjoy any of them. They loved me, but I was burned out after my first year there, so I resigned. They offered me a lucrative offer to stay, which I considered, but I was dying inside … and out, for that matter. I looked at myself in the mirror, couldn't believe how sallow and gray my skin looked. I was gaining weight and was, I guess, just numb.

"I'd saved every cent I made from a good salary. My only real expense was rent, very high rent, and bus fare. I didn't own a car. So I got rid of what few things I owned except what would fit in a backpack and hitched east. I ended up here and never left. I love it here.

"I'm filling journals with notes about all my adventures,

the people, the quirkiness, the places, the desert. I'm working on it now, turning it all into a book, maybe several books of fiction. I've the plots set for several stories and numerous characters already outlined. I have the first chapters for my first one down and have been circulating it to various agents, have one that seems interested, but so far, nothing is for certain."

Jenny considered that he'd asked her about herself and ended up with it all being about him, but she tried to let it go. "Wow, Chris! I'm embarrassed that I ever said anything to you. I just can't seem to get anything going, no ideas, no possibilities, nothing. I'm a failure before I even get started."

"Now wait a minute, Jenny. Do you journal at all? Do you write down your thoughts, your experiences? People you meet? People you know? Things you see? Everything, anything, can be an influence for a story. Just build an arsenal of observations and experiences, and make some into some short stories. Short stories are a great place to start and can lead you to longer stories, even novels."

Jenny nodded. "I know what you're saying. I've told myself the very same things. But I'm always seeing everything as my own personal drama. I guess I've never thought anything I see or do as anything interesting or important story material."

"But Jenny, we are where stories come from, from our experiences, our view of the world around us, our own fantasies about that world, and the characters we create to populate our world. It's a lot of fun just making shit up as you go."

She laughed. "You actually make it sound fun. But I just get lost in my crazy reality and don't see how anyone would ever find it the least bit interesting."

"Yeah, I can understand, but you'd be surprised. I'm sorry I blathered on about myself way too long. Please tell me more about yourself. Tell me everything."

Jenny now felt able to continue giving him more information about herself but realized how little she wanted to share, so she gave him a short, guarded version of her history about growing up in California, going to college in Boulder, and living in Durango, skipping over anything about her problems. By then, they'd met several other people along the trail, making her feel more relaxed.

After hiking a few miles, she felt the total absence of any sound, no breeze, no animal sound, nothing other than the sound of their footfalls, her breathing, their voices, and maybe the far-off call of some bird. The desert was rocks and sand but alive with sage and piñon pine. After walking without talking for another mile or so, Jenny felt like she was almost in a meditative state.

Chris broke the silence. "Here we are at the place I wanted to have you see and possibly feel. I found it to be a pretty high-energy spot."

"One of the famous vortices?"

"You might call it that. Let's sit over there." He pointed to a flat rock alongside a low cliff wall.

Following him over, she sat with him on the rock. She looked out in a westerly direction over the vast desert until it ran into faraway mountains. The air was cool, but the sun-warmed rock made it comfortable to sit and bask.

"Do you meditate, Jenny?"

"Yeah, I have at yoga class and sometimes in the morning. Why?"

"I always like to sit and meditate at these places. It can be pretty amazing. Want to try?"

"Sure, why not? Then a little lunch."

Closing her eyes and taking a deep breath, she entered into a state of quiet bliss like she'd never had before. Her mind opened into a spaciousness of light; her breathing became shallow, and she simply sat in peace. Shortly, she had a very clear image of her being somewhere, like in a field of light, and dressed all in white. The vision faded and then there was nothing but emptiness.

She heard Chris's voice whisper, "Jenny, it's time."

She slowly came back to reality, blinking her eyes to what was, to her, a new, wonderful, beautiful day. She sat for a minute, bringing herself back into reality, then looked over at Chris, who was still sitting there with his eyes peacefully closed. She knew she'd heard his voice, but he was still far away somewhere.

She said softly, "Chris, it's time."

He wiggled a little and slowly opened his eyes, turned, and smiled. "How was that?"

"Nice, very nice," was all she said, remembering her vision.

Chris checked his watch. "Oh my, we've been here for a little over an hour."

Jenny raised her eyebrows. "Really?" It had felt like five minutes.

After a snack of protein bars, trail mix, and some water, they headed back to the Jeep.

"Thanks for bringing me here, Chris. It's beautiful. I don't know if that was a vortex, but it was the nicest meditation I've ever experienced. Usually my mind is racing, filled with a grocery list of thoughts. At that place, my mind just went completely quiet. I really loved it. Thanks."

"Hearing you say that makes me happy. We could go out again tomorrow."

"Yeah. Maybe." She silently pondered the request but didn't want to commit.

They spent the rest of the hike lost in their own thoughts.

On the way back to town, Chris asked again whether she wanted to go out again tomorrow, to which she responded the same. "Yeah. Maybe. I'll call you tonight."

As soon as she dropped Chris off at his truck, she left to go to Amanda's, hoping it wasn't too late to catch her. It was right at five thirty when she got there, and a Closed sign was being hung. She ran up and knocked. Amanda noticed her and unlocked the door, letting her in and then re-locking it. As always, being in a locked space made Jenny feel trapped and uncomfortable. She took a deep breath. "Can we talk for a minute?"

"Are you okay? Something wrong?"

"No, I'm fine, just confused about something that happened. Hey, I'm hungry. Can I treat you to dinner, if you don't mind my desert dust?"

"Don't mind at all, and that would be nice, but you don't need to do treat."

"I'd like to. Please?"

They left for a quiet restaurant Amanda knew about a block away. Out of the store, seated with drinks ordered, Jenny felt more comfortable and told her about the day with Chris and her meditation vision. Amanda listened quietly and seemed nonplussed by her story.

After she finished, Amanda said, "That's pretty cool, don't you think?"

"Not really. It sort of freaked me out. It makes no sense, but it felt so real. I'm not sure what I think."

"Well, Jenny, I deal in this sort of thing in my work all the time, among other things. But visions like that do have meaning. You were transcending all your problems and were in that state of perfect bliss we all, knowingly or unknowingly, are striving for, a place where there is nothing but pure happiness and peace."

"It was that for sure. It ended all too soon."

"I can understand. It's hard coming back to reality from a blissful experience like that.

Also, I've been thinking, and I see you and Chris may have a spiritual connection of some sort. I saw that when you two were together at the store. There are all kinds of connections, and there are many books written about them. I don't know whether or not you have much faith in this sort of thing, but I do. I've seen lots of things of this sort, and I think it might be good for you to explore that connection to whatever degree you might be comfortable with. Of course, it's totally up to you to do as you choose."

"I think I told you I'm not comfortable around men," Jenny said. "I was abused as a child, and I'm dealing with it all right now. It's like a festering sore that never goes away. I just get scared with new men, and women too."

Amanda remained silent for some time, staring blankly somewhere beyond Jenny. Finally she focused, put her hand on Jenny's, and said, "I knew there was something bad when I did that session with you. I'm so sorry. Is there anything I can do to help? Anything at all?"

"I don't know what. Whatever you did that first day seemed to make things different somehow. Things didn't seem so bad afterward. But it all didn't go away. It's still there."

Their food came, interrupting their conversation. They then spent their time talking more about themselves and their backgrounds as they ate. Jenny was always careful about what she shared with others, but she detected that Amanda was doing the same, glossing over a lot of her past. Once finished, Jenny paid, and they bid each other good night.

Back in her room, she cleaned up and spent the next hour

writing in her journal about the day and the strange things and people she was encountering in this strange place. Before she went to sleep, she called Chris and made plans to go back into the desert the next day.

CHAPTER 28

Chris took her to a new, more remote area, and, this time, Jenny felt more at ease with him. In some ways, he reminded her of William when they'd first met.

They hiked for miles on a trail that followed different terrain than yesterday, through some canyon areas where he showed her ancient petroglyphs. They chatted more about writing along with other topics about their lives and the stunning area through which they hiked. Jenny learned a lot more about him than he did about her. The trail ended back at the parking area about six hours later without any vortices or meditation stops.

Tired and hungry, they decided to have dinner together when they got back to town. They chose a Mexican restaurant and ordered drinks and food.

"So, Jenny, how long are you going to hang out here?"

"I don't know, maybe a few more days. I'm not wild about being back in Durango for Christmas. My friend, the guy whose cabin I live in, is planning a big deal, and I'm not really wanting to be there. Presents and all? I'm just not into it. I'll probably move on somewhere to camp, maybe farther south."

"Well, don't get me wrong here. I'm not trying to be pushy or anything, but I have an offer. I enjoy your company and would like it if you would hang here for a while. You could stay at my place. I'd sleep on the couch, and you could have my bed. I promise, everything will be on the up and up. I'm not trying to be too forward or anything. I'll respect your space and maintain a proper distance. We could do some writing and spend time in the desert, and you wouldn't have to pay for a hotel room. If you don't want to, I understand. Please don't think I'm being stupid. Maybe this all sounds stupid. I'm sorry. Maybe just forget it."

She thought of the talk she'd had with Amanda. "It wasn't stupid, Chris. Actually, it was a nice offer, but I'm not ready for a relationship. Aren't there any girls in this town you go out with?"

"There are, but they all want to get serious, get married and have babies. Or there's the opposite, others who just want to party all the time. I'm not tuned into either right now. But you're different, not threatening either way. You're just who you are, and you're fun to be with."

She smiled. "Somehow, I think that might be a compliment. I don't know. I'm not sure how to react to your offer. I'll consider it, but I don't think so. Okay?"

"Yeah. If you do, great. If not, that's okay."

Drinks and food came. They ate without broaching the subject again. They split the bill and Jenny took him back to his truck.

He left, and she went to her room and cleaned up. She found her two-piece that Kelly had insisted she buy, thinking about a soak in the hot tub, but, instead, she sat thinking about this strange journey she was experiencing, trying to make sense of it all. Chris seemed nice, and she felt okay being around him, but it was hard for her to trust him. And stay in his house? That seemed a bit too much. She decided to call Joan and seek her counsel.

"Hi, Joan, it's Jenny. I'm so sorry to bother you in the evening like this, but I need to talk if you have a few minutes."

"Of course I do. What's going on?"

Jenny told her everything that had happened since the last time they talked, including her vision. Joan paused for a minute, and Jenny could almost hear the wheels turning in Joan's head.

"Wow," Joan said eventually. "I wish you were here so I might read you better than long distance, but knowing you as I do, my advice is not to do this. If you like him, give it time. You don't need any more trauma in your life right now. The desert hikes you've been doing sound fine, but take it slowly. Okay?"

"Okay, I hear what you're saying. I will. Promise."

"When are you coming back?"

"Not sure yet. Maybe after Christmas."

"You know, Will is planning a big Christmas dinner."

"Yeah, but I'm really not into the holiday thing. Just as soon not be there right now."

"Well, I talked to him a few days ago, and he's hoping you'll be back by then."

"I'm sure he is. I'm still not sure how I feel about him right now, or even if I want to stay in his bunkhouse anymore."

"Jenny, I don't want to lecture you again, but you need to let that go. It was a misunderstanding on his part, that's all. He deeply regrets that he upset you. Call him again and just talk. Try to let your anger go. It's not doing you any good."

"Okay, maybe tomorrow. I need to let you go. I'm taking up your time when you need to be not working. Good night and thank you so much for everything. Can't wait to see you again and get back to the group session."

"You're being missed by everyone. And thanks for calling. It must be getting easier."

"Yeah, it is, sort of."

"Good night, Jenny."

Already after seven, she headed for the hot tub and slipped into the 104-degree water. It felt great to be soaking under the stars on a clear desert night. After about an hour, she dragged her tired and fully relaxed body back to her room. She lay awake with her head telling her she should bail out of Sedona and head somewhere else and be by herself. But her heart wanted to further get to know this man. Finally sleep came with dreams as confusing as she felt when awake.

The next morning, she awoke earlier than she wanted. She dressed and went for breakfast, still unsure of what she would do.

She called him after breakfast. "Chris, I'll head your way if your offer still stands."

CHAPTER 29

She found his little house from the directions he'd given her the night before. It was a small rustic cabin nestled in cottonwood trees by a creek. He answered her knock, opened the door for her, and escorted her in. The inside was surprisingly neat and tidy, other than the dirty dishes in the sink. In many ways, it resembled her bunkhouse, smaller, less modern, but with a similar layout.

"Welcome to my humble abode."

"Nice little place, Chris." She noted his writing desk with a laptop, yellow tablets, and a large china cup storing pens and pencils, and he had a lot of bookshelves. "You look pretty well read."

"Yeah, I read a lot, mainly the classics and a few recent authors who I like. Can I get you something? Iced tea? A beer? Wine?"

"Some tea would be nice but only if you have some made, or else just water."

"I'll make some tea then. It'll only take me a minute."

"Please, just water," she insisted.

"Okay, but I could make tea."

"Water will be fine."

He brought in glasses of water and motioned for her to sit. She sat on the sofa, and he sat opposite.

He said, "Do you maybe want to go out camping for a few days? Maybe tomorrow? There're some places we could go to that we can't really do justice in a single day. The weather's supposed to stay reasonably warm."

"God, Chris. Why are you so determined to get me camping in the desert?"

"Because I know you'd love some of these places I have in mind, and I ruined it for you the first time. I just feel like I owe you, like I want you to really enjoy more of the beauty and mystery of it. I want to share it all with you."

"Maybe. What about today?"

"It's a little after noon already, and I have to get myself organized if we're maybe to be out for three days."

Jenny felt rushed, but she did want to go out and spend time camping as she'd originally planned. Clearly Chris knew places. He's already taken her to some amazing spots. "Maybe. Let me think on it."

"You'll love it. I know you will."

Jenny began to feel uneasy being there. After fidgeting a little, she said, "I want to thank you for your offer, but I'm going to pass. Sorry."

"Where're you going? Can I come?"

"No! You can't come! I don't know where I'm going. I need to be on my own for a while. I'll probably go out camping like I originally planned."

"By yourself? I could come and show—"

"Yes. By myself. Thanks for everything. I'll call when I get back."

CHAPTER 30

She found a grocery store and replenished her supplies. Then she studied her map, headed southwest, found the backroad she wanted, and drove down it until she felt she could have solitude. It was already dark, and she set up her camp with the light of her headlights. She took a deep breath. It felt good to be alone.

After a glass of wine, her nerves began to quiet. No one was around. No hairy guys interrupting her space. She wrote in her journal for a while in the light of her headlamp, then crawled into her sleeping bag and fell asleep. She dreamed of her being the sole person left on the planet. No one was left to threaten or hurt her.

She spent the next two days exploring around the nondescript area where she was camped, then she moved on to another place farther down the backroad and set up her camp again. After roaming the desert for the next few days, she began to feel bored and lonesome. She missed seeing Helen and Kelly and Joan. She still felt pissed at Will, but that was subsiding. She thought of Chris. He probably knew some other places to explore that were more interesting than what she'd found.

She remembered the pendulum she'd gotten from Amanda. She rummaged through her things and retrieved it, then held it like Amanda had showed her and asked for a yes direction. It wiggled for a moment and began to move in a clockwise rotation. She stopped it and then asked about staying at Chris's place. It again wiggled for a moment and began to move in a counterclockwise rotation. The longer she held it, the harder and faster it rotated, a definite no. She then asked about camping with him and got a "yes." As weird as all this seemed, she felt better, more confident, trusting Amanda and what she'd just experienced. She packed up, headed back to Sedona, and called him from the convenience store.

"Hey, Chris, it's Jenny. I'm sorry I took off like I did. Would you mind if I camped in your yard tonight? And would you still be up to show me some of your haunts in the desert?"

"Jenny, hi, of course I would. Come on over. I was just starting to make some dinner and I'll make enough for two. But you can stay inside."

"Thanks, but I'll be more comfortable in my tent."

"Are you sure?"

"Yes, I'm sure. My tent will be fine but dinner sounds great. Can I bring anything? I'm right on the edge of town now."

"No. I have everything I need, so just come."

"See you in a few." She took her time driving out to his cabin, thinking through her decision. It seemed okay.

He answered on her first knock, "Hi. Great to see you again."

"Yeah, thanks," she replied. "I'll pitch my tent over there."

"You're welcome to stay inside here where it's warm."

"I'm sure I am, but all the same, my question was, can I pitch my tent over there?"

"Sure, of course. I'm getting dinner ready. Come in when you're done."

"Would you mind if I used your shower? I'm a little gamey after three days."

"No problem. It's the first door on the right." He pointed across the room.

Jenny emerged from her shower to a dinner Chris had prepared of chicken and veggie stir fry over quinoa. Jenny had only water while Chris had a glass of wine. She helped clean up and said good night and then left the warm cabin for her tent and cozy sleeping bag. Her dreams took her back to her days spent in the mountains and the freedom she'd believed she'd had back then. The reality of her life came with her waking at dawn.

Chris took her to some of his favorite haunts. The desert and some of the energy places he showed her made her buzzy. At two of the places, they stayed for a while and meditated together, without visions, just quiet, peaceful experiences.

They spent their time hiking and talked more about themselves, their thoughts about life, books they'd read and, of course, more about writing. Chris kept encouraging her to do at least a short story to see how it would go for her.

After another day together, Jenny realized she liked him and enjoyed talking with him. She found him as Amanda had said, genuine, sensitive, and kind. She actually was beginning to feel somewhat safe being with him.

One evening after they'd set up camp, had their dinner, and the sun had set, leaving a chill settling in, Jenny excused herself and went off into the dark to pee. She came back to find Chris ready to light a little pipe.

"Want a little hit? It'll help you sleep."

"A little hit of what?"

"Just a little marijuana."

"I've never tried it. What'll it do?"

"Just mellow you out, but no more than a little hit, especially if you've never tried it before. Okay?"

She considered it for a moment. "Sure."

He showed her how and handed over the pipe and lighter. She followed his instructions, then coughed and sputtered. "Gaaaak! That was harsh!"

He laughed. "Yeah, it can be pretty harsh the first time."

They each took another hit, the second being easier for her. He put his stash away and then looked at the sky. "Man, look at the stars, so beautiful, so clear, no city lights out here. It's so amazing."

She'd been so wrapped up in her chill that she hadn't paid attention, but now she looked up. "Wow, just like my nights in the mountains, so clear, so beautiful. It always makes me feel so small and insignificant."

"Truly so, but we're all children of the universe. We're not insignificant but an integral part of this wonderful creation we're part of, and we all participate in the constant creation and re-creation just by being who we are."

"I'm cold. I need my fleece jacket."

Returning a few moments later, she sat for a while, pondering Chris's philosophy. Starting to feel a little strange, very mellow but tired, whether from the marijuana or the hiking or both, she said, "I think I need to turn in."

As tired as she was, Jenny lay awake for a while. Eventually she heard Chris's tent zipper.

She started to giggle, considering the weirdness of everything that was happening, then she drifted off to sleep and dreamed she was flying. She looked down and saw herself sleeping in the tent. A silver cord from her solar plexus connected to herself in the tent. It was strange, but exhilarating. She could see the lights of Sedona. Then a larger area of lights appeared to the south. Prescott? Phoenix? Weightless, in total bliss, she suddenly felt fear. Maybe she'd died and this was what happened. She'd left her body behind. Suddenly the silver cord began to reel her in, like a fish, until she returned to her still breathing sleeping body. She awoke in a panic and screamed, "Chris. Help. Please help."

He was there in an instant. "Jenny. What's wrong? What happened?"

On the verge of tears, she told him her dream, of how wonderful it was until she thought she had died.

He nodded thoughtfully. "Have you ever heard of an out-of-body experience? I think that's what you might have had. Do you remember a silver cord? They connect your ethereal body to your mortal body. Your physical body was sleeping. It's hard to explain. Amanda would do a way better job of explaining this than I can. It was like your soul or spirit was free of your body and experiencing who we truly are. You were able to experience the freedom. Oh, man, I think I'm so screwing this up. I've had the same experience once myself. I was so freaked out. I hiked for twelve straight hours to get back to town. It was late, but I went to Amanda's anyway and woke her up. I was so freaked. She explained it to me and got me calmed down."

"Quit shitting me, Chris! Seriously, just quit."

"Jenny, please trust me. I am not shitting you. Please talk to Amanda when we get back. Please, for my sake anyway. I'm sorry I can't do a better job of explaining this to you. Just let it go as a bad dream for now and talk to Amanda when we get back."

She thought about it, but it was still an unnerving

experience. It had been fun until it wasn't. "I'll talk to her. Thanks. Right now I gotta pee again."

When they were getting things together for breakfast, he said, "Do you feel like a little drive today? We could head up to Jerome. It's a funky, old mining town hanging on the side of a mountain not too far from here. We could have lunch."

"Sounds fun. We can get some supplies and ice for the cooler to stay out a few days more. Maybe we should pack up and spend the night up there. Are there any hotels or anything?"

"There's the Miner's Hotel. I've stayed there It's rustic but really nice, sort of pricey. We could check it out. We could always camp if that doesn't work."

"I want to do some more hiking and exploring, but yeah, sounds fun. Let's do it."

CHAPTER 31

They packed up their camp and headed out on a mild sunny day to Highway 89A, then due west through the desert toward a mountain range and up a winding, steep road to the old mining town of Jerome. The quaint little town had narrow, windy streets, houses, stores hanging precariously on steep slopes, boutiques, antique shops, art galleries, a few restaurants, and the requisite T-shirt and souvenir shops.

Jenny and Chris spent the rest of the morning roaming various shops, coming to rest for lunch at an Italian restaurant. Some light food and iced tea later, they continued exploring shops and enjoying themselves, laughing and talking. They did some shopping at an outdoors store, each buying some new clothes. A short time later, they found themselves in front of the Miner's Hotel, and it was getting late, so they went in to book rooms. The only thing available was one room, a double queen suite.

They looked at each other, smiled, and nodded approval.

"Okay, with me," she said. "My idea. I'll buy."

"Oh, come on. We can split. I have some money."

"Then get a haircut and a shave."

"What? You don't like the way I look? I'm not that bad after only three days. That's harsh."

Jenny cracked up. "Giving you crap. Sorry."

He laughed back. "Yeah, I'm a bit scraggy. I hear ya, but I still want to split the bill."

"Well, okay, if you insist."

They walked up to their room, a spacious suite with great views of the desert floor below, a luxurious bathroom with a huge spa-size tub, and a minibar.

"Wow, this is pretty amazing. The lap of luxury," she said.

"Not too tacky at all," Chris remarked. "Hey, can I shower first? I'll be quick. Then I'll head out to a barber shop I saw and try to get a trim."

"Sure, go ahead. I'm planning on taking a long, hot bath."

Jenny threw her bag on the floor and fell onto the nearest bed, relishing the comfort.

Chris showered and put on his new clean clothes. "Back in a few," he said.

She reluctantly arose from the comfortable bed, went into the bathroom and started filling the tub. She threw in some bubble bath, got some of her new clothes from her shopping bag, took a bottle of wine from the minibar, went in, locked the door, stripped off her clothes, and got into the steaming, hot bath. *Yum,* she thought, as she soaked away the last few days. She soaked until the water started to cool, then toweled off and got dressed in her new, clean jeans and T-shirt. She emerged from the bathroom just as Chris came back, transformed with a haircut and a shave.

"For a desert rat, you clean up pretty good. You even smell good," she said.

"Got the full treatment."

They sat with a minibar wine each, enjoying the view of

the desert, and talking about how much fun they'd had.

"Let's go out and look for someplace for dinner. I'm getting starved," he said.

"Me too. Let's go."

The town was alive with Christmas lights. Festive groups roamed the streets. They found a restaurant that looked like it had come directly from the eighteen hundreds and went in. The interior carried the theme of the exterior, making them feel as if they'd stepped back into the time when the town and the Cleopatra Mine were in full swing—though more upscale, with linen tablecloths and napkins, crystal glasses, and full settings of silverware. They ordered a bottle of bordeaux, lamb chops and salad for Jenny, and steak and salad for Chris.

"This beats a tent and freeze-dried food any day," Chris said.

"Yeah, but it lacks the ambiance of the desert or the mountains, just being outside. I love the solitude, love being away from people. I feel safer, more secure."

"I like a balance of both really. I like being out for a few weeks, but then I'm ready to get back to civilization. I like my little cabin where I can write, where I can go into town for coffee, see a few folks I know, browse the bookstores, and eat some decent food. Even though I like camping in the desert, I like being warm and sleeping in a bed."

"Beds are overrated. I hardly ever slept in a bed over the last two years up until last October. It was just my tent, sleeping pad and bag. I miss it. I liked that everything I owned fit into my backpack. It was total freedom. Now I seem to be accumulating stuff, furnishing my little house, new clothes, linens, blankets, towels, a car. Where does it end? Our society seems to be so dependent on stuff. Everybody has too much stuff, way more than is necessary to live. Sometimes I want to just shed everything and go back to living out of my backpack again."

They continued chatting and drinking their wine. Their food came, and they enjoyed a delicious dinner. Finished, their table cleared, each ordered a dessert and an aperitif. After all that they were both stuffed and a little drunk.

They left the restaurant and walked toward the hotel. He reached for her hand, but she pulled away despite the nice warmth rising inside her.

It was getting late, and they decided to call it a night. They went to their room, fell into their beds, lay there, and giggled. Jenny felt alight with happiness, with a giddiness she couldn't ever remember having before. She really liked this guy. He seemed to take her as she was, and he seemed to enjoy being with her. There was no judgment. He made her feel safe. It was nice.

In a quiet voice, Chris said, "Jenny, I really, really like you. I think I might be falling in love with you."

She took a sharp breath; her mood changed in an instant, her whole body tensing. Her old demons flew out of the walls and circled around her like the merciless, black, awful creatures they were, laughing hysterically at her, taunting her. All her memories began to flash in front of her eyes. You can't ever love anyone. Nobody will love you, ever. You are damaged goods. You are worthless; you are a shameful, pathetic little slut.

She bolted upright and looked over at him. "You think you're falling in love with me! Falling in love … with me? Hah!" she spat out, continuing in a sarcastic voice, "Oh, Chris, thank you so very much. You are so incredibly sweet and wonderful and totally stupid!"

Then, in a more caring, serious voice, she apologized for her outburst. "I'm sorry. You didn't deserve that, you didn't. But please don't fall in love with me, Chris! I repeat, please do not fall in love with me. I haven't really told you the whole story about my crazy, fucked-up life; it's ugly, scary, not pretty."

Chris sat for a minute, then said, "Tell me, if you want to. I'm a good listener. I told you I'm not judgmental or critical. Give it a shot if you want. I'll just listen."

"Just forget it. Me? I'm just a fucked-up crazy girl who doesn't trust the world. A crazy recluse. Please. Just fucking forget it. Just let it be said my childhood was far from anything you could imagine."

He didn't say anything, but got up and stood staring out the window into the night. Then he turned to her, "Jenny, I can't forget my feelings for you. But I won't push. I'm sorry I said what I did. I didn't mean to upset you. There's no way, no way, I could ever imagine what you must have gone through to make you feel this way. But Jenny, maybe this should be your story. You have to write this. It could be therapeutic maybe. There are probably other women out there and so many more who need to know your story. Do it as a memoir or a novel. Do it third person. However you do it, you need to get this story out there."

She laughed at that remark. "You really think anyone would want to read this crazy shit about my crazy life? It's way too stupid and scary. Anyway, I just don't think I could ever do it."

"Yes, you could. Really. It would be a wonderful story. You can add characters or make it any way you want, as fiction. No one would ever know it's about you."

"Except for everyone who has ever known me." Her voice dripped with sarcasm.

"How long are you planning to stay in Sedona? You could come crash at my place. We can write. Do you have a laptop with you? I'll help if I can. Do whatever I can do to help you.

What do ya think?"

"Whoa, slow down, Chris. What the hell! One thing I do not fucking need is any pressure. I do not need fucking pressure right now. And I don't want to stay at your place. How is it you just said you wouldn't push? Please!"

"Wait! Wait! I'm sorry. I tend to get excited and go overboard. I'm so sorry. I can act pretty nuts sometimes. I'll slow down and shut up, okay?"

"Chris, you're a good guy, but I'm damaged goods! It's not a great story. The truth is, I'm unlovable. It's just the way it is. It is all fucking true! I can never love you back like you need to be loved. Never. Just don't. I don't know how to love anyone, so please don't. I just cannot be your girlfriend!"

Chris thought about all he'd heard. "Jenny," he said very gently and passionately, "please, just let go of your baggage shit. It doesn't do you any good. It doesn't make any damn difference to me. This is now. That was then. What don't you get about that? This is now, right now. This moment is all we have. The past is only memories. Neither of us can know what is in the future. There is only right now, this moment, this moment you and I are experiencing together. I've only known you for what, three, four days? Already I can't imagine ever being without you. You are amazing, wonderful. I love being with you. What don't you get about that? You're too hard on yourself. Please?"

"Oh, you make it sound so easy, like going and giving away your old clothes to a charity or something. You don't have a clue. It's not that fucking simple. You somehow presume that you have some sage knowledge about what it's like. You have no fucking idea. You have all these happy notions about something you have absolutely no clue about. Live in the moment? My moments are mostly living with the memories and with fear. Just forget it. I'm going to bed. We're outta here tomorrow."

The next morning she awoke and saw that he wasn't there. His bed looked slept in, but he and all his gear were gone. She shrugged, packed her gear, went down to the lobby and grabbed a banana and a coffee to go, then checked out and started out of town. There he was, with his thumb out for a ride.

She stopped and said, "Get in," and then headed back down the switchbacks toward Sedona.

"Jenny, I—"

"Please just shut up. I don't want to talk."

They rode in silence and arrived at his cabin. As he was getting his things from the Jeep, she said, "I apologize for being so hard on you last night, but you need to stop thinking you know everything. I'm working with some people who are smart and know what they're doing. Not some New Agey bullshit. Goodbye."

He was about to speak when she reached over, closed the door, and drove away.

Jenny pulled over at the convenience store south of town and looked at her map, deciding to follow her original plan and head south to the Sonoran Desert. She hit I-15 and headed toward Phoenix and Gila Bend.

Three hours later she stopped for gas at Gila Bend. She noted how quiet the old wind-swept desert town was and wondered what it'd be like to live there: few people, probably cheap real estate and few distractions. It would almost be like living in the mountains only with no winter. She'd be far away from everyone. With a full tank, she continued south toward Mexico through the towns of Ajo and Why to Organ Pipe Cactus National Monument.

At the Visitors Center, she found out she could camp there and decided to stay for a few nights. The area for tent campers was fairly deserted. Apparently most people were at home to celebrate Christmas. It was perfect.

She pitched her tent, then went for a short hike through the barren desert filled with tall Saguaro Cactus and many other cactus specimens, all of which looked both beautiful and scary with their sharp needles and thorns. Afterward, she sat in the quiet desert stillness, spending the rest of the day reading and with her journal. After a light dinner, she crawled in and snuggled in her sleeping bag, emotionally drained from the last few days with Chris. Dreamless sleep came easily.

The next week she spent in welcome solitude, reading through her journal, trying to decipher everything that had happened, her feelings along with exploring this mysterious uninhabited desert land of cactus, rattlesnakes, and scorpions.

Morning meditations stretched from the usual twenty minutes to over an hour some days. The quiet on the desert enhanced the quiet in her mind, giving her more clarity. In her empty space of surroundings and mind, Jenny tried to come to terms with herself. She remembered the dream she'd had of freezing in the snowstorm when she saved herself. The realization came that maybe, with her need to escape, she was simply running away from herself and needed to get back to the idea that she would need to save herself from the trauma of her life. But she also knew she needed help from Joan, from the group sessions, from Helen, and Will. She also had her grandparents and Kelly, and Amanda. And maybe Chris? Maybe not. Chris had been written out of her scenario.

One week extended into two weeks. She made a few trips back to the town of Why for supplies, but other than that, she maintained her hermit status. Then she had a very vivid dream.

She was out hiking in a barren desert, when she came upon what looked like a pile of very large, black, gray, and red-striated boulders that looked surreal and out of place in the otherwise flat, barren landscape. The boulders varied in height from maybe ten feet to some about twice that size. She walked around the maybe one-hundred-fifty feet circumference. It was like some giant machine had located them precisely or like they'd grown out of the desert floor.

She discovered a small space she could fit through and crawled into another world, a deceptively large space enclosed by the boulders. Some of the rock surfaces had strange writings on them, some crudely drawn pictures, and a circle of small stones sat in the center of the space. She felt strange and disoriented, but at peace. She sat, closed her eyes and was suddenly gone into another place, into a deep meditation.

She saw strange people, all in white, glowing like they were just light and nothing else. They gently, quietly led her down a glowing white corridor, slowly, like in slow motion. A woman waited for her. She looked just like Jenny, only older—maybe her mother. The woman reached out to Jenny, hands at arm's length, and looked deep into her eyes. The woman's gaze told Jenny how much she loved her, and that she was always with her. It was the most beautiful thing ever.

Then some dark, ghastly, scary entities appeared and circled around her. This woman, who Jenny thought was her mother, extended her arms, and something like electricity shot out from her fingers. The dark, horrible things evaporated.

The woman told her she would find someone to share her life with, that she would be a successful writer, and that her demons would die in the light.

The woman told Jenny she would always be with her, though Jenny may never see her. She bade her goodbye and disappeared into light. Then Jenny saw Chris, standing at a far distance, looking at her. She felt great desire and felt herself become sexually aroused.

She awoke with a start, seeing it was already light out. The dream was so real she had a hard time separating then from now. She struggled to reorient herself, feeling confused, happy, and still aroused by the last part with Chris. She took some deep breaths to calm herself, and decided to go back to Sedona.

CHAPTER 32

Her first stop was Amanda's store. It was shortly after ten and Amanda was just opening. "Jenny, hi. What's going on?"

"Do you have some time to chat?"

"Sure. Let me finish opening up first. Go grab a chair in the reading alcove." After getting the cash register set up for the day and a few things in order, she joined Jenny. "Mornings have been slow, so let's talk. I haven't seen you in a while. I thought maybe you'd gone back to Durango without saying goodbye. Have you been out with Chris?"

Jenny told Amanda where she was and the dream she had the night before. "I still remember everything, like it was really real. It was so vivid. I know that woman was my mother. She was beautiful. I was talking to her. She chased away my demons, and I felt so good and so free. I didn't want it to end. And then there was Chris and my desire for him. But I really went off on him." She told of the night in Jerome and what happened the day after. "I don't know what to think." She finished almost out of breath, her heart racing from sharing the recollection.

Amanda didn't respond for a few moments. "Let's talk

about the dream. I guess what you had is called a 'lucid dream' where everything feels real, like you aren't just observing but interacting in the dream. I've only ever read about them, never experienced one myself. Putting our perceived reality of existence aside, I would say that indeed, your mother was there, as were all the entities you encountered, the light beings as well as the dark beings. I would also say that the dark beings or entities, as you called them, were some of your demons that you've been dealing with, primarily the demons of your abuse. Your mother did annihilate them with her energy, with her undying, never-ending love for you. As an aside, we might talk about souls sometime but not now. Have you felt any different since then?"

Jenny pondered this, pausing to wipe a few tears. "I don't know how I feel. I'm just trying to sort it out. Really? You think that these demons might finally be truly gone? It seems too easy. My therapist would say that it was too easy, that I needed work to get beyond all my past crap."

"Yes, I believe you might be free of those demons, but the dregs, the scars, the memories of it all will still be with you, probably all your life. It's how you deal with those memories that will make the difference now. You can choose to let them dominate you, or you can choose to work on accepting and releasing them.

"I've worked with all this metaphysical stuff for the last twenty years and have seen lots of weird, crazy stuff. I've also heard many things from others. But I'm also a realist. You'll have to see how your life is or has changed … or not. Please, please do not give up on your therapy. Keep with it. From what you've told me, and what I saw when working on you, there's a lot of stuff you've been carrying, and you need to keep working on. I believe that the experience you told me about is a wonderful beginning. But, and a big but, pay close attention to your feelings and your life. Be aware. Be mindful. Use your pendulum, like I showed you, to help you with answers when you need them. Trust yourself. Trust your intuition."

As Jenny was trying to absorb all this, Amanda asked what her plans were. Jenny again went back to her time with Chris and her little breakdown after telling him everything and about how understanding he seemed to be, and how angry and dismissive she was of his feelings.

"Chris has never experienced anything like what you did in his life," Amanda said. "From what he's told me, he had a pretty normal childhood with good parents, school, and college. His parents weren't wealthy, but were comfortable and sent him and his two siblings to college. I'm guessing you gave him some comeuppance for his assuming he knew how to run your life. He deserved it. Are you going to see him again?"

"I don't know. After that dream I feel there's something we need to resolve." And, she thought, some physical desires.

A customer came in and Amanda excused herself.

Jenny sat for a few minutes, then went outside to call him. "Hey, Chris, it's Jenny. Can I come by and talk?"

"Yeah. Sure. I'll be home all day."

"See you in a few." She stuck her head back in the store and said, "Thanks Amanda, I have to go but need to talk to you sometime about something called OBEs. I'll see you later."

Apprehension built in her as she drove out to his cabin—more than apprehension; it was sexual desire. But in the back of her mind, something she couldn't grasp floated around just under the surface. She felt the desire, but there was something dark and foreboding surrounding it, like something deep in her memory.

He answered her knock and she threw her arms around

his neck and said, "Kiss me."

An hour later, they lay, spent, naked in his bed. Jenny lay there confused by her desire for Chris but not understanding at all why she'd just done what she'd done. A wave of shame rolled over her as she considered this new experience and found it to be not that exciting. It was a little painful, and then nothing so great. She didn't think it was horrible but, on the other hand, she didn't feel good about it and decided it wasn't anything she needed to do again. And there was that niggling thought bouncing around harder than ever in her mind. She wanted to take a shower.

Later, showered and dressed, sitting inside his cozy cabin with a cup of tea, Chris asked, "Do you want to talk about what just happened?"

"No. But I again apologize for being so hard on you, but as I said, Chris, you don't have a clue how to fix my past. It's gonna take more than just moving on. I have to deal with it, heal it, and that's going to take time and effort."

"I understand and I apologize for being so presumptuous. I just want to see you happy and thought I could fix it, but I see now that I was being overbearing and stupid. I thought a lot about all that the last few weeks, did some research and now see how some things like you've experienced need to heal, and it takes time. I'm sorry."

Jenny nodded. "Okay. Still friends?"

"I hope so after what we just did. Need more tea?"

She ignored his comment and slid her teacup toward him.

He poured more tea. "Remember I invited you to stay here for a while and the offer still stands. New Year's Eve is two days away. Why not hang out until after the new year? We can just hang out together. I'm happy you're here and don't want you to leave. How about it?"

Jenny thought for a few moments. "Well, I am wanting to go home. I need to see William, my landlord, mentor and one of the best guys I've ever known. I want to see my friends, and I've a lot to discuss with my therapist. The reason I left was that I got really pissed at William when I accidentally saw an outline he was writing for a story, a story about me, about my life! It blindsided me, and I was really pissed. He said it was a surprise. I realize now he meant well, but I guess I just had to get away to think it all through. He's really a great guy, and I truly love him, like a father.

"I don't want to get involved with you. I have such crazy trust issues thinking that everyone I meet wants something from me and is going to betray me and hurt me. I'm always on edge. I know it's all my own fears, and I need to understand that not everyone is out to get poor dear Jenny. But it's hard for me to reconcile. I just don't want to hurt you or get hurt." She stared off into space. "I do find it interesting that both you and Will are trying to get me to write about myself."

"I guess we both apparently think you have a story to tell. And, you know, I can understand that you might feel this way from all you shared with me. From what you've said about how you want to write but have no stories and can't get started, I think you're just blocked and maybe he thought his outline might help.

"And again, I'd like to spend more time with you, be together. I promise I won't hurt you or betray you. If things ever go sour, which I know they can in any relationship, I'll talk with you about it. I'll always be honest with you and I won't screw you over."

She thought on this for a few minutes. "I don't know. You talk about 'relationship.' I know nothing about being in a relationship. Maybe I can just hang out with you. And, yeah.

I think I'd like to hang out for a few days. New Year's Eve?"

"That'll be great. There's some of my friends getting together for a party in town. It should be a blast, and we can go if you want."

"I never celebrated New Year's before. It always seemed just like another night before you changed calendars. Let me think on it."

"Yes," Chris exclaimed, pumping his fist. "You can sleep in my bed. I'll take the couch."

She thought about sleeping with him and something told her to take the couch. "Thanks but I'll sleep on the couch. I'll get my sleeping bag."

She saw a look of expectation fade into disappointment. "I'll help you bring in what you need. We can go into town to the grocery store to get some supplies. I need a grocery list. What do you want?" He was excited and starting to ramble on.

"Okay, Chris," she said, not sharing his excitement. "Slow down. Give me a few minutes, and I'll be ready. I'll get what I need from the car."

"Sure. I'll see what's in the fridge. Be thinking of what you might want for food and drink."

Jenny went out to the Jeep and brought in what she needed. She unpacked her personal items and put them onto a bathroom shelf where Chris cleared a space for her.

Then they were off, planning the food list as they drove the short distance to downtown.

The next day, Chris needed to do some errands and Jenny wanted to see Amanda again. While Chris went to the bank and the bookstore to pick up a book he'd ordered, Jenny walked over to Amanda's store.

"You're back," she said when Jenny entered the store.

Jenny smiled. "I have some more questions for you. What

are OBEs?" She tried to explain what had happened that night.

Amanda confirmed what Chris had told her and that she herself had had such an experience a few years ago and wished she could do it again. "Things like that are not uncommon, especially out in the desert, especially this big, red, mysterious desert. From what I understand, an OBE can happen during meditation or when you're completely relaxed and open. So a little marijuana probably didn't hurt," she said with a smile.

"Thanks. This is really a strange place. I'm happy I came here and met you and Chris, but I'm getting antsy to get home where things are not so paranormal."

Amanda laughed. "We don't realize it, but we're always surrounded by the paranormal. But the paranormal becomes magnified in a high-energy area such as this. Some think the paranormal is completely normal while others, even some who visit here, are so tuned out they don't even notice anything but an interesting town surrounded by amazing scenery."

"I'm going to be staying with Chris until after New Year's. I really like him, Amanda, but I don't know love. I can't remember ever feeling love. I guess my grandparents love me. I guess I love them. But it's a different feeling with him, different from what I feel for my grandparents. I like seeing them and all, but it isn't the same feeling when I'm with them. It's nice but not the same. With Chris, it's different. Am I making any sense?"

"Yes you are. You have to understand that there're different forms of love. There's parental, like what you feel for your grandparents. Then there's passionate love for someone you want to be with, to share everything with. The latter would be what you're maybe feeling for Chris, especially now, in the beginning of a new relationship where everything seems new, alive, and magical."

"Alive and magical? I enjoy being with him. But love? I don't know. And there's another thing, he keeps pressuring me, just like my friend William, to write a book about my weird life and my crazy experiences as a child … and as an adult, I guess."

"I'd agree with him about the book. Write it. There are tons of self-help books written by professionals who try to help. But you're 'first person.' You have the story, the real story. I would encourage you to do it. I think there are many out there that could relate to it." She smiled. "What you've told me is very powerful stuff. Pay attention and stop and say goodbye before you leave."

"I absolutely will. Thank you. I appreciate you and your help. I'm going to be around until after the new year, so I promise I'll see you before I leave."

"I look forward to it."

The next morning she awoke on Chris's couch, wrapped in her sleeping bag. "Good morning," a smiling Chris said. "Bacon, eggs, toast? I got the coffee on. Hope I didn't wake you."

"No. I was awake and ready to get up. Coffee sounds good. And I'm hungry. Thanks. Back in a minute."

She appeared a few minutes later and went for the coffee, fully dressed for the day. She felt safe with him, but there was something not right. She sat down at the table, facing his back as he prepared their food, wondering what she was doing there.

After they'd finished, she helped clean up. Then she went outside to call Will. "Hi, Will, it's Jenny. How's things?"

"Doing well. How about you?"

"I'm doing great. I've been exploring the desert down here and loving every bit of it. I really wanted to call and tell you again that I'm sorry for the way I overreacted to that outline you did. I realize you're only trying to help, and I responded badly. And I'll be heading back after New Year's. I'm missing you all."

"It is okay, Jenny. I understand. I should have talked to you about doing that. And you're heading back? Great. I was beginning to worry you were gone for good."

"Well, there's this guy I met, and I wanted to spend a little more time with him before I come back. I like him. We've been roaming the desert together. He's a writer also. Between your and his encouragement, I've set my mind to start on a project. I think I'll be wanting to see that outline when I get back, unless you've burned it."

"Not a chance. It's still here waiting for you. I'll email it to you if you want. Do you have wi-fi somewhere so I could send it?"

"That'd be nice, and I'd appreciate that. Thanks. Hold on just a second … yeah there's wi-fi here, so just send it to my regular address."

"I'll send the outline as soon as I hang up. But I thought you and Peter—"

"Will, all I can say is that Peter hesitated a bit too much when I told him a little about me, like I was someone he'd rather not have to deal with. I couldn't handle that. I need someone who can accept me for who I am."

"I understand. He is a lawyer you know. And he'll probably be a good one who'll be sure to rely only on solid evidence."

Jenny chuckled. "Thanks, Will. I love you. See you after New Year's."

"I love you too, Jenny. Be safe."

"For sure."

She was on a roll and called her grandparents, letting

them know what was going on and where she was. She asked about Michael, and the report wasn't good. The assault charges from the women in Colorado Springs were very solid. DNA evidence linked him to the victims of his attacks. Then there was his altercation with her at the restaurant. Dean had contacted a good attorney, an ex-colleague in his old firm, to represent Michael. The best defense was going to have to be insanity. There was way too much condemning evidence against Michael.

"He's not doing himself any good either," Dean went on to say. "His bail hearing judge was a woman, who, probably rightfully so, denied any bail, saying he was both a danger to society and a flight risk. He went ballistic, calling the judge names I don't wish to repeat, screaming how it was all your fault. Ever since you were kids together, you caused all his problems, how he would teach you and all women a lesson. He then threatened to kill you. The bailiffs had to forcibly remove him from the courtroom. His attorney wanted to quit right then and there. It was hard, but I persuaded him to continue to represent him."

"It sounds like he has totally lost it. I've no idea why he'd blame me for all this. This is really scary!"

"I am sure it's frightening for you. Understandable, but he's locked up and will be until trial, which most likely won't happen until sometime in the spring at the earliest."

Dean asked about Peter, to which Jenny replied that things hadn't worked out without going into any detail. She didn't mention Chris. She again invited them to come to Durango in May or June. Dean said they were planning on it.

"Thanks for calling, Jenny. It is so good to talk to you. Thank you again for being in touch, keeping us up to date. We appreciate it."

"You're welcome, Grandpa. I want to apologize again for being out of touch for those years. I had a lot to sort out in my life and needed that time of seclusion. I think I'm able to finally be a good granddaughter, especially after all you've done for me. Without your help," she paused, choking back a sob, "I would probably be dead. I love you both so much."

"We're happy we could help. We love you too, Jenny. I have to go."

"Me too. Give Grandma my love. Call you soon."

And they clicked off.

Jenny stood there for a long while, pondering what Michael had said about everything being her fault. She had no idea why he'd think that. Then there was that small niggle which was now bouncing harder against the surface of her consciousness. There was something there, something hidden, like it was on the other side of a gauzy curtain, a thin barrier, existing just beyond her realization. She could almost feel it, taste it, and smell it, but it remained elusive.

CHAPTER 33

Chris received a big package delivered from UPS. He opened it, and there were four gaily wrapped Christmas presents along with a card from his parents. "Ha, I was wondering if my parents had forgotten about me," he said. "Only about a week late."

Jenny said, "Amanda mentioned that you have a brother and a sister."

"Yeah, I have an older brother and sister, who live in the LA area close to my parents. I was home last Christmas, and my mom and dad visited me here last summer. My brother and sister are almost ten years older, so we were never close as siblings. I told them I wanted to spend my off time from work here and in the desert and told them last month that I'd be staying here for this year's holidays. Of course, they were disappointed, but I told them I'd get to LA maybe next summer."

"Maybe I'll get to meet them all someday," she said, feeling a twinge of jealousy.

"I hope so. They'll love you if they think you might get me to settle down and quit being a bum."

"You're far from a bum," she said.

Chris getting a box of presents from his parents made her think of her friends. She decided to get them a late present. The next day she went to Amanda's store where she selected three nice crystal points, a smoky one for Will and two clear ones for Helen and Joan. She was about to go and pay when she thought of Kelly. She found another smaller one for her. She was missing everyone and wanted to be back home in Durango.

Jenny received Will's outline shortly after they talked, and it did give her some inspiration. It mainly laid out a rough timeline of her life, with few details. It would be up to her to fill in the blank spaces. If nothing else, it was a beginning.

She drummed up the courage to sit down with her laptop the day before New Year's Eve. She started the manuscript as a memoir but soon switched to a third-person narrative with different names, circumstances, and locations. Removing herself from first person helped free her up from being personally attached. This technique worked better for her, and the story started to flow. She was really writing! She did some revisions to William's outline as she went along and created each character's persona. Once started, she became almost obsessed.

Consumed with writing, she forgot all about New Year's Eve the next day. Chris interrupted her by telling her he'd made dinner reservations at a restaurant in town for a seven o'clock dinner before the party. Jenny realized she had no dress-up clothes to wear. She grabbed him and took him shopping to help her select a party outfit. After two boutiques, she found a dress. She couldn't believe she was really buying a dress, a little black dress, cut above the knees with a scooped neck and back with wide shoulder straps. Next came shoes, with sensible heels. And then there were some costume-jewelry bracelets and a faux pearl necklace.

She stopped by a beauty salon and made an appointment for the next morning and then took Chris to rent a tux, complete with a bow tie and patent leather shoes.

Morning came, and Jenny went off for a hair trim, style, and makeover, feeling like she wanted to be beautiful for Chris. She felt so much excitement, she could hardly contain herself.

Chris picked up his tux, and they were ready. Late afternoon they cleaned up, got dressed in their duds, and observed each other. They burst out laughing, simply because they both looked so great, and it was so incongruous for them to be playing dress-up.

"Oh my God, Jenny, you look so radiant, absolutely beautiful. You are stunning. I can hardly stand it."

"And you look so good I could eat you."

"Fine with me. Let's go and party."

She grabbed her down puffy jacket. "This jacket doesn't work very well with the rest of me, but it's warm and'll have to do."

Chris laughed. "You look fabulous. Not to worry."

They had a slow, relaxed dinner by candlelight with wine and quiet talk. After their chocolate mousse dessert, they left around nine thirty for the party. Chris had reserved a table for them with two of his friends and their dates, who were already there, seated, having drinks. Chris introduced Jenny and his friends to her, Carla and John, Amy and Bill. He worked with John and Bill at the landscaping company.

They were happy to see Chris after wondering where he'd been hiding out since they hadn't seen him for almost three weeks. He held them off with tales of his desert adventures and of how he'd met Jenny. Their attention turned to Jenny, asking her about herself. All she told them was that she was from Durango and had come here for a brief respite.

"So where're you staying?" Carla asked.

"Oh, with Chris," she replied matter-of-factly, noticing raised eyebrows. "Be assured, I am sleeping on the couch. We were hanging out and hiking. We went to Jerome for a night. Chris has been showing me the desert and his haunts."

"Are you guys together or what?" Carla asked back.

Chris interrupted the exchange. "Yeah, I guess we are. At least we're heading in that direction, I hope." He looked back at Jenny like a moonstruck teenager with a big, silly grin.

Amy said, "Wow, this is awesome … and fast."

Carla added with a chuckle, "So you snagged the illusive Christopher Holdsworth. Never thought it'd happen."

"Yeah, it's fast, we know," he said, "but it seems right, and we're going for it."

Jenny shot him a glance, and he shut up.

The music started, and people started to move to the dance floor.

The others got up to go, to the relief of Jenny, who didn't want to get into anything further on their relationship.

Chris took her hand. "Come on. Let's go dance."

She froze. "I've never danced. I guess I didn't know people danced at these things. I haven't a clue what to do and don't want to embarrass you."

"You've never, ever danced? No problem, it's not hard. This is a slow one. I'll show you. Just follow me. Come on."

She reluctantly got up and followed him out to the floor. She watched others move, noting how they held each other, and imitated what she saw.

"Now," Chris said, "just watch my feet for a second and then do the same, only backward. I'll lead you. Just listen to the music and the rhythm. Just feel the music."

After a few minutes, she found herself actually dancing. Chris was a good dancer, and he led her gently around the floor. She felt almost part of him, and the dancing felt good and natural to her.

"This is fun, Chris."

"You're a quick learner."

"You're a good teacher." She moved in close, her face buried in his neck as she'd seen others do.

The night went on with lots of joking, laughing, dancing, and chatting about local gossip. The women decided to go to the powder room, leaving the guys to chat.

Amy said, "So Jenny, how did you manage to lasso Chris? We've known him for the last few years, and he only ever dated someone once, maybe twice and that was it."

Jenny shrugged. "Well, as strange as it might seem, he appeared as a big, hairy guy at my campsite and scared the hell out of me, and I packed up and came back to town. I ran into him the next day in a shop I'd been in the day before, and he knew the owner and we got introduced. He felt bad and took me to lunch, and, well, you know, we've been hanging out ever since."

"So how's he in bed?" Carla asked, smiling, along with an eager-to-know Amy.

"What do you mean?" Jenny asked, feeling heat rush to her cheeks.

"You know. You're 'doing it,' aren't you?" Carla said.

"Doing what? You mean, having sex?" Jenny asked. "No, no! We're not! We haven't … just not." Sensing how uncomfortable she was, they let it drop.

The women returned to their table with Jenny feeling flushed. Chris looked at her with a questioning gaze. She sat down, took his hand and gave him a quick kiss on the cheek.

Midnight approached, and champagne was served to all the guests. A lot of folks donned silly hats and excitement built. Jenny felt herself being caught up in it all. She was having the time of her life.

Boom.

A loud report sounded outside somewhere, reverberating through the room. Everyone in unison hollered, "Happy New Year!" The band started playing "Auld Lang Syne," and people sang.

Chris pulled her into his arms and kissed her. "Happy New Year, you wonderful, sweet girl."

"Same to you." She put both of her arms around his neck and they shared a nice long kiss.

The party went on. After about another hour, Jenny told Chris she was ready to go home. He'd also had enough partying. They bid their goodbyes and went to the Jeep. Jenny, who'd had only water and a glass of champagne, drove home. They were both silent, lost in their own thoughts about the night.

Jenny finally said, "I like your friends."

"They like you too." He reached over and put his hand on her neck.

She responded by rolling her head to his touch.

They got to the house and went in.

Jenny grabbed Chris around the neck and kissed him. "Thanks. This was a wonderful night."

"You are so very welcome. It was my pleasure, and you deserved it. Thank you for being with me. It was the best New Year's Eve ever. I'm ready for bed."

He went into the bathroom first.

They hadn't had sex since that first afternoon, and after a bit of processing, she came to the conclusion that maybe sex could be good. It offered her an intimacy she hadn't experienced before. The night had amped up her desire for him, and she wanted to try again.

Chris was in bed and had already turned off the light when she quietly came into the bedroom and slipped in beside him, snuggling up next to him.

Chris rolled over. "What are you doing? Jenny, you're naked!"

"I know. I want to have sex with you again."

He sucked in a breath. "You seemed pretty uncomfortable after that first time, I didn't know how you felt. Are you sure about this?"

"It's okay, and I'm ready again, only more slowly this time." She took his hand and brought it to her breast. She shuddered with his touch, with anticipation.

She so wanted him and, trembling with passion, focused on the intense desire filling her body. Her thoughts went to Lady Chatterley, thinking about what she'd read about her passion, wondering whether this was what she'd felt, this intense need, a need to have her fulfilled as a woman. At that moment, there was nothing else in the world that mattered other than having Chris inside her.

He fumbled with his pajama bottoms and T-shirt. She moved an exploring hand to him and felt his erection. He moaned. He reached for the side table drawer, fishing for a condom, unwrapped it, and slipped it on. He moved a hand between her legs and felt her wetness.

"Oh God, Chris. Now, right now. Please, right now."

He rolled onto her and entered her. She could hardly breathe. With that first clumsy time out of the way, she tried to let herself go, to get into the moment, but her mind was getting in the way. That buried thought was there, interrupting everything.

Chris's body stiffened, and he drove so deep into her that she thought all of him was inside her. He breathed like he'd just run a marathon. But she felt nothing. She started to cry.

"Jenny, are you okay? Did I hurt you?"

"No. No, you didn't hurt me. I was expecting something, but there was nothing. I thought sex was supposed to be fulfilling or something. Pleasurable. But there was nothing."

"I'm sorry. I thought you wanted to do it."

"I did. Maybe there's something wrong with me. I don't know. I'm sorry. I need to go to the couch and go to sleep."

She got herself out of his bed, dressed and went to the other room and got into her sleeping bag. When she closed her eyes that same small niggle began teasing her brain. After a while the niggle quieted and sleep came with dreams of being lost in the desert without water or food. A pack of feral dogs chased her, and she became trapped in a cave with the dogs coming closer, sniffing, growling, drooling. She awoke with her heart racing and in a cold sweat.

She unwrapped herself from the sleeping bag and went for a shower to wash away the dream. Afterward, she made some coffee and sat, thinking of last night and how much fun she'd had until she got into bed with Chris.

She had to get out of there. Everything seemed off, and she wanted to be home. She was gathering her things when Chris staggered out.

"Man, too much champagne. I got a splitting headache."

"Did you take some aspirin or something? There's coffee."

"Yeah, took some Advil. And I need coffee."

He poured himself a cup. "Are you okay?"

"Yeah. I decided to head home today."

"What? I thought you're leaving tomorrow."

"I really want to get home. Anyway, I have an appointment with my therapist the day after tomorrow and want to get settled back in. I have a lot to talk about and need to see her. And I want to get back to the group sessions. I've missed too many and need to be there. And I'm starting to teach some yoga classes next week and have to get back into the groove. You could come up to see me."

"Oh, man, I'd love to, but I have to start work again next week. My boss landed this huge contract at some mansion on the edge of town. Some wealthy guy from San Diego just bought it and wants the whole area around the house xeriscaped. The previous owners had lawn all around like a freaking golf course. Took a zillion gallons of water to keep it green. This guy wants it to be like the desert. Probably going to be two to three months of work and good pay. I'm getting to a point that I need the money. Then maybe? I've been to Durango … liked it. Can you get back here sometime? Sometime soon?"

"My schedule's full between my therapy sessions and teaching yoga which I've never done before. I have a lot on my plate. You could find work in Durango."

"Jenny, this job'll set me up with money for a while. My boss pays me really, really well, and I need the money. I'm about broke. Our last job was over the end of October so I've been living on my savings, which are getting low. We can be apart for a little while. Just knowing we'll be together soon will be enough to keep me going."

"I don't know, maybe I could get back in a few weeks. But there's my brother. I haven't had time to process a lot of what my grandpa Dean told me was going on with him. I'm really worried about him. Please understand. It's hard for me to go, but, but I really need to head back."

She said the words, but wasn't sure about them. She knew she sounded cold and indifferent despite what she felt for him. She really wanted to be with him, but part of her wanted to be out of there, away from him.

She put her things in the Jeep, said a brief goodbye with a quick kiss, and then she was gone. She stopped by Amanda's store, but it was closed for the holiday. She'd send her a note of apology. It was about a six-hour drive, so she'd be back in Durango late afternoon. She felt empty, confused, and emotionally drained.

CHAPTER 34

After an uneventful drive, she turned into her driveway at three thirty.

Her little bunkhouse, her comfy hideaway, felt welcoming. She turned up the heat and unpacked her stuff. She held her new dress up to her breast, remembering every detail of the last few weeks. The crystal she set by her bed, then she called Chris.

"I made it home safe and sound. I wish you were here with me."

"Yeah, me too. My cabin feels empty without you being here."

"Let's try to talk often."

"We will. Promise! You've totally changed my life, changed it for the better."

"Yeah, me too. We'll talk tomorrow night?"

"Absolutely. Be well."

"You too."

They clicked off.

Someone knocked on her door. She answered it to find William.

"Hi, stranger. Welcome back. How are you? Missed having you around. So did Helen and Cat." The cat ran over and rubbed against her legs, happily meowing.

"Happy New Year." Will gave her a hug, which she returned, hanging on for a long time.

"Happy New Year to you."

"Are you okay?" Will asked. "Did you get the outline I sent?" After a pause he added, "Are we okay?"

"Yeah, I'm good. I did get your outline, and it is a big help. Thanks. And we are absolutely good. Your outline got me off my ass. I started and have written over a thousand words so far. Once I got going, it just seems to flow."

He smiled and hugged her again. "Congratulations, author."

"Thanks, Will. Thanks for everything. I love you."

"I love you too, Jenny."

"I missed you and all my friends here, but my trip was good. No, better than good, actually fantastic. I told you I met a guy. I really like him. We spent my time there together. I had some great adventures and experiences being in the desert. It was, like, mystical? Magical? That's as best as I can describe it." She turned and threw her arms around him. "Just hold me for a minute."

She broke away. "I have a present for you." She went to her bags and rummaged around until she found the crystal. "Hope you like it." Then she told him all about Amanda and her store.

He looked at it for a long while, wiping his eyes with his sleeve. "It's the best present ever. Thank you. I'll treasure it always."

"I'm happy you like it. I've never bought presents before and wasn't real sure." She went on and eagerly explained all about crystals to him, then suddenly said,

"Will, please hold me again for a minute. Please. I'm feeling something is wrong, very wrong, and I'm scared, and I don't know why."

CHAPTER 35

After a fitful, dreamless sleep, Jenny got up, did some yoga, and a short meditation. Then she went for a short run and then to her appointment with Joan, who greeted her with a warm hug and a, "Happy New Year. I missed you."

They sat and Jenny unloaded everything in vivid detail. Joan listened with her eyes wide, doing everything she could to keep her mouth from dropping open. Jenny finished by talking about her "niggle," that there was something very familiar and weird about having sex, and how un-meaningful her sexual experiences with Chris were.

"Jenny, you've left me speechless, and that is hard to do for me. First, I'm happy for you, I truly am. But are you sure about this Chris? It's only been like, what, three, four weeks? How're you feeling deep down? I understand the newness and the excitement of falling in love. There is a very wonderful high that comes with all the newness of discovering someone. And, let me add, that to love someone, you have to totally trust them. Do you trust Chris?"

"I understand what you're saying, and strange as it may seem, yeah, I do totally trust him. I like being with him.

He's considerate and supportive. He makes me feel secure, protected, and between him and Will, I've started writing. I'm excited to be actually getting words out."

"That's good, Jenny. It is. I just want you to be very careful. You're treading in new waters here; you're still very vulnerable. And what if you never saw him again? Would you feel so energized about writing?"

"Hmm, yeah, I think so. I wasn't going anywhere much with any writing until he got me going, along with Will's assistance, of course. Also, he accepts me, reassures me, and makes me feel safe and cared for. That's something I'm not used to, except from the few friends I've made here. But this is different. It's a different feeling from how I feel about everyone else, even my grandparents, even Will. I've told him a bit of my past, but no details. I'm not sure how he'll handle the awful truth of my past.

"I guess I have some things to think about. But what about this thing about sex that's rolling around in my brain that I can't grasp? It's so there, but I can't access it. It keeps haunting me, driving me nuts, like a dream you know you had and still feel its effect, but you can't remember the dream, only the effect it had. I just can't understand where it's coming from or what it is."

"That is interesting. There are such things as blocked memories, especially if there was any trauma involved. Have you ever tried hypnotism?"

"Hypnotism? No, I always thought that was some sort of magic trick or something."

"Not at all. Sometimes you can uncover blocked, hidden, or repressed memories, like possibly what you're experiencing. I believe from what you're telling me that there might be something you've repressed for whatever reason. If you want to try, I have a psychologist friend I've referred clients to before. I'll go with you if you'd like."

"Sure, why not? Anything to make it go away. It's always there, like right now, and it's driving me crazy. I want to find out what's there, to get rid of it."

"I understand. Let me give her a call, see when she might have time." Joan picked up her phone and tapped in some numbers. After a brief conversation about what she wanted, she thanked the person on the other end, and clicked off.

"She had a cancellation and is free tomorrow at nine?"

"Great. Where should I go?"

"Come by here at about a quarter to, and we'll go together. Mallory's office is a short walk from here."

"I'll be here at eighty forty-five. Thanks. Appreciate you hearing me out."

Jenny gave Joan her crystal, which Joan loved, then she continued to talk more about her Sedona experience until Joan's next appointment. They got up and had a goodbye hug.

Jenny stopped by to see whether Helen was in her studio, but she was gone for the day. She picked up some groceries, went home, and spent the rest of her day in front of her laptop, writing.

That night she used her pendulum to ask about the hypnosis. The answer was a strong yes. Then she asked about Chris and got another strong yes.

She experienced a deep sleep with dreams of unlocking doors and being very frightened by what she found. She awoke with a start, happy to have the dream gone. Cat was snuggled in with her reassuring purr.

She arrived at Joan's office at 8:45, apprehensive about what was going to happen and, what, if anything, she might uncover from possible repressed memories. They walked two blocks and took the elevator up to the third floor of a bank building.

Mallory Palmer, an attractive woman in her fifties, wearing jeans and a nice white blouse, met them in the reception room. Jenny noticed a big diamond on her left hand. The office had windows looking out to the west with abundant natural light. Walls were a pleasant off-white with photographs of the Animas River and posters of Durango events from previous years. Mallory seemed pleasant enough but all business. She took Jenny into a quiet room adjacent to her main office.

Mallory explained what she was going to do. "You'll be awake and alert. With my direction, I will try to bring you to a state of intense concentration and total relaxation. Once you get into a trance-like state of mind, with my help and guidance, we'll see if we can uncover what might be hidden in your subconsciousness. Once there you'll be able to talk to me without any reservations. Be assured, this is not a treatment that will erase any hidden issues, only uncover them, so you will need to continue to work with Joan. Understood, and are you ready?"

"Understood and … I guess I'm ready. Let's do it."

Mallory directed her to a straight-backed chair, pulled up another chair and sat facing Jenny. Once Jenny was seated, she told her to take a few deep breaths and relax.

Mallory held a pendulum in front of Jenny and asked her to follow it with her eyes as it swung gently back and forth, back and forth, back and forth. Mallory gently coaxed her to relax and focus, and soon Jenny felt herself relaxing into an altered state. For an instant she flashed on her time in the boulder place in Sedona, except this time she was awake and alert. Through questions and direction, Mallory led Jenny deep into her memory bank to see what might be buried deep within her psyche.

After establishing a basis, she asked, "So tell me, Jenny. Have you ever had sex before?"

After a long pause: "Yes, I have."

"Recently?"

"Yes."

"Was your first time?"

"No."

"When was your first time?"

"I was fourteen years old."

"Was it consensual?"

"No, it wasn't consensual. I didn't want it. I was forced."

"Who were you with that forced you to have sex?"

Another long pause, then she screamed, "Michael! My God, Michael. Stop!" She began screaming for him to stop, screaming, crying, screaming. "No! No! Michael! Don't! Stop! Please! Stop!"

Mallory snapped her finger. "Jenny! Jenny! Wake up! It's time. I'm here, and you're okay. It's all right. Michael isn't here. You are just remembering something from your past that you'd forgotten. You're safe."

Jenny's wild eyes regained focus. She looked around for a few moments and took some deep breaths, remembering. She screamed, "That fucking son of a bitch! My own fucking brother! That bastard. He fucking raped me, his own sister."

She let out a guttural moan and started sobbing uncontrollably, almost falling off her chair. Joan had apparently heard her and rushed in, grabbing her and holding her as she cried and screamed all at once, body wrenching with convulsing sobs. She beat on Joan with her fists. After maybe ten minutes, she started to calm down and relaxed into shuddering sobs. Finally she collapsed onto Joan, holding on to her like she was a life raft.

Joan motioned to Mallory that she could leave them alone. They sat there, not saying a word for almost thirty minutes when Jenny loosened her grip and looked up. "I feel tired. I need to lay down now. I need to sleep. I'm really tired … so tired." She started to fall asleep in Joan's arms. Joan got her onto a couch, covered with a throw and left her to rest.

Joan had to go back to her office, so she called Helen, who came in to stay with Jenny. Jenny slept soundly and quietly until almost noon, and then she woke with a start.

Helen said quietly, "Hi, sweetheart. I'm here with you."

"Where am I?"

"You're in Mallory Palmer's office. Do you remember anything about what happened?"

Jenny wiped her eyes. "What time is it? I remember being hypnotized. I think. Oh shit! Oh shit! What did I say? I think it was about Michael?"

Helen said, "Just a minute. I'll get Mallory."

She stuck her head out and called Mallory in. Mallory told her receptionist to call Joan and was in the room an instant later with a bottle of water. "Hey, Jenny, how're you feeling? Here's some water. Do you remember any of what happened?"

Helen excused herself and left, going back to her studio, knowing Joan would be there shortly.

Jenny thanked her for the water, opened it, and drank most of the bottle. The cold water helped her recover some more. "It was about Michael, right? It was him, right? He raped me, right? My brother raped me!" Her voice sounded hollow, as if coming from deep in a cave, but hard and mean with anger. "I'm remembering it all. It was him who walked with me into the forest that day. I didn't escape from him like I thought I did. He hit me really hard, and I remember that I wasn't unconscious but dazed from his fist. He ripped off my shirt and bit my breasts, ripped off my shorts and rammed himself into me. God, it hurt so bad. I was crying, screaming, asking him to stop, to please stop. Please stop doing this to me! I'm your sister!"

She stopped for a moment to get her breath from crying and talking at the same time. Mallory handed her some tissues. She took a deep breath and settled herself down for a moment before continuing. "All he said was that I was a 'a fucking slut' and deserved it. You should want to be fucked. You are just getting what you know you want. It's all bitches want. It's all any of you are good for, you stinkin' whore. All girls stink. I remember it all now so vividly. It hurt so terrible bad. He just kept ramming himself into me.

"'How do you like this, you bitch?' he said. 'You are just a stupid bitch.' He just kept saying that over and over and over. I think I passed out for a few minutes. I vaguely remember him jerking and having spasms, laying on me for a minute, then getting off and hitting me again with his fist. He told me that if I told anyone, he would kill me. He got up and walked away, just leaving me there. God, I hurt so bad. I hardly could walk back to the yurt. My face was bruised. My nose was bleeding. No wonder I always felt uncomfortable being around him. Maybe this is why he blames me for all his problems and hates me.

"He's totally crazy, Mallory. He's nuts and should be locked away. I'd testify against that son of a bitch at any trial in a heartbeat. Thanks for listening to all that. Pretty crazy, huh?"

"Not crazy, Jenny, not crazy at all, just very hard and sad. It was so very, very wrong what happened to you. And it's certainly not surprising that you hid that away in your memory for so long. Victims tend to block out such severe trauma sometimes, and what happened to you was very, very severe. You'll need to rehash all this again with Joan. She's here now and will take you back to her office. Are you okay to walk?"

"Yeah, I'm good. It'll probably get easier, won't it? I guess I've a lot more to work on now. So much seems to be coming back, like the proverbial floodgate has opened. Thanks, Mallory, thanks for everything. I hope to see you around, hopefully under better circumstances."

"You are most welcome, Jenny. I hope to see you too."

Jenny and Joan left. The day was bright and wonderful, but Jenny felt dark inside. She just wanted to float away with the south breeze blowing gently up the street and never come back. She took Joan's hand and squeezed it, holding it until they reached her office.

"I have time, Jenny, if you want to talk now. Or we can wait. There's no rush now. Apparently you've gotten through the hard part with Mallory. It's up to you."

"Let's do it now. I want you to know every shameful, ugly detail."

She sat with Joan for two hours, repeating everything she'd told Mallory. "And I remember I was bleeding and my face was battered. I went back to the yurt and Dory said, 'So what happened to you?' I was too ashamed to tell her what happened. I knew she wouldn't care anyway. I remember I told her I was hiking down a steep slope and stumbled and fell. She just grunted, 'You should be more careful.' I went and cleaned up and fell into my bed and slept until next morning. When I woke up I hurt everywhere, and all I could remember was that I fell down a steep slope. But I didn't understand why my bottom hurt so bad.

"Then Michael told everyone I was nothing but a fucking bitch slut, that fucked her own brother. I didn't understand why he was saying that. I knew I'd never had sex with him. From then on, I had no friends … nothing new; I never had any in the first place. All the kids there at the Farm laughed at me, taunted me, bullied me. I thought about suicide but was always too afraid. I just wanted to run away, to leave. The only place I could find any peace, any solace was in the books I scrounged. I was able to hide in the stories and fantasized my life into the stories. Then my grandparents found me and gave me a way out." She was crying softly by the time she finished.

They both sat quietly for a while, Joan evaluating all she'd heard. Jenny, whose mind had just stopped thinking, realized she was thirsty and hungry.

Joan finally broke the silence. "Jenny, I want to start seeing you twice a week, Tuesday and Thursday as before. And I want you back at group. There's a lot we need to work on after all this. No more trips for a while."

"I know. I promise. Do you think I'll ever get over this?"

"As I've said, you will over time, but there's a lot we have to do."

"Yeah, apparently so. Hey, I'm starving. Do you want to have dinner with me? I'll treat. We could call Helen."

Joan called Helen who said she'd meet them in ten minutes. They headed toward one of Jenny's favorite places, got seated, and ordered drinks. Helen joined them in a few minutes, and they avoided anything about the day, talking, eating, and imbibing, which Jenny did a bit too much of. Helen took her home with her. They sat up, and Jenny unloaded everything on her. Helen listened, and they both ended up crying. She'd completely forgotten to call Chris.

Helen put Jenny into her guest room, where she dreamed of how happy and grateful she was to have the good friends she'd found.

CHAPTER 36

January was over. With her life beginning to settle down, Jenny moved into a routine. She met twice every week with Joan and went to group on Tuesday night. As hard as it was, she'd shared her story of her rape with the group.

She found out that night that several of the women in group had also been raped or sexually abused, not by siblings but by their fathers or other family members, such as uncles. Her therapy was going well. She was beginning to heal about what had happened with Michael all those years ago.

Under Helen's tutelage she enjoyed teaching the three beginning yoga classes at the studio. It started slow, but she had more students coming to her class as weeks went on. She continued going to Helen's intermediate classes three days a week, still managing to get in some running.

She'd given Kelly her crystal, which made her cry, and they started running together every Saturday. Kelly got her up to the high country for some snowshoeing, which was pure happiness for Jenny, being in her beloved mountains.

Jenny told Kelly all about Chris and her time in Sedona together. Kelly was excited for her and couldn't wait to meet him. Jenny didn't share anything about Michael.

She managed to spend time writing every day. William reviewed her work and helped her, encouraging her.

She enrolled in the Mindfulness Meditation class, which met once a week for six weeks.

She hadn't heard from Chris since they talked after she got home over three weeks ago. She called him a number of times, but her calls kept going to voice mail. *Guess I was just another roll in the sack for him.*

One Tuesday after her session with Joan, Jenny went out for a run. By a few miles in, she felt great. Running always cleared her head. Her phone buzzed, and she saw it was Chris. She answered, heart pounding.

"Chris, where've you been? I thought you wrote me off."

"Aw, I'm sorry. I dropped my phone into John's hot tub right after we talked that day you got back. Fried it. Started to work on this project the next day, sunup to sundown. I just got to the phone store.

"My boss is under a strict deadline for completion and wouldn't give me two fucking hours off. Finally this morning, I went to work and faked being sick after lunch so I could leave for the afternoon. I'm really sorry. I miss you so much and want to see you. I got the new phone and saw all your calls. I'm sorry."

"I was worried. I thought you wrote me off as just another fuck," she said with a nasty tone in her voice.

"No. That is so not true, not true at all. Everything I told you is true. Please don't think that you were a one-time deal. I've never been as serious about anyone as I am about you."

"Yeah, I'm sorry. You didn't deserve that. I was just so damned frustrated and angry, not hearing from you after everything and our time together. So much has happened.

But, hey, I'm out running, and I'm cooling down and getting chilled. I need to get my butt going. I'll call ya tonight?"

"Yeah, for sure. Miss you." They clicked off.

They talked that night for over an hour. Jenny didn't tell him about the hypnotism or what she'd found out about her and Michael. She wanted to do that face-to-face. They talked or texted almost every night from then on.

By February the weather had changed from a bright balmy January to almost constant snowy weather, especially in the mountains. Skiers and snowmobilers were happy, but it seriously hindered Jenny's running schedule, so she was focusing on doing yoga, teaching, and learning.

The day before Valentine's Day, Jenny received a big box of chocolates and a beautiful card from Chris. She'd never celebrated Valentine's Day before and hadn't given it any thought. She called him, apologizing for being such a slacker.

Two nights after Valentine's Day, she went to Helen's class and it started snowing heavily. The roads were bad so Helen invited her to stay in town.

She dreamed she was naked, tied down with rope, spread-eagled on a table. There were thousands of Michaels lined up, taking their turns raping and beating her, calling her "slut bitch" and worse. She saw it as if she were above herself, watching. Then it all ended and Michael reappeared. He covered her with a blanket, cut the ropes binding her, and tenderly massaged her wrists and ankles with salve and lotion. "I'm the final one and will be the last. I'm sorry, sis. This is all over. I'll be gone forever. Now you can heal."

She awoke in a cold sweat, trembling and nauseous. She looked around, not knowing where she was. The alarm clock showed 8:20. She remembered she was at Helen's, and she'd be at her studio by now. She checked her wrists. They were fine, but she felt a knot in her gut. Something was wrong. Very wrong. She shook off the feeling, got out of bed, went to the bathroom, and washed her face.

On the way back to the bedroom to get dressed, she checked her muted cellphone and saw she had several voice messages, all from Dean. "Jenny, please call me. You need to call immediately." She thought one of them had gotten sick or worse. The knot in her gut was now becoming almost nauseous. She called.

Dean answered. "Jenny, thank God you called. Are you okay? Is there anyone there with you?"

"I'm alone. I just got up. Why? What's going on? Are you okay? Is Grandma okay?"

"We're fine. Please sit down, Jenny. It's Michael. It's not good. I'm sorry. It's not good at all, Jenny. They found him this morning. Oh God, Jenny, Michael committed suicide last night." His voice shook. "He somehow was able to cut his wrists and that's all we know."

She stood for a moment absorbing what she'd just heard and then crumbled to the floor in a heap, unable to breathe. Her phone fell from her grip. Her nausea grew. She crawled back into the bathroom and wretched into the toilet, but there was nothing but bile. She wretched and wretched until she collapsed on the floor. She lay there, whimpering, all her strength gone. All the joy, the lightness, and the power she'd been feeling were gone.

Thoughts rolled through her like a fast freight train: *I feel like everything inside me has been scrubbed out with a stiff brush, like my soul was scrubbed away. Maybe I'm dying. Maybe this is what dying feels like. It's really not so bad. All my life is really all a sham anyway. My brother raped me and told me I wasn't worth anything, soiled, spoiled. All his problems were my fault. Maybe*

I really did kill him. Maybe I was there and cut his wrists. I just want to die like he did.

She lay there almost like in a coma. She couldn't move, as if all her bones were gone. "No wonder I can't get up. When my soul left, it took all my bones with it," she whimpered to no one.

Helen came home a little after ten and called for her. Her Jeep was still outside. With no answer, she looked into her guest room and was starting to go back to the living room when she heard the whimper from the bathroom.

"Oh my God, Jenny!"

Jenny moaned, her speech thick and garbled. "Get away from me. Don't touch me. I'm a filthy, filthy whore. Don't touch me. Just let me lie here and die. That's what I deserve. I killed my brother, my twin. It's my fault. I killed him—" She trailed off and became silent, her breathing ragged and shallow.

Helen called 911, then got a cold wash cloth, went back to Jenny, and rubbed it over her forehead. She called Joan and told her about Jenny, then returned to wiping Jenny's face and forehead with a cool washcloth, trying to console for what, she had no idea.

"Oh, Jenny! Oh, Jenny!" was all she could say as tears ran down her face.

Jenny passed out, unresponsive.

CHAPTER 37

Around two thirty, Jenny came around. Joan was there with her and buzzed for the nurse.

"Hi, sweetheart. It's Joan. I'm here with you. You're in the hospital. You're going to be fine. Can you hear me? Can you understand me?"

Jenny nodded and looked over at her with sad eyes. After a few moments, she said, "I remember everything. Oh, God, Joan. He killed himself. My twin brother fucking killed himself. How could he just fucking do that? I think he took part of me with him. I feel so empty, just so empty of everything. I think I'm dying. Please hold me and keep me here with you. Please hold me. I don't want to die."

"You are not going to die. I'm right here with you."

The nurse came in and took vitals and said the doctor would be around shortly. Joan asked whether the others could come in. The nurse nodded. "Yes, but only for a few minutes." Then she turned and left.

Joan reached down and did a bed hug, holding her for a long time. Helen and William came in and did the same, trying to reassure her that she would be okay. Jenny appreciated it all but felt like she was drowning in an angry, dark, bottomless sea.

Helen had called Dean and Susan, who were able to catch an early afternoon flight to Durango and were arriving shortly. William left to pick them up at the airport and was back with them at the hospital an hour later.

They all left the room so she could be alone with her grandparents. Susan and Dean, each to one side, sat and held a hand, not able to say anything.

Jenny would stay the night in the hospital. Visiting hours were over, so everyone left except Joan.

"I'll be here with you tonight, Jenny. Since I'm your therapist, I'm allowed to stay. You should be released in the morning. Helen's getting things you might need."

Jenny gave a weak smile and said, "You don't have to—" and with that she fell asleep.

CHAPTER 38

William, Dean and Susan arrived at the hospital at ten o'clock the next morning to get her. When an orderly wheeled her out in a wheelchair, they noticed how haggard, frail, and pale she looked, like she'd aged overnight.

They arrived at William's compound where Dean and Susan would be Will's guests. Jenny went toward her bunkhouse, announcing that, after she took a shower, she was going to bed. Susan accompanied her. Dean went back over to William's house.

Joan came out to Jenny's around three thirty. She chatted with Susan a few minutes, then woke Jenny. "Hi, I see you're getting some rest. Do you have any questions for me? Do you want to talk?"

"Yeah, what are the drugs I'm taking? I hate drugs!"

"Just a mild antidepressant. Please take your dose as prescribed. It will help. Please. You'll need to take it until we see how you recover."

In a hollow unexpressive voice, Jenny said, "Recover from what? From all the shit that my fucking family has given me. I hate all of them. I actually feel glad that Michael is fucking dead. He deserves it. I hope my father rots his ass off in prison. And I hope fucking Dora dies of syphilis. I fucking hate them all." She stared blankly straight ahead, without facial expressions.

"Okay, Jenny. It's okay to feel angry—"

"Angry doesn't even fucking begin to cover how I feel. I've been so fucked over by all of them. They were supposed to love me and care for me, and all they fucking did was treat me like shit and rape me. I hate all of them!" Her voice rose, and she almost screamed, "I just want to go hide from everyone. How can anybody ever love a bitch slut like me?"

Joan placed her hand on Jenny's shoulder and just sat, not saying anything, letting her anger cool.

"Oh, Joan, I feel horribly empty, so lost, like my life is done, like there's just nothing left in me. I just want to go back into the mountains or desert. Things were easier when I was away from everyone and everything. I hate the way I feel. I hate it! Hate it! Hate it!"

"I cannot begin to understand how you feel. I've heard from so many women who were in the same place as you, and they've all recovered. Once again I'll say it, it's going to take a lot of hard work on your part, and I'll do everything in my power to help you, but it's going to be up to you. You're going to have to want to. I know it sucks right now, but it will get better. I promise. I know I keep saying that, but trust me, it will get better. I want you in my office tomorrow at nine for our session. Are you up for it?"

"What choice do I have? I'll get over this or I won't. If I don't, I'll be destined to live in the mountains and desert by myself for the rest of my life."

"You will heal. I promise. I'll get you through this. Please hang with me. You have a lot of people who really love you.

Remember that. Okay? Promise?"

"Okay then. I'll see you tomorrow morning. Let all the fucking fun continue," she retorted with sarcastic meanness in her voice.

Joan squeezed her shoulder, got up, and left. She met Susan on the way out and said, "Take good care of her. Will you stay with her at night?"

"Yes. Of course I will."

The next morning Susan took Jenny to town to her appointment with Joan. Susan left and went for coffee and did some shopping, but when she returned, she still had to wait for over an hour. Finally, Joan and Jenny appeared. Joan looked concerned. Jenny looked very drained and pale with dark circles around her red eyes.

She walked straight out to the front door. "Let's go, Grandma. Get me out of here!"

"I'll be there in a minute. Just wait for me in the car."

Susan went in to talk with Joan and asked what she thought about Jenny. Joan explained that Jenny had had a very abusive childhood, emotionally and sexually with no other specifics, and that her brother's suicide had exacerbated her otherwise tenuous condition which they had been dealing with since October. While they'd been making some headway up until now, this was a severe setback for her. Essentially, she couldn't handle any more and had simply had a nervous breakdown.

"She has borderline serious depression and is extremely fragile at the moment. She will need help and will need to have someone monitor her to make sure she keeps to a schedule and is taking her meds. She'll need a lot of tender love and care, no fawning or pity, but just wholesome genuine direction and caring."

Susan replied, "I'm planning on staying with her for as

long as she needs support. Dean's flying back to Denver and returning in a few days. He's driving back and will bring what I need for an extended stay. Jenny is now my only grandchild, and I'm going to do everything I can to help her to have a happy, normal life."

She left and went to the car. She found Jenny sitting and staring straight out the windshield, seemingly in a trance.

"Are you okay?" Susan asked, getting into the car.

"No. I'm not okay. Just thinking, Grandma, just thinking."

"Anything you want to share?"

"Yeah, maybe. Let's go and get some coffee, maybe sit and talk."

"Okay, where to?"

Jenny gave directions to Raven's. They got their drinks and sat down at a table.

"Want to talk about anything in particular?" Susan asked.

"I want to share everything with you, Grandma, if you want to hear all the crap that has been my life."

"Whatever you want to share, Jenny, I'll be happy to listen."

Kelly appeared. "Hey, Jenny, where've you been? Missed you at yoga." She started toward their table. "Are you up for our run on Saturday? There's a trail I've been wanting to do for a while. I have a couple of other people who want to go too. Hey, I just bought some new running tights. You've got to see them. They're really cool."

"Not now, Kelly! Not now! Please. Please just leave me alone. Just go away. Please just get the hell away! And stay away!"

Kelly held up both palms. "What the hell. Screw you! Please just excuse the hell out of me. Sorry. So sorry to intrude on your private space. I thought you were my friend. Screw you!" she retorted bitterly, turned, and walked away.

"Who was that?" Susan asked.

"Nobody, Grandma, just nobody. Sorry. Let me continue."

Jenny began telling her grandmother the whole story, her voice shaking, from her earliest recollections, including the sexual abuse, Old George, Michael, everything. It felt good to tell her grandmother her story and why she was in the state she was in. By the time she finished, she felt more in control of herself and stronger with a sense of some of the power she'd once had.

Her grandmother had sat stone silent, absorbing every word and pulling tissues from her purse to wipe her eyes. Jenny had talked for over an hour, capturing the essence of her living hell in California.

"That's about it, Grandma. That's my story. Nice, isn't it? What a fucking happy life I've had!" she said with a hard, sarcastic note.

Susan took a few deep breaths and sat for a long while. "I can't believe this, Jenny. This all cannot be true. It just can't be."

"Believe me, Grandma, it is, way truer than I want to believe myself. I've gone over this so many times in my mind and with Joan. And yeah, it's true … very, very true. I'm sorry to have told you all this. I'm really sorry. You were surely not prepared for it, but I wanted you to know."

"But Dory, your father, those other people. They were your family. They should have protected and nurtured you. I just cannot believe that Michael, that Michael—"

"Yeah, Michael, dear, sweet Michael. I couldn't believe it either, Grandma. I guess that's why I buried it so deep, so deep that I couldn't remember it myself. I'm sorry. I'm really sorry about him, sorry that he was so messed up, sorry to drop this bomb on you, sorry for everything. I'm trying to be a good person, Grandma. I really want to be a good person. I just want to be free of all this. I'm tired, really tired. We need to go. I just don't have anything left."

"I don't think I can ever understand all of this, but rest assured, we'll do everything in our power to help you, to help you heal from all this. I just can't imagine. Let's go."

When they got back, Jenny went into her bed and fell asleep, dreaming of being with Chris in the desert. Amanda was there. She did some sort of ceremony. A raven came and landed on Jenny's shoulder and whispered in her ear that she would find peace.

CHAPTER 39

Susan took Jenny to her next appointment with Joan on Thursday. Afterward, Joan pulled Susan aside and told her Jenny needed to get back on some sort of schedule with her yoga classes, running, and writing. And she told her to make sure Jenny made it to group next Tuesday.

When they got home, Jenny paced around the little house with restless energy. She knew she was making her grandmother nervous but just couldn't help the restlessness she felt, as if there were snakes inside her, trying to get free.

"Jenny, why don't you get out of here? You like running. Get out of here and get some fresh air."

"Yeah. maybe a little run would do me good. Yeah, I need to get out. It's a beautiful day."

She changed her clothes and went out for a four-mile run.

"I'm home, Grandma," she said on her return. "It felt great to move. Running always seems to help me clear my head. Thanks for getting me going. I'm heading to the shower."

"Good. We can plan dinner when you get out."

After dinner, she went to her bedroom and called Chris.

"Jenny, are you okay? I haven't heard from you. I've tried

calling you, but I just went to voice mail. What's going on?"

"I'm sorry, Chris, but to make a long story short, my brother committed suicide. Then there's the other shit I found out a while back too. I haven't shared any of it with you. I can't talk about it right now. Let's just leave it for now. I don't want to talk about it on the phone. I ended up in the hospital. I guess I had a nervous breakdown."

"My God. My God, Jenny, this sounds like serious business. I'm coming up tomorrow."

"But, Chris … your job!"

"Fuck my job! You're way more important! I'll quit. I'll find something in Durango. I'm packing up and will leave in the morning."

As much as she wanted him to, she replied, "Wait, Chris. There's really nothing you can do. I have so many people fawning over me right now, taking care of me, and worrying about me. It's almost a little much, really. I'm afraid you'd be in the way and frustrated. My plate is essentially full."

"But, Jen, I'm concerned about you."

"Oh, Chris, please don't be. Stay with your work till it's done. Maybe I'll try to get down there in the next few weeks."

"Yeah, okay, That'd be great. But I'm really concerned."

"I know you are and thanks. You mean so much to me, especially right now. Just talking to you makes me happy. I miss you so much."

"Yeah, me too. Let's talk tomorrow night?"

"Promise. Later." She clicked off.

She went to bed, feeling happy, and slept with dreams again of being in Sedona with Chris and Amanda.

Susan got her up early for her yoga class. "Why don't you join me this morning, Grandma? I can lend you some clothes. It'd be fun to have my grandmother in my class."

"I'd like to, but I'm not up for any advanced class. My classes in Denver are geared for people my age."

"Oh, come on, it's a beginner's class, and I'll be easy on you. There're several other women around your age that come all the time. I never expect more than anybody's able to do. It'll be fun. Promise."

"Okay, okay then. I'll come but you might have to haul me home."

"Naaaah, you'll do fine."

Susan smiled at her exuberance, seeing a little change for the better.

And so off they went. Jenny was gracious to Susan, helping her with some of the poses she wasn't familiar with. Susan liked the class and met several other women afterward, one whose husband was there with her. They all wanted her to join them for coffee. Susan declined, wanting to get Jenny home, but Jenny, overhearing, insisted that they go. She wanted to go as well. They spent the next hour having coffee, talking about themselves and getting to know one another. The group finally got up and said their goodbyes with Susan committing to be at class again on Monday. She and Jenny left for home.

On the way home, Susan said, "That was really nice, Jenny. You're a good teacher. And everyone there likes you. I'm so proud of you."

Jenny's heart swelled like it would burst. "Thank you, Grandma. That means a lot to me for you to say that."

They got to the house and made lunch. Afterward, Jenny excused herself, wanting to sit and do some writing in her journal, something she'd neglected ever since she heard about Michael's suicide. She spent most of the afternoon writing and trying to make some sense about her brother and their mixed-up relationship.

Friday and the weekend passed with Jenny working on her book, running, and enjoying Susan's companionship and care. Jenny, Susan, and William enjoyed weekend dinners together with Helen joining them.

Susan went with Jenny to yoga again on Monday. On Tuesday night, they went into town for Jenny's group session. Susan said she was going to the bookstore and then for some coffee or tea and would be back at eight thirty. Jenny went into the group room and took a seat. Several women were already there. The rest followed shortly, including Joan. And they began.

Jenny said she wanted to go first and started with, "Well, I found out that that my twin brother, who I told you about raping me when I was fourteen, committed suicide about a week ago … and it really sucks."

Everyone sat stone silent until Joan finally asked, "So … anyone want to comment?"

They all started talking at once, all wanting to express their concern for Jenny as well as relating to her some of their own stories of loss. After Joan finally got them under control, the night went on with continued stories of loss of loved ones. At eight thirty, Joan called for an end to the discussion.

Joan said, "Well, this turned out to be an interesting and very lively night. Thank you, everyone, for sharing and showing support. Any final words?"

Jenny, who hadn't spoken since she'd dropped the bomb that started it all, said, "Thank you, all. You're all my sisters and," she paused, choking down her tears, "you've all helped me realize I'm not alone. Thank you."

They all got up and had a huge, long group hug.

"Anyone want to go out for a drink and some munchies?" Juanita asked.

Shelly and Ann were game, but Mary and Barb needed to get home. Jenny and the drinks and munchies group left, found Susan, and went and had some beers, wine, coffee, and two plates of appetizers. They chatted about everything except what had gone on that night in group.

During the drive home, Susan said, "I really enjoyed meeting those young women. It was fun. I'm loving being in Durango; it's such a beautiful place, and everyone is so nice and friendly … makes me feel at home."

Jenny just smiled and said, "That's exactly why I love living here. This is a place where the energy from the desert and the mountains joins together. And it's good."

CHAPTER 40

Dean returned on Wednesday, driving his big black Mercedes, bringing everything Susan had requested and what he would need for an extended stay. Jenny was writing, and Susan was reading when he came into the bunkhouse looking for them. Happy to see him, they each gave him a long hug, then asked about his trip.

"I've news about Michael. The coroner completed the autopsy, and it was ruled a suicide as we suspected. I had the body sent to a mortuary for cremation and am having the ashes kept there until we can pick them up. I suppose we maybe should do a memorial service."

Jenny shrugged. "Why should we? It'd probably be just you two. I wouldn't go for sure. Dad's in prison; Dory's who knows where. Anyway, the idea of sending him off with anything other than disgust doesn't appeal to me at all."

"I understand," Dean said, "but shouldn't we do something?"

"Maybe simply scatter his ashes somewhere and be done with it," Susan added.

"We don't have to make a decision right now," Dean said.

"Let's all just think about it for the time being and figure it out when we get his ashes."

Dean camped out in William's guest room, and Susan continued to stay with Jenny. A routine developed for Jenny and Susan. Three mornings a week they went together to yoga. Jenny met with Joan twice a week as well as for group.

She continued to write in her journal, work on her book every day, and meet regularly with William, who went over her work with her. He liked how the story was developing and was editing and encouraging her along the way.

In the second week in March, there were still snowstorms in the mountains with chain laws in effect on the high passes. But the weather at lower altitude had started to warm enough that Durango and the north valley received rain. Daffodils, crocuses, and other cold-weather plants emerged from the winter.

Jenny began to feel better and more stable, and Susan moved over to William's. She, Dean, William, and Helen were becoming close friends, sharing time together as couples, going out to movies, concerts, and dinners.

Chris called her almost every night. She continued to put off getting down to see him, still feeling unstable emotionally. He wasn't going to be done with his job until April sometime. She wanted to see him as well as pay a visit to Amanda and decided it was time. Monday night, when she made her almost nightly call to Chris, she mentioned joining him for the next weekend.

The next day Jenny announced, "I'm planning on going to Sedona this coming weekend."

Susan looked concerned and said, "Jenny, I'm not so sure that would be a good idea right now. You've settled into a good routine, and maybe you should just stick with it for a while without bringing in an added distraction. A trip to Sedona? I don't think it would be a good idea at all. Have you talked with Joan about this?"

Jenny argued. "Thanks. I appreciate your concern, Grandma, and no, I haven't talked with Joan about it. But I want my to see my friend Chris, who I haven't seen since New Year's. I want to see him, and that's it. Period."

"Well, why can't he just come here instead?" Susan asked.

"Because of his work. We want to see each other. It's really important to me." She proceeded to tell Susan about her adventures with him, excluding the magical experiences in the desert and her sexual experience.

"Maybe I could go with you," Susan said.

"I'd love to have you, but it would be awkward since I'll be staying with Chris. His place is really small, smaller than the bunkhouse even. You'd be left to your own devices."

"Maybe Dean would come, and all of us could go. Dean and I could stay at a hotel and leave you two to do as you wish."

She called Chris that night with the proposed plan, explaining her "grandparent dilemma," saying that both of them wanted to come with her. Chris thought that it would be great if her grandparents came. He would love to meet them. They could have dinner together Saturday night and maybe do something together on Sunday. Jenny responded that she selfishly wanted him all to herself. Maybe dinner, but that would be it.

The rest of the week dragged on slowly for her. She told Joan of her plans at her counseling session, and Joan thought it would be okay as long as Susan and Dean would be with her.

They left on Friday morning, and Jenny found it pleasant to just ride along. She looked out on the stark emptiness of the Navajo Nation, and then at the tall pines south of Tuba

City, after which they drove to Flagstaff, and down I-17 to Sedona. She was filled with anticipation and dread. What if it was different? What if her time with him earlier had really not been as great as she thought? What if he really wasn't what she remembered? What if she really couldn't stand to be around him?

They arrived at Sedona and Dean found the hotel, where he'd made reservations. They had time to kill, so they went to a coffee shop. Afterward, they still had time, so they took a walk down Main Street. Jenny stopped by Amanda's shop, took them in, and introduced everyone. She asked Amanda whether she might have time tomorrow for a session, and Amanda had an eleven o'clock time slot that would work. After they left, Susan asked all sorts of questions about Amanda, including what the session was about, all of which Jenny answered vaguely with Susan finally giving up and dropping the inquiry.

Dean suggested that Jenny and Chris should get rooms at the hotel so they could all be together.

Jenny replied, "Maybe tomorrow night. I'll ask Chris, but if we do, we'll only want one room." That remark raised the eyebrows of both grandparents. "You might as well know. We slept together when I was here last winter. He's a very special guy, and I plan on being together with him as much and as long as we can stand each other."

"But Jennifer," Susan responded, "don't you think this is too sudden, too quick? You hardly know this young man."

"What's too quick, Grandma? He and I are both unconventional people living somewhat unconventional lives. And truth is, I know him far better than you can ever imagine. I really feel as if I've known him forever," she finished with an inward smile.

"Jennifer, it's just that you've been through so much and

are dealing with so much right now."

Jenny responded, "I know. I sort of told him some about what's going on now, but nothing else. I have to tell him the other stuff at some point. I dread the thought and what he might think."

"Yes you will. The sooner the better. Does Joan know?"

"Yep, told her everything, how I feel, that we had sex, and she seemed okay with it all. So—?"

Susan smiled. "I can't wait to meet this young man. Apparently, you're quite smitten."

"Totally, and it's time I head to his house. Will you take me?"

"Of course, let's go," said Dean, who'd been listening quietly to the interchange with a big smile.

When they got to Chris's house, he wasn't home yet from work. Jenny got out and grabbed her bag. "Chris works tomorrow, so we can go shopping and exploring in the morning. I want to see my friend Amanda at eleven, and then we can have lunch afterward and go from there. Can you pick me up here around ten? I'd like to go for a short run first."

"Sure. We'll see you then," Dean said.

She found the key under the rock and bid her grandparents goodbye.

Jenny went in and felt at home, everything was familiar, the books, the bedroom, the smells. She took it all in, savoring it all, both excited and nervous to see him. She curled up with her journal until Chris arrived around five thirty.

"Oh my God, you're here. You made it," he said as he walked in.

She ran and threw her arms around him, and they kissed. But she knew something was off, and the kiss she gave him was hesitant and cold. If he noticed, he didn't say anything. All her anticipation faded, leaving her strangely uncomfortable.

"Dinner? Want to go out for a bite?"

"Ah, yeah, sure, whatever's easiest."

He cleaned up from work and was ready in twenty minutes. They took his old Toyota pickup into town to a Mexican place, had a quiet dinner, and caught up on the last few weeks, mainly small talk. Jenny avoided the hard stuff.

Back at Chris's, he opened a bottle of wine, and they both sat on the couch, one on each end, facing each other to talk.

Jenny said, "Okay, ready for some more of the really bad shit?"

"Yeah, I guess. Sure, go ahead."

She told him everything that had happened, the hypnotism that brought up her rape, then her brother's suicide, her trip to the hospital, her therapy. Then she delved into her childhood, telling him every sordid detail.

Chris listened, not saying a word.

Jenny finished with a weak smile. "So there you have it! Wonder why I'm messed up?"

He sat for a few long minutes and finally was able to speak. "God, Jen … I don't know what to say. I'm so terribly sorry about all this. It's hard to wrap my brain around it … all this stuff. I can't imagine how hard it must have been, how hard it must be for you right now. It makes me feel, I don't know, numb, angry, sad."

"That's why I didn't want to tell you any of this on the phone. I've a hard time imagining it as well, that all this stuff keeps coming down on me. I think I might actually be done with having any more surprises, like all this recent shit that happened since I left in January. I'm feeling a little better and more in control of my life. Grandma's like a mother hen, and I'm afraid she'll never leave me alone again. She was reluctant to leave me here with you," she finished with a chuckle.

"I don't know what to say."

"Don't say anything."

Chris said, "I guess I want to say that this doesn't make any difference in how I feel about you."

"Just as long as you don't feel sympathy. I don't want sympathy. Okay?"

"Nope. No sympathy from me. No way! I promise," he said with a little laugh.

She knew he wanted her closer to him, to have her snuggle next to him, but she couldn't bring herself to do it. Thinking of being close to him made her anxious.

After an awkward silence, they moved away from that topic, and Jenny talked to him about tomorrow, about her grandparents' wanting to have dinner with them, about getting a room tomorrow night. Chris liked the idea as long as they'd be allowed to share a room. Jenny explained that she'd already set them straight as to sleeping arrangements. Chris said he would be off work at three o'clock and would meet them at the hotel at four.

They sipped at their wine slowly until Chris said, "I need to get going early and would like to turn in. Ready?"

But the very thought of him touching her made her skin crawl, felt repulsive. Jenny began to panic and knew she had to get out of there. With clipped words, she said, "I need to leave. I just cannot stay here. I'm sorry. I want to go to the hotel where my grandparents are. I can't be here. Either you take me or I'll call Dean." Panic rose in her voice. She was almost shouting.

"What? I don't understand. What's wrong? Did I do something?"

"No, you did nothing. But I have to go." She got up and

picked up her bag. "I'll call Dean to come and get me." She put on her jacket and headed for the door.

"Jenny? What's wrong? Did I say something to upset you?"

"No, no. You didn't say anything wrong. I'll call you."

"But I don't understand."

"Neither do I."

"Wait. I'll take you."

They rode in silence as Chris took her to the hotel. She said good night, no hugs or kisses, and went inside, leaving a confused Chris watching from his truck. She was able to get a room, and the first thing she did was call Dean to tell him the plans had changed and to call her in the morning when they were going for breakfast.

"Are you okay? You sound like you're scared. Did Chris do something?"

"No. He didn't do anything bad. I just couldn't stay there tonight. I needed to be here by myself. I'm fine. Really. Call me in the morning."

She had a troubled sleep with dreams of evil looking men grabbing at her and trying to touch her, staring at her with lust, anger, and hatred in their eyes. She awoke trembling to her phone chirping. She answered and told Dean she'd meet them in thirty minutes after she'd a shower, a cold shower.

Dean and Susan were seated in the restaurant when she arrived with her hair still wet. As soon as she sat, Susan asked, "Jennifer? What's going on?"

Jenny shook her head, trying to get her bearings. She caught a waiter's eye and said loudly, "I need coffee, please." Now her hands were shaking. "I don't know what's wrong, Grandma. I want to go home. I'm sorry. We shouldn't have come here."

"Did Chris do something to you?" asked Dean with a

tinge of anger.

"No. He was just kind and gentle Chris as always. I made him bring me here. He was as upset and confused as I was. I had to get away from him. I started to panic. I couldn't stay there. Can we go back this morning?"

"What about your appointment with Amanda?" Susan asked.

"I'll call and cancel."

CHAPTER 41

They rode in silence with Jenny lost in her thoughts and Dean and Susan listening to classical music. Dean decided to go on I-40 from Flagstaff to Gallup and then head north as an alternative route that would take them through western New Mexico. After about an hour of silence, Susan asked Jenny how she was doing.

"I miss him, Grandma, but I can't be with him. I don't understand what I'm feeling."

Jenny thought about Chris and wondered how his day was going. She was pretty sure it wasn't going well considering the way she left him last night, telling him, she couldn't be with him and to please leave her alone. She dozed off waking now and then to look out at the barren land of western New Mexico, as empty as she felt.

"I'm really liking it out here, Susan. I love the emptiness," Dean said as he was coming into Durango. "I think I might like to move here. We've talked about getting out of Denver. We've lived there long enough. What do you think?"

"I like it here too," Susan said. "It's so much quieter and easier than the city. Jennifer's here, and we've met some wonderful people."

Jenny, now fully awake, said excitedly, "It'd be really nice to have you here. Do you think you would really consider doing it? You've, like, been in Denver forever."

"Personally, I've been in Denver long enough," Dean replied. "I'm done with the firm at this point. Most of the partners would most likely be happy if I were farther away and not hanging around the office all the time, looking over their shoulders. Unless they need my advice on some case, of course. Then it's a different story. But I can usually get them straightened out on the phone or with a video conference. There's really nothing holding me there anymore."

"Maybe we should look at property then," Susan said.

"It'd be so great if you were here. Then I could have a real family for once."

They arrived at William's compound. William wondered what they were doing back so soon, after only one night when they were to be gone for three. Jenny explained that it was too soon for her to be doing any traveling and to see Chris. "I should've waited for a while. I thought I was up for it, but I guess I wasn't," was all she offered.

After William grilled some burgers, which they had with salad, Jenny called it a day. She slept deeply with dreams of her and Chris camping in the San Juans at one of her favorite places, a meadow covered with wildflowers: reds, yellows, whites, purples, magentas.

On Tuesday, Jenny met with Joan for her session and told her of her short weekend with Chris, her feelings of being repulsed by the thought of sleeping with him, even by just being there. "God Joan, I don't know why, but the thought of him touching me made me almost sick to my stomach. I had to get away." Then there was the dream.

Joan sat back, looked at the ceiling, then said, "Jenny, you were dealing with the sexual abuse as a child, but I think your discovery of your being raped by your brother, then his suicide has shaken you to the core and has made you feel extremely vulnerable, especially to any intimacy, so your rejection of any physical contact with Chris is understandable,"

"But I like to hug you and my grandparents. I like hugs from Will and Helen."

"Yes, but they and myself are safe. You had sex with Chris and didn't find it very rewarding as you told me. Your abuse as a child is one thing, but finding out you were cruelly raped is quite another. And now, knowing where any physical contact with Chris might lead, I can understand your reluctance. It's a new thing we need to address. It will take time for you to fully heal from everything you've experienced, so be patient. Don't rush. We'll work through it. Okay?"

"Yeah, Sure. Whatever you say. I'm just tired, tired of everything, tired of being angry, tired of being fucked up. I hate feeling this way."

"I understand. It's sort of like peeling an onion. There's all these layers. I'm thinking and hoping we may have stripped away all the layers now. Hopefully there are no more left, and we can now deal with what we know without any more surprises."

Jenny paused for a thoughtful moment, then said, "I can't imagine anything more. Hopefully there are no more. I think I have enough by now to last a lifetime. Do you think I might ever be able to have a normal sexual experience? Whatever that might be?"

"Yes, I certainly think so. Be patient, and we'll get there. Are you taking the antidepressant meds?"

"I am, as you advised. I hate them, but yeah, I'm

taking them."

"That's good. Please stay with them. The other thing I'm concerned about is PTSD. Are you having any thoughts about harming yourself? Are you sleeping okay?"

"What's PTSD?"

"Sorry, it's an acronym for Post Traumatic Stress Disorder. It can cause depression, anxiety, a need to harm oneself or lash out at others. Are you sleeping okay?"

"I think so, but some of my dreams are disturbing and scary."

"Okay. Any eating issues?"

"No. I have a good appetite."

"That's good, being active as you are is beneficial for dealing with anxiety and depression. I know you're angry which is totally normal. But do you feel like hurting yourself or others?"

"No, not at all. I love the people around me and would never want to hurt anyone."

"Good. If you ever think you might, please, please call me or someone for help. Promise?"

"I promise," she said with a wry smile.

"I'm serious, Jenny. Please don't think it's funny. There's been too many cases of people with PTSD acting out with aggressive behavior, even murder. It's not funny. With all you have suffered, it could be a possibility."

"I'm sorry. I can't comprehend ever wanting to hurt anyone."

"All the same, you carry a lot of anger and resentment. What would happen if you came face-to-face with your father or Dory?"

"I'd probably tell them what low-life bottom-feeding scum bastards they are and walk away."

Now Joan had to hold back a chuckle. "And you have indicated that you think the problems with Michael were your fault. What about his raping you?"

"No, I now realize his raping me wasn't my fault. I never did anything that would've warranted him raping me. He got caught up in circumstances beyond his control. I somehow managed to avoid becoming involved in the whole shit circus. But the rape and the bullying are still all on him. And, yeah, I am angry. I'm so angry it's hard to describe. I feel so much pain, betrayal. I'm pissed off that my life is being so crazy weird. I just want to be normal. Oh, Joan, this is all so much. I don't know what I feel anymore. Sometimes I just don't think I care anymore."

"I understand. But how about power? Do you feel powerless?"

"No. Right now I feel strong and in control … well, not really when I think about it, like not wanting to be touched by Chris. I just don't know anymore. After hearing others in group, their lives, their issues of abuse and drugs and whatever, I think of Dory. I keep wondering what her childhood might have been like. Was she abused and never had the resources like I and others have? I think of myself and where I might have ended up if not for my grandparents. Maybe I need to realize that Dory might have been a product of circumstances she had no control over, what she might have been like with different circumstances. Deep down, I can't completely blame her and want to forgive her. Am I making sense here?"

"Those are great observations, Jenny, and make perfect sense. I think you're ready to let her go. It was a bad time for you. Not being there, I can't say, but I'd venture to guess she had no hostility toward you. She was most likely operating with the poor skill set she had. To forgive her would be a big step."

"Thanks. I don't want to carry anger anymore, but there's my father and Michael. I don't know if I can ever forgive Michael or my father, for the matter."

Joan said, "From what you've told me, your father was suffering from grief from the death of your mother and didn't know how to grieve, drowning himself in alcohol and drugs. He was a product of circumstance. And Michael … the same can be said for him. Like you just said, he was a product of circumstances beyond his control. If you can look at these three individuals with that understanding and with compassion, you will have overcome a huge hurdle in your recovery. You can then forgive yourself for whatever guilt you might feel and come to realize none of this is your fault."

Jenny didn't respond, and a silence hung over the room. After a long few moments she said, "You're right. I finally see the bigger picture. It's just a bunch of crazy people who weren't able to make good choices and went down a different road, hurting people along the way, not realizing what hurt they were causing. It's gonna take me a while, but I think I can maybe really absorb all this and get on with it. This has been the best session we've had, Joan."

"It has been good. It may take a while, but I believe your path to forgiveness is now more clear for you. Stay with it."

With that, their time was up. Jenny went home to rest up for group at six thirty. Everyone was out doing errands. She spent two hours writing in her journal about her session. Then she went on about where she wanted to go with her life and how her new friends, her grandparents, and Chris all fit into the picture.

CHAPTER 42

Weeks went by, and by early April spring wanted to arrive, but the continuing cold coming off the mountain snowpack pushed it back.

Jenny had talked and texted with Chris several times a week. She kept trying to explain why she'd left so abruptly, but he couldn't understand why she couldn't just get over it. He desperately wanted to see her, but she couldn't deal with him right now. She was barely able to deal with herself.

He called one night and said, "Jenny, I can't understand why you're so distant all the time. I miss you and want to see you. I understand you had some trauma, but isn't it time you just let it go and get on with your life? Just live in the moment."

Jenny felt her anger rising. "You understand nothing. Nothing! You have no clue about what it's like … what it's like to realize you were raped … raped and beaten by your brother. No you wouldn't 'cause you're a guy. You have not a fucking clue. So don't give me that same line of shit you tried back in Jerome. You can live in your own fucking moment. My moments are filled with that memory. And 'just let it go'? Just let go? I wish it could be that easy."

She took a breath, and Chris interrupted, "But, Jenny, it's been a few months now. I miss you—"

Somewhere between crying and shouting, she said, "Go see Amanda. You need help." She clicked off, shaking with anger and wishing she could've slammed the phone onto a receiver. She sat for a moment, then stood and after several deep breaths, shed her clothes, put on her swimming suit, grabbed a towel, poured a glass of wine and wandered over to Will's hot tub to enjoy the soft pine forest glowing in the moonlight.

As she was relaxing and her head cleared from her anger, she realized how much anger she still held inside her, like anger was now part of her DNA. She didn't hear back from Chris.

Jenny occasionally saw Kelly at Helen's advanced yoga class, but Kelly made it a point to avoid her. Jenny didn't blame her after the way Jenny had told her to leave her alone. After one Friday's intermediate class, Jenny made it a point to corral Kelly and apologize. She begged Kelly to join her for a cup of coffee. Kelly frostily accepted. They walked in silence to Raven's and got some coffee, found a table, and sat.

"Kelly, I'm really sorry, so very sorry for the way I treated you. I feel like such a drama queen, but I've had so much shit dumped on me, and the time I dissed you, I thought I was losing any remaining grip I might still have on my life. Seriously. I was in a really bad place … still am for that matter. Sadly, you happened on me at a really bad time. I'm so sorry about what I said. You are the best friend I've ever had. Please believe me."

Kelly said nothing, and Jenny continued, "I told you about being attacked by my brother in Denver and that he was arrested and was in jail. What I was never able to tell you is that I found out through hypnosis that he actually raped me when I was fourteen. That was bad enough, but then he committed suicide about three weeks ago. All this shit in just over eight weeks.

"I ended up in the hospital in shock. I'd just gotten out when you saw me, and I was so awful to you. My grandmother stayed with me for weeks and just recently moved out of my house. I'm on antidepressants and been under close observation ever since. I am so sorry if—"

Tears ran down Kelly's face. "Holy shit, girl. Holy, holy fucking shit! This is so awful! Oh my God, I can't believe this. I had no idea about all this. This is all so fucking nuts. How're you doing? Are you able to cope? How are you able to cope? I cannot believe all this. I wish I'd known." She dug into her pack for some tissues.

Jenny, for once, wasn't crying. She reached across the table and took Kelly's hand. "It's okay, Kelly. I'm doing a lot better now after the initial shock. But I have to tell you. I went to Sedona before Christmas and connected with a guy. His name's Chris. He's such a great stabilizer for me. I think I might be in love, Kelly. I really do. I had no idea I could ever feel this way about a guy, ever."

"Wow, so what's gonna happen? Are you moving down there?"

"No, he wants to move up here when this landscaping project he's working on is done, probably in maybe two or three weeks. It all sort of makes me nervous, wondering how it will be with him around all the time.

"But we had a big argument the other night, and I haven't heard back from him. He thinks I should simply move on from everything, like it didn't happen. It did happen, and I'm working on it. He just doesn't get it and until he does, he can stay there."

"Wow. So what're you going to do?"

"Wait 'til he gets his shit together I guess. Until then I don't want him around preaching how I need to let it go. I've found out these things just don't go away. These traumas cling to you, like they become part of your DNA or something."

"I can't imagine or even come close to understanding how you must feel."

"It's hard, but getting better slowly. Even with his not fully grasping what I'm going through, I still miss him and want him here. Guess we'll see what happens."

"Where'll he live?"

"With me for a while, I guess. I asked him to, until he finds his own place.

Kelly said, "I'm sorry, Jenny, for the way I acted as well. Sometimes I'm too overbearing and too wrapped up in myself to pay attention to what's really happening around me. I shouldn't have barged in on you that day like I did. But I was so happy to see you. I'm sorry I didn't respect your space."

"It's okay, Kelly. You didn't know. How could you? Still friends?"

"Forever!" Kelly replied. "And I hope it works out with Chris. I'd like to meet him."

"Yeah. Thanks. We'll have to see."

The two of them chatted on for another thirty minutes. Then Kelly had to leave for work. They parted with a long hug, and Jenny committed to go trail running with Kelly on Saturday, depending on the weather.

CHAPTER 43

The days warmed, but the nights continued to be cool, and occasional snowstorms gusted in over the mountains, falling as rain in the lower valleys.

Jenny's therapy was going well. She was down to seeing Joan just once a week, hopefully moving soon to every other week. Group also was going well for her. She felt better and stronger and could feel her deep-seated anger beginning to release its hold on her and slowly being replaced with compassion.

Dean and Susan decided to move to Durango and made an offer on a nice Victorian on the pricey Third Avenue two blocks east of downtown. They called a realtor in Denver, put their penthouse on the market and already had two offers.

William had been helping her with her writing. One day when at his house, going over some ideas with him, she said, "Will, have you thought about writing another book yourself?"

"It's always in the back of my mind. Any ideas I have generally go back to the template I've made my living at, nothing very new or inspiring, same old stuff and same old formula. Did you ever bother to read any of my books? You've never said."

Jenny reluctantly responded, "Yes, I have, part of one anyway."

"So what did you think? Honest opinion."

"I'm sorry, Will, but to be honest, I wasn't much impressed. I'm far from any sort of literary critic, but what I read, well, it was well written, but the story, it was just all fluff. Pretty inane, to say the least. I'm sorry."

William sat there for a minute, thinking, finally saying, "Thank you for being honest. I know exactly what you're saying. I guess I was able to help you get over your block, but I can't do it for myself."

"So maybe I should write a 'secret' outline for you?" she said with a coy smile.

"Touché. I deserved that."

Jenny laughed. "Sorry, but I couldn't resist; it was too easy. But seriously, is there anything I can do to help? Maybe you should write another romance, but take it in a different, more serious direction. Maybe incorporate some sort of self-discovery along the way. Maybe a road trip. Did you ever read *Zen and the Art of Motorcycle Maintenance* by some guy, let me think, yeah, it was Robert Pirsig, I think. I can look it up. But it was about a road trip with his son and another couple from Minnesota to California. There were a number of intertwining plots along the way plus a discourse on quality versus quantity, as I recall."

"I've not read it. Do you have a copy?"

"You're in luck, because I still have mine from when I was in college. It wasn't an assigned reading. Just one I happened to come across, took me three readings to get it. But I thought it was brilliant. I'll find it and lend it to you."

He thanked her, and they moved back to reviewing her writing.

Life was rapidly changing for Jenny. Chris had called back a week after their blowup, eating humble pie. He'd gone to see Amanda and told her what had happened, and she apparently raked him over the coals for being so stupid and insensitive. He was finally beginning to understand the trauma and gravity of what Jenny had experienced.

On that Saturday Jenny went on her first trail run with Kelly, and loved the freedom of running on the hilly challenging trails around Durango. There were miles and miles of single track and hiking trails all around the town, all waiting for her to explore.

A week later, after their second Saturday run, while having a beer at one of the brewpubs, Jenny said, "Kelly, thanks for getting me out on these trails. I love it."

"Yeah, I know just how you feel. That's why I do it. I'm just happy we're running buddies and friends. I like sharing time with you. Thanks."

"And I thank you. You're really a very special friend and a confidante, I might add. My first-ever girlfriend."

Chris called the next day. "Good news, we're wrapping up this job in about two weeks and I plan on heading your way. I'm getting excited now."

Anxiety washed over Jenny. "That's great."

There was silence until Chris said, "Are you still there?"

"Yeah."

"You don't seem very enthusiastic."

"Sorry. It's the reality of it hitting me I guess. Knowing you'll be here permanently. Are you sure you want to do this, leave Sedona, your desert, your friends?"

"There's no problem with that. I'm looking forward to getting out of here, having a new adventure, having you."

"The thing is, Chris, you don't have me. Maybe you'll

never have me. Right now the thought of you touching me, having any physical contact with you makes my skin crawl. It's not you, but it's the product of my rape. Physical contact with any thought that it might lead to anything else makes me anxious, and I panic, just like what happened when I was there in Sedona and had to leave. So you may be disappointed."

Now he didn't say anything.

"Are you still there, Chris?"

"Yeah. I guess I understand. So what do we do? I still want to move up there, to be there with you."

"I don't have any answer as to what we do. If you still want to move here, that's fine, but I can't guarantee anything. We'll have to play it by ear and see what happens."

"Do you even want me to come?"

"Of course, but I want you to know where I'm at and what to expect. I don't want pressure, and I don't want you to be disappointed."

"I got it. I still want to move up there and be with you. I'm willing to see where it all leads … and be patient."

"You may need a lot of patience," she said with a chuckle. "It may be a long while, if ever. If you're willing to hang in there, I'll be happy for you to be here. We're just gonna have to take it slow and easy."

"Agreed. I'll see you in a few weeks then. Okay?"

"Okay. Thanks for understanding. I have to go."

"'Til later."

Jenny sat there digesting the conversation. He was coming. Her anxiety level rose a few degrees. She had a session with Joan on Tuesday and wished it was sooner.

When she met with Joan on Tuesday, she'd barely sat down when she started relating Chris's phone call and their conversation. "I feel kind of excited but really anxious, Joan.

I'm not at all sure about this anymore. I really like him, but the thought of a relationship really scares me. I thought I was ready, but now, I don't know."

"Jenny, slow down. It's not like you're getting married or anything. Just take a breath and realize that you'll be spending time, getting to know one another. You both may find you want to go further into a commitment … or not. Time will tell. Being anxious won't help anything."

"Thanks. I'm not sure what I'll do with him around all the time."

"What you'll do is maintain your schedule and routine as best you can with bringing him in as you see fit. Don't let his being here distract you from what you do, who you are, what your goals are."

"Thanks. That helps. Good advice as always."

CHAPTER 44

Chris called on the Wednesday night of the last week of April. They had finished the project that afternoon, and he was loading his stuff, heading out tomorrow, and would see her probably mid to late afternoon.

She thought Joan's advice had settled her nerves, but her anxiety level rose once again, and she didn't sleep well that night. She met Kelly the next morning for an early morning run, which helped clear her head.

They went for coffee afterward and Jenny said, "It's happening. Chris is arriving this afternoon, and I'm really nervous. Do you think I'm making the right decision, Kelly?"

"Well, all I've ever really done is go out on a few dates with guys, except for one I liked and thought we were getting serious, but he split for a job in California and I never heard from him again after he left. But none of them ever clicked with me. Most of them just wanted to party, try to get me drunk and into bed. I'm afraid, girl, you're on your own on this one. But you know I'll always be there for you and for sure try to help you sort out anything you might want to talk about."

With the day seeming to drag on forever, Jenny tried to write but couldn't focus. She went over to William's, but nobody was there. Then around three thirty, the old Toyota pickup pulled up to her bunkhouse, and he was there.

"So here we go," she whispered to herself.

When she went out to greet him, almost all the fear she'd been feeling melted away into the warmth of her feelings for this guy, but her greeting was less than warm as expressed by her quick embrace and light kiss.

All she could say was, "Want a beer?"

Chris either did not, or pretended not to, notice the physical coolness. "Sure. I'd love one. Wow, this is a beautiful place."

She led him inside her bunkhouse, cracked two longnecks, and invited him to sit. "Chris, I have to admit, I've been a bit nervous and scared about this, but I'm happy you're here. I've so much to show you and friends for you to meet."

"Well, to tell the truth, I'm a bit nervous myself, but I'm happy to finally be here with you. It does feel a bit weird. We can see each other every day, all the time. It's like we are committing to something, and it's kind of scary."

"Yeah, I know what you're saying, but I want you to know, I'm not committing to anything. But, good news, I'm feeling so much better; though I still have a long way to go. I still have difficulty with decisions sometimes. I still need structure and predictability in my life, so I'm not going to be constantly available for you. I know I've said this before, but I don't want to get hurt or to hurt you. I can't ask you to be my caretaker or babysitter. I've got to learn to be good with myself before I can be a decent partner. And I'll need you to respect my boundaries, I'll need you to understand where I'm at. I'm far from being normal, whatever that might be, but I'm working on it. Just be forewarned."

"I understand and promise to respect your boundaries. I'm looking forward to getting into a new place and a new life. I was just biding time in Sedona, but now I feel like I'm maybe settling into a place, who knows, maybe forever. I guess it's something I'd never really thought about. I just know I want to be with you."

"Yeah, I'm happy you're here," she said, looking at him with happy eyes. "Hey, let's go over to William's. I think I just heard him pull up. I want you to meet him. He's the greatest. Bring your beer." She got up and took his hand to lead him next door.

William answered her knock, and she introduced the two men. William invited them in and had them sit. He and Chris started talking like old friends. William got some more beers, and they chatted for over an hour. Susan and Dean came back from doing their errands, and William suggested that they all have dinner together. There were some steaks in the freezer and what was needed for a big salad and some potatoes. He called Helen to join them.

Dean had brought a dozen bottles of wine to replenish William's supply, and he opened a bottle of red and found a bottle of white that was already chilled. They all moved to the kitchen to help, chatting and laughing.

Helen arrived. "I hear there's a party."

"I guess so," Jenny said. "Helen, this is Chris."

"Great to finally meet the mystery man." She leaned in for a big hug and whispered in his ear, "I love Jenny like she's my daughter. Do not ever hurt her, or I will kill you. Understood?"

He backed away, eyes wide and with a forced smile. "No worries, Helen," he said quietly. "Understood."

She smiled back and winked at him.

After dinner the group broke up around nine o'clock.

Jenny helped Chris carry in the bags he needed for the night. The rest could wait until the next day.

"That was a fun night," Chris said. "Everyone made me feel welcome. They're some great people."

"They're the best. Hey, Susan and I are going to go to yoga in the morning. Why not join us?"

"Me? I never did yoga in my life."

"No time like the present to start. You could come to my eight-thirty beginners class."

"Probably not tomorrow. I have to start looking for a place to rent. Any suggestions?"

"Don't have a clue. You'll have to check the paper or call a rental agency I guess. Let me show you where everything's at. The place is about the same as your Sedona place. Make yourself at home. There's food in the fridge. I'll be leaving at about seven-thirty, and I'll see you when I get back around one. Will you be okay?"

"Yeah, no problem. I might go into town and explore while you're out."

"Why don't you ride in with Susan and me? You can take the Jeep while we're in class if you want or just walk around. We can meet after my class, around eleven, for coffee or an early lunch."

"Yeah, that sounds like a good plan. This is a very cool, little house. I'd love to find something like it," he said as he opened his bag, took what he needed, and headed toward the bathroom.

When he returned, he saw that Jenny had made up the couch for him. If he felt disappointment, he hid it well.

"I'm sorry to make you sleep on the couch, but right now, I'm not able to have physical contact with most everyone. I just can't. It makes me nervous and scared and nauseous. I hope you can understand."

"I can. You warned me, and so did Amanda, about what to expect, so I understand and will respect you on that."

Thanks, and thanks for being here."

"I'm happy to be here and together. It'll be great to be close, to see each other, and not to have a six-hour drive every time."

She said goodnight and went into her bedroom and closed and locked the door. Sleep came easily, and she dreamed that she was on top of a mountain, looking out over yet more and more mountains, all waiting for her to cross.

They woke early, had a quick breakfast, got Susan, and headed to town.

"Here's the keys. Let's meet at Raven's. It's a coffee shop about two blocks that way, right on Main Street. Say about eleven."

"I'll see ya then."

After class, Jenny and Susan walked down to Raven's. Chris wasn't there, so they each got something to drink and sat, chatting about the class.

About fifteen minutes later, Chris found them and sat down. "Hi, sorry I'm late, but I've had a stroke of luck."

"No problem. We're just talking. So what's up?"

"Yeah, I found a place to live already, right up on Third Avenue, a guest house, great guy, great rent. I can't believe it. He needs a part-time caretaker for when he and his wife are gone during the winter. Six hundred dollars a month. From what I've heard, this is a real steal here in Durango. It's small but furnished. It's big enough for my writing desk and bookcase. It's quiet. I love it."

Jenny smiled. "Let's see it."

The next day Chris and Jenny took his things to his new

place and got it all arranged. Afterward, they went to Walmart and got what other necessities he needed. Then after grocery shopping, they headed back to his place and got everything put away, with the bed made and towels hung.

"Want to spend the night?" he asked.

"Hmmmm, I'd consider your offer, but there's no couch, so maybe not," she replied. "Tomorrow's Saturday, and I'm scheduled to go for a run with my best friend, Kelly. It's our girl time together, with breakfast after. Sorry, but no boys allowed."

"Guess I'll have to live with it then. I've never been a runner anyway."

"I'll text you when I'm free and see what you want to do. Okay?"

"Sounds good. See ya tomorrow."

Next morning, she was up and off and met Kelly for their run at the trailhead they'd decided on. They did a ninety-minute trail run, then went for breakfast.

Dean and Susan had left for Denver that morning to close on the sale of their penthouse, and to pack and get everything ready for their move to Durango. They'd sold the place furnished, so they had only personal things to get together. They were coming back in five days, along with the moving van, to the restored Victorian they'd bought on Third Avenue.

That night Chris went out to Jenny's for dinner. He was all excited. "You won't believe this, but I was driving by this nursery and decided to stop to see if they needed anyone. I talked with the owner, and he liked that I had experience and hired me on the spot. He wants me to start Monday morning. Low pay to start, but he said he'll adjust it according to how I work out. I simply cannot believe how all this is working out."

"Maybe it was meant to be," Jenny replied.

CHAPTER 45

May arrived, and Jenny was delighted to share all the flowering trees, bushes and flowers in and around Durango with Chris. The city had come alive with beautiful color and new life. They walked Animas River Trail, observing rafters and kayakers who were enjoying the high water from spring runoff from the mountain snowmelt. Jenny got him to events like the spring art walk, the Taste of Durango, and the Farmers' Market, just to name a few.

They were enjoying their time together and only apart when they were busy or working. Chris worked five and a half days a week and stayed out on Jenny's couch Saturday nights.

Jenny continued to meet with Joan on every other Tuesday, with group on the same night. She did her yoga classes on her three-day schedule, and she had her Saturday-morning runs with Kelly. She and Chris enjoyed nights out with her friends. She had her chats with Helen and lengthy literary discussions with William about her book, on which she diligently worked and which was growing word by word, page by page, chapter by chapter. It was now over seventy thousand words and drawing to completion. All that was left was for her to get the ending right. William continued to help her craft it and kept on encouraging her. He'd contacted a few agents he knew about the possibility of getting it published and had sent off the first three chapters to them.

After reading *Zen and the Art of Motorcycle Maintenance*, William started his own project, a romance centered around a physics professor and a woman who was a new-age psychic healer—who reminded Jenny of Amanda in many ways. He struggled with the discourse of science and metaphysics and did a lot of research into these subjects, but he was happy to have finally branched out, and he liked what he was writing. He never stopped telling Jenny how much he appreciated her advice.

May sped on by, and suddenly it was June, arriving with warm sunny days. After graduating from law school in May, Peter moved to Durango where he interned at a small law firm. He and Kelly struck up a friendship that rapidly escalated into something else, and they now spent time together as couples.

Since Jenny had returned from her ill-fated trip to Sedona, Joan had been helping her with some therapy exercises to overcome her inability to handle physical affection, especially from Chris. Jenny had no problem with Will and Dean as she didn't feel sexually threatened by them. Chris also met several times with Joan soon after he moved there to better understand Jenny's trauma and treatment.

During the second week in June, Jenny and Chris were walking on Main Street one Friday night, and she reached over and took his hand. He responded by looking at her with a smile and gently squeezing her hand. It was a start.

July brought afternoon thunder showers the locals called monsoons, and Jenny and Chris spent several nights a week enjoying the downtown ambiance, the food, and the live music on open patios at the bars and restaurants. Hardly a weekend went by that they didn't try to do a day hike or go camping together, at least for a night, in the mountains by themselves or with friends.

They'd always slept in separate tents, and if it was an especially nice night, Jenny would sleep out under the stars. One particularly nice night, she asked Chris to sleep outside beside her and, strange as it was, it was the first night that she was able to sleep close beside him. Along with that, she found she was able to kiss him more warmly and allow him to show some affection back, like letting him stroke her face or her hair.

By mid-August, Jenny felt stronger, more balanced, more stable with herself and with Chris. But a new issue arose: where was her father? Was he really in prison? Was he even still alive?

A dream she'd had about a man she recognized but didn't know brought this up. He smiled and radiated an aura of love toward her, saying, "Jenny, oh Jenny, I'm sorry." His words made her feel warm, like she did with Chris and Will. From deep inside, she felt a deep love for this man. He faded away into a white mist.

She awoke with a start to the dawn and lay in her bed, remembering the dream, trying to understand. Then it hit her. Holy shit! It was Julian. *He's alive.*

At her session that same morning, she excitedly told Joan about her dream and what she'd figured out. She boldly announced, "I'm going to find him and go see him. I want to see my father. I know I can find him. I just have to. All of a sudden, I feel a warmth and love for him. Why, I have no idea. I just know."

Joan looked at her for a moment and then said, "Your

father? What do you think seeing him might accomplish?" She was hoping to see where Jenny might be going with this.

"Yeah, my father. It was him in my dream. I know it. More than anything, I know it. I think he's in prison in California for drug trafficking, according to one of my brother's letters from a few years ago. I've asked Dean and Susan, but they don't know any more than I do."

"If you do find him and see him, what do you think you will gain?"

"Closure. Final closure to all this. Don't you see?"

Joan smiled. "Yes, I do. I'm just concerned that what you might find might not be helpful. What if he's crazy or mean, or doesn't want to see you? He might not even remember you. Then what?"

"I don't care, Joan. Then at least I'll know one way or the other. No matter, I have to forgive him."

"You're determined to do this?"

"Yes, I am. I don't think I ever realized how much I need to at least let him know I'm still alive."

"Do you think he knows about Michael?"

"I have no idea how he would know. But Joan, it's just … I don't know. I just want to see if he's okay. I want to see if I can forgive him. He's my father, and I feel like I need to try to, to what … to hopefully reconcile, maybe."

Joan sat considering all this for a few moments. "Maybe that could be one of the last pieces you need to finally get on with your life. It might be a good thing for you to do, but it might also be hard. It could be really hard. I'm also thinking you're now strong enough to be up for it. I'm just worried about any setbacks you might encounter in seeing him."

"I think I can handle it. I know I need to do this. I really do. I could use a road trip. There are several stops I want to make on a journey to my past. Want to go with me? I might need a therapist."

"I don't think so, but thanks for the invite. It would be nice for you to have someone to travel with, though. Chris maybe? Any idea where he might be incarcerated?"

"Chris is busy, but I'll ask. And I have no clue where he's at. California's all I know for sure, so I'll start there. I'll go home and see what I might find on the Internet."

With that, they ended the session, and Jenny left for home on a new mission. She made herself a cup of tea and went online. After about two hours of researching prison registries and making a few phone calls, she located her father, Julian Morse. He was at the California Men's Colony in San Luis Obispo, serving ten years for drug trafficking. The prison apparently accommodated minimum and medium-security inmates, providing a mental health system as well as a mental health crisis unit. The facility provided inmates with programs for self-improvement, such as academic and vocational education, prison industry work skills, and inmate self-help group activities. She called and found out visiting hours and the protocol for visitation.

She consulted her pendulum; it gave her a definite yes to make the journey.

She knew how busy Chris was with work but decided to call anyway and ask whether he could go with her to California. They could go see his family maybe. She wanted to meet them.

"I'd love to go see my family," he said. "I've been trying to get a week off all summer, but we're just swamped. There's no way I can get any time off right now. Probably won't until later in the fall when things start to slow down a bit. Why do you ask?"

"Well, okay, this might sound weird." And she told him her plans.

"Wow, I'd love to go with you. Can you hold off until we can go together? We could fly out. You thinking about flying?"

"Flying would make sense, but I had planned on driving. I want to stop to see Amanda on the way. I also want to go back to the Farm."

Since her plan started to evolve on seeing her father, she had also started thinking about the Farm and seeing it again, if it still existed, to see who might still be around. It was a visit she dreaded, but she strongly felt she needed to go. She wanted some closure to that part of her life as well.

"I really want to drive; it'll give me time to think, prepare myself."

"So … driving? It's like two full days, you know. Why not wait until I can go with you? It would make sense. Then we could see my parents. I don't think it's wise for you to go by yourself anyway."

"What? Not wise. I'm not sure what you mean by that, Chris. I can take care of myself, thank you very much. I don't need a chaperone!"

"Hey, I'm sorry. I just don't want anything to happen to you."

"God, Chris, get over it. I survived on my own many years before you came along. I don't need you to be my guardian."

"I'm not trying to be your guardian. Can't I be concerned?"

"Oh, just forget it! I've already plotted my route. I know where I want to go, what and who I want to see, and I'll be going solo," she finished, angry and disappointed that he couldn't go.

"I'm sorry, Jenny. It seems like I just got here, and now you're leaving."

"Dammit, Chris, what don't you understand? I fucking need to do this! I fucking want to see my father who is in fucking prison. If you can't handle my life, maybe you should go back to Sedona. Then you wouldn't have to try to run my life for me. I'm sorry, Chris. I'm just a little on edge about this, but I have to do this. I just have to. Please understand."

"I know. I'm being selfish. I'm sorry for the way I reacted."

"Yeah, me too." She gave a little laugh.

That night, feeling strong, confident, and filled with an unquenchable desire, she brought Chris to her bed and made love to him, and it was good. She couldn't believe how beautiful it was, now that it finally happened.

The next day Jenny packed for her trip and included camping gear just in case. She went into town and loaded up on trail mix and PowerBars. She went to see her grandparents to tell them about her plans. They were hesitant but didn't try to dissuade her. Then she talked to Helen whose only concern was that she'd be okay and not get into something she couldn't handle emotionally. She said she'd keep in touch.

She went home, found William, and told him she'd be gone for at least a week, if not two. Then she went to her computer and wrote. Chris came out after work. They had a light dinner, read until nine, and then went to bed and once again made love.

Jenny had a restless night, filled with dreams of trying to get to an unreachable destination. Always in slow motion, she was never able to focus, always finding herself on unfamiliar roads leading nowhere.

CHAPTER 46

Up at dawn, she said goodbye to Chris and was on the road across the Navajo Nation to Flagstaff, then down to Sedona to see Amanda. She called her on the way to make an appointment, but Amanda was busy all day. However, she invited Jenny to her house to have dinner and spend the night. She reached Sedona early and walked Main Street looking into some familiar shops until it was time to head to Amanda's.

Her house was on the same road a little beyond where Chris used to live. Jenny drove by his place and stopped. It was empty, everyone, everything gone, but the memories still remained of last Christmas. She felt an empty ache in her chest and tears came. She sat for a few minutes, dried her eyes, then drove off.

She pulled into Amanda's, grabbed what she needed for the night, and started up the walk to the house. It was like entering a shrine, with carefully placed stones, a few very large crystals, and statues of Buddha, Ganesha, and other entities all interspersed with cactus and other desert plantings. Amanda greeted her with a long, tight embrace, and Jenny went into a warm, inviting house with tapestries and artwork on the walls, soft furniture, colorful pillows, and smelling of the succulent aromas of food cooking. Amanda gave her another huge, long, warm embrace. The house seemed filled with magical energy, making her feel like she had entered another dimension.

Amanda had some wine ready to pour, and they sat. She asked how things were. Jenny gave a short version of what had transpired with her therapy, of Chris, and of where she was headed and why.

"Jenny, are you wearing that protective talisman I gave you?"

"Of course." She pulled it out from under her top and showed it. "I've been wearing it ever since you gave it to me. If nothing else, it reminds me of you."

"Thanks for the thought, but I think it does more than that."

After more conversation and another glass of wine, dinner was ready.

Jenny felt happy being there. "Amanda, I somehow feel I have known you forever. Thanks for your kindness."

"Maybe we have known each other in other lifetimes. I'll have to check on that," Amanda said, smiling.

They cleaned up after dinner and sat to finish their wine. Amanda asked, "So you're on your way to see your father? How're you feeling about that?"

Jenny laughed. "What do you see in my aura?" She turned serious. "But to answer your question, I've really no idea. Maybe I should have just written him a letter. But I really need to see him and let him see me. I guess I need to confront him. I just want to try to come to terms with him and everything that happened to me. What do you think?"

"Well, this is something I can't see; maybe things might surprise you, anger you, and shock you, but I think it will definitely be beneficial in the long run. I can't elaborate, but maybe some things will unveil themselves and give you a better perspective."

Jenny nodded. "So Amanda, do you always show such concern and hospitality to your other clients?"

Amanda hesitated for several moments, had several sips of wine, took a deep breath, and responded, "No, I don't. The truth is, Jenny, I have a special empathy for you." She took a few more deep breaths and continued. "I was also abused as a young girl. Only you and one other person know this, so please—"

"Oh my God, Amanda. I'm so sorry! I promise I'll never tell anyone. I'm so sorry. How many abused women must there be?"

"I don't know, but I'm guessing there are many of us."

Jenny asked gently, "Do you want to talk about it?"

"If you don't mind."

"Of course I don't mind. I've learned from my therapy how healing sharing can be. Please tell me whatever you want."

Amanda began, her voice now shallow, "It was my father. It started when I was around twelve or thirteen. He came into my room one night." She stopped, choking back a sob and taking a deep breath. "I told my mother, but she said I was lying. She ignored my pleas for help. She just ignored me … but I know she knew. She just didn't care.

"After that first time, it continued more and more frequently. I had nowhere to turn, no one to talk to. I couldn't stand it anymore so I began systematically stealing money from my parents in small amounts, trying not to cause any suspicion. It took a long time, but when I had what I thought I might need, I sneaked out and ran away one night. I was sixteen. I hitchhiked out of Columbia, Missouri, where I grew up, and headed west. A woman picked me up. I lied and said I was nineteen. She believed me. I said I was going to California.

"I wanted to get as far away as I could from my parents. This woman, Rachel, God, I so love her, she became my mentor and rescued me from my life. She believed in me. She was coming here to Sedona. I rode with her all the way, using what money I had to share gas and buy a little food. I had my driver's license and was able to help her drive.

"I was broke when I got here. She gave me a job at her shop, now my shop, and a place to stay. I bought it from her ten years ago when she retired. She taught me everything I know." She stopped to get some tissues and wipe her eyes.

"She became my surrogate mother and still lives nearby with her husband. I see her often. I'd like you to meet her sometime. You'd like her. I love her dearly."

Jenny smiled. "I'd love to meet her, Amanda. That's some story. Wow, did you do any counseling?"

"Regretfully no. I should have. Rachel was my only counselor. She helped me so much. She did work much like I do, only more so. She has the real gift. I am still working on getting to her level. But I regret not having worked with a counselor. I know it would've helped. I am forty-three years old, and I've never had a relationship with a man. I've had ample opportunity but sadly could never trust men. And that's my story. That is why I care for you so much. I went through similar abuse."

They remained silent for a long time. Amanda poured them more wine.

Jenny finally said, "Maybe it's not too late, Amanda—for counseling, I mean. As scary as it was in the beginning, it's helped me so much. You should truly do it."

"I know you're right. I just never had the courage."

"It's hard. Trust me on that. But once I got through sharing the really ugly parts with my counselor, Joan, the rest sort of started to fall into place. It's not been easy, but I'm not sure where I'd be right now without her help and yours as well."

"Okay then, enough about my past," Amanda said. "Let's come back up to the present. Tell me more about what's going on with you."

Jenny told her about Chris's move, and Amanda asked how it was going.

Jenny replied, "Well, good news is I'm finally able to receive and share affection. We had sex, and I actually enjoyed it; no, I loved it. He's a great guy, and I'm in love with him, I guess."

Amanda said, "You guess?"

"Yeah. I'm not too sure what love is, but all I know is I'd like to spend every hour of every day with him."

Amanda laughed. "I think that's close enough. I'd say that you are probably soul mates."

Jenny smiled. "Pardon my ignorance, but what is a soul mate?"

Amanda explained that Jenny and Chris were both separate parts of the same soul, separated sometime in some other lifetime; they had both incarnated in this life to become one again for either a short time or forever.

Jenny's eyes widened. "I'm going to have to try to wrap my brain around this concept. Wow, really? I think it'll be forever."

"It is a strange concept. I know I have this book somewhere. Give me a moment to find it." Amanda got up and returned shortly with a book. "This will explain it better and give other information about souls that may or may not be of interest to you. Keep it, and you can return it the next time we see each other. We can talk more about it then."

It was getting late, and they both said good night. Jenny's room was comfy and small, also decorated with tapestries and artwork as well as stones and crystals. It felt so warm, and she felt very safe and protected there. She slept soundly with dreams of flying, her body being simply pure energy and light. She awoke early, her first thought being how much she liked being here with this woman.

Amanda was already up and had made coffee and toast. Jenny ate quickly, anxious to be on the road. She grabbed her things and hugged Amanda long and hard, thanking her for her kindness and hospitality. "I wish we lived closer so I could have you for a friend."

"We are friends, my dear young woman, very close friends, even with the distance factor."

"I love you, Amanda."

"Love you too. Be careful out there."

"For sure. See you soon. Promise."

CHAPTER 47

Jenny went back up I-15 to I-40 at Flagstaff and headed west, pushing hard to get to Bakersfield for the night. She called the prison at a gas stop and asked about visitation on Tuesday, knowing there were no visitation hours on Monday.

The person at the prison told her she'd be the first person to visit her father since he'd been incarcerated there eight years ago. Jenny asked her not to tell Julian she was his daughter.

She made it to San Luis Obispo at midday Sunday, found lodging in the town proper, and spent the rest of the day walking around the little city. Then she went out by the seashore to roam and think. The gently rolling waves coming to the shore and salt air did little to calm her nervousness, with her being just short of being terrified of what she was planning to do on Tuesday.

After dinner, she went to her room and called Susan and Dean, Chris, William, and Joan to tell them she'd arrived and was all right. Joan wanted to talk and find out everything about her trip so far, including how she was feeling and so on. It was turning into a phone therapy session, but Jenny just wanted to be left alone and was gracefully able to cut her off and bid her a good night.

The next day, Monday, she drove up the coast, taking her time to pause and enjoying the different beauty of the place. Jenny stopped at some of the little towns along the way, visiting various shops that caught her interest. In the late afternoon, she returned to her little hotel and went out for the early evening, enjoying a glass of wine in a little bistro.

After a light dinner, she went back to her room. She called Chris and talked for thirty minutes, then curled up in bed with Virginia Woolf's *A Room of One's Own.*

After a dreamless but restless night, she awoke early, did her meditation, went for a run, and had breakfast at the hotel. Then she waited, with nervous anticipation, to go to the prison and see her father.

CHAPTER 48

Jenny arrived at the main gate, and a guard checked her over at the guard station. She had to leave everything she carried on her body, except the clothes she was wearing. She followed a guard into a banal green waiting area, where there were a number of people already sitting on cheap plastic chairs. No one spoke; everyone was singular and subdued in his or her thoughts and probable anticipation. Jenny's heart pounded like a jackhammer, and she consciously struggled to do some deep yogic breathing to avoid passing out.

She was soon called and directed to a booth with a phone handset, and there she waited. Shortly a man appeared on the other side of the heavy window, wearing an orange jumpsuit. She hardly recognized him. He was thinner than she remembered. His face was lined, and gray streaked his hair, but he was definitely her father, Julian.

He sat without looking up and got situated, then he looked up. Bewilderment and shock filled his face. They sat there for what seemed like a long time, but in reality it was only a few seconds. Finally, Jenny reached for her handset. Julian followed suit.

"Hi, Daddy, it's Jenny … your daughter," she said in a quivering voice.

He sat there, just looking, and finally replied, "Jenny, oh my God, I can't believe it. Jenny! Jenny? My beautiful daughter?" He dropped the handset, buried his face in his hands, and broke into convulsive sobs.

"Daddy, it's okay; it's okay. Please don't cry," she said as tears ran down her cheeks.

Once Julian was finally able to talk, he said, "Jenny, my beautiful, beautiful daughter, it's been so long. How've you been? Where have you been? Tell me everything. I'd given up all hope that anyone even knew I still existed, that I'd ever see you, or anyone, ever again."

"It's been a while, hasn't it? I've so much to tell you. There's just so much … so much …"

"Have you seen Mom and Dad? Are they okay?"

"They're great. I see them a lot. We're all living in Colorado, in Durango. They send their love," she lied.

"What about Michael? Do you see him?"

"Saw him before last Christmas. Let's talk about him later, if that's okay?"

A sense of foreboding clouded his face. Jenny dreaded the moment she'd have to tell him about Michael.

Julian replied, "Sure, Jenny, sure. Later then. I'm so happy to see you. You're … you're like a vision. You look just like your mother. God, Jenny, I loved her so much, and then … and then she died. It broke me, broke my heart, broke my spirit, literally killed me inside. I just wanted to die too.

"I was lost. I had you two babies, and I didn't know what to do. Then I met Dory. She was wild, fun, and crazy. She knew about this commune in California where everything was paradise, so I took you two and went with her to that damned place.

"I was already drinking too much, and there at the commune, drugs were plentiful. I let her be in charge of you two kids while I stayed drunk or stoned almost every day. I needed money. I started hanging out with a couple of guys. We'd go to San Diego and pick up a 'shipment.' We'd take and distribute it to people in San Francisco, Sacramento, even as far as Vegas sometimes, and of course we had a good trade going on out of that fucking commune. There was so much money involved.

"I'm so sorry. I've had so much time to think in here, you can't imagine the guilt, the regret, and self-hate I have about your childhood, about everything that happened. I was such a rotten father."

Jenny started to say something, but Julian held up his hand to stop her. "I finally got busted shortly after you disappeared. Me and seven others. Thankfully I ended up here rather than one of the harder places. I got cleaned up and went through a lot of rehab, AA, and such. There's good support here, and I was once again able to face life. I had no contacts for anyone. I didn't know of any way to reach anybody to let them know where I was. I didn't think anyone would care anyway. And now you appear, and an empty hole just got filled. I never thought I would ever see you or any family again. And I couldn't blame you. I can't believe you're here … I can't understand why you would, after the way I neglected you and Michael … what Dory did to you. Why did you even bother?"

Jenny sat for a few moments, digesting what she'd heard. "I came, Daddy, because I needed closure. Now I see maybe you do too. It's good. It's okay, Daddy. We've both had it tough."

She started to tell him about her life. But their allotted

time was soon up. She had to leave. The guard came to escort Julian away.

"I'll be back tomorrow, Daddy. Is that okay?"

"I already can't wait. I want to hear everything about you and Michael. I love you so much! I'm so happy you came. I'm sorry to have rambled on so. I just needed to unload. It's been so long. I've so many regrets. Can you ever forgive me for being such a waste?"

"I already have … and I love you too, Daddy." She got up and left, tears streaming down her face.

After she returned to her hotel room, she sat for a long while, simply thinking about her father after seeing him after all these years and digesting their hour-long visit. She was happy she'd made the effort to come and see him. They would never have those twenty some years back, but they could have this time to reconnect, to be a father and daughter.

She went back on Wednesday and Thursday. On Friday, Julian pressed her about Michael. Knowing she couldn't avoid the truth any longer, she braced herself, took a deep breath. "Daddy, he was really messed up. When I saw him in Denver and we were going to have dinner together, he just went off on me, started screaming at me in this restaurant, threatened to beat me, said I was just another stupid woman who needed to have some sense slapped into her."

She related the rest of the incident to him, and finally, they came to what she dreaded saying. She started feeling sick to her stomach, and she wailed, "And then he killed himself! I'm so sorry to have to tell you all this, Daddy. I'm so sorry."

The color drained from Julian's face. He remained silent for a long time, then finally said in a hollow, monotone voice, "If I would've just been a father to you kids … I wasn't! I'm so sorry, Jenny, so damned sorry. I can't ever forgive myself …

never!" He sat quietly, tears also running down his face.

"It'll be all right, Daddy. You still have me. We can be together when you're released. I'll get you to Durango. You'll be fine. I have some great friends there."

"Jenny, I can't ask you to do anything for me. I haven't earned anything from you. You don't owe me anything. You owe me nothing."

"You aren't asking. I'm offering. I want to have my father back. I need him back. I'm being selfish. I want you close, to be together."

"It might be strange. After all, we don't really know each other, do we?"

"But you're my father, and I want to know you. Please believe that!"

He was about to speak when the guard came. "Sorry, Julian, but we really have to head back. I've let you go overtime as it is."

"Yeah, I understand and thanks." He got up to leave.

"See you tomorrow, Daddy," she said with a smile and blew him a kiss.

She went back every day. They talked about Dean and Susan and Michael. He wanted to know every detail of her life. They had so much to catch up on. Jenny asked about Dory. He had neither seen nor heard from her since right before his arrest.

Jenny left him on Sunday, promising to be back later next week. She had another place she needed to visit and would see him before heading back to Colorado.

While she and Chris talked most every night, she realized she hadn't called Joan all week. She went out by the ocean, found a rock to sit on, and called her at home. Joan picked up right away. Jenny apologized for not calling sooner and for calling her on Sunday. But she wanted her to know she was fine and that seeing her father and reconnecting were very hard and bittersweet, but also rewarding. She kept it brief, said a goodbye, and clicked off.

Jenny went back to her hotel. She got her maps out and plotted a route to Sacramento. She wondered whether she could find the Farm and whether there would be anyone there she still knew—if it still even existed. She hoped so; she needed more answers for closure.

Early Monday morning, Jenny went to see the warden to discuss Julian. She found out he was a model prisoner and would be up for parole shortly. With his good record, he would certainly get released. Jenny asked what the process of being on parole entailed. She found out he'd need to go to a halfway house, have a guardian or overseer, couldn't leave the state, and meet with his parole officer regularly. He'd need to join a local AA group, and, hopefully, he'd find work.

Jenny asked, "Do you think I could be his guardian?"

The warden replied, "It could be a possibility if you lived in California. Parolees generally aren't allowed to leave the state."

"Okay, thanks for your time. I'll be back in a few days for another visit." They shook hands, and Jenny turned and left. As she walked to her Jeep, she considered what the warden had said about Julian leaving the state.

Before she left the parking lot, guessing Dean wouldn't want to help, she called William and told him what was going on and that she needed an attorney. Could he recommend anyone who might help? William gave her two names and the numbers to call. After she ended the call with William, she called the numbers. The first one said he couldn't take on anything more right then. The second was busy with a client but would call back. She got her call back about forty-five minutes later and pulled to the side of the highway to answer it.

The lawyer's name was Cynthia Davis, and after Jenny explained the situation, she said she'd be interested in taking the case. They discussed fees, which Jenny was comfortable with. Cynthia would proceed to look into the possibilities and be in touch. Jenny thanked her and continued on to Sacramento.

CHAPTER 49

Jenny got to Sacramento and used her memory and Google Maps to backtrack her escape route from almost eight years ago to find her way back to the Farm. She found the train station and from there located the road she'd come in on all those years ago. She headed out and began to recognize some landmarks along the way.

Close to where she remembered the commune to be, Jenny stopped at a convenience store at an intersection and asked the grizzled older man behind the counter whether he knew of a hippie commune anywhere nearby. He said he knew of a bunch of folks living together up north, about ten miles away. He thought for a moment, then gave her directions.

It was getting late, and Jenny asked if he knew of any place to stay nearby. He gave her directions to Interstate 5 and said there was a motel at the interchange. She thought about camping and, deciding against it, drove another fifteen miles and found a Quality Inn, a gas station, and a restaurant by the intestate. She got a room, got situated, and went for some food. Afterward, back in her room, she thought about what and who she might find, if anything was even left after these years. She slept a dreamless sleep.

She got up early the next morning, headed back the way she'd come, and then followed the directions the man had given her. She came to the little village she used to walk to as a little girl. Then everything came back to her.

Two miles up the old lane, there it was, still the same, only things looked better, cleaned up. There was a large garden area and a new grow dome. People were busily going about their day. She recognized everything like it was only yesterday, but it all seemed so much smaller now.

She parked, got out, and started walking around. The old yurt where she lived was still there, only it looked so much better. She saw Buddhist prayer flags fluttering over the door as well as everywhere else. A young man she didn't recognize came up to her and asked whether she needed help. Jenny told him who she was and said she'd grown up here and wondered whether any original residents might be left.

"Do you remember Annie?" he asked. "She's one of the originals from what I know. She lives right over there." He pointed to a place Jenny recognized.

Jenny's face lit up. "She was one of my few favorite people. Oh my God, she's still here."

"Yeah. She's probably around her cabin somewhere."

"Thanks so much. Appreciate your help." She turned, strode down a familiar path to a cabin, and knocked on the door.

A woman opened it and looked out with a confused look that turned into a broad smile, "Oh my God, Jenny. Is that you? Oh my God, Jenny, it is you, all growed up. Come in! Come in! I'm making tea. Want some tea? Please sit, but first, give ol' Annie some love. Then I want ta know everything about you. Oh, come here, you sweet girl." She grabbed Jenny and hugged her so hard, Jenny could hardly breathe.

"I'd love some tea, Annie. Thank you. Great to see you."

Annie proceeded to pour their tea, offered some cookies, and sat, facing Jenny. "Jenny, dear sweet girl, you look great, absolutely wonderful. Where've you been, for what, ten years?"

"Almost eight, Annie, and you look wonderful yourself. Has life been good to you?"

"Actually it has … after the big bust, that is, but I'll get to that. Please tell me, are you still in California? You just up and disappeared, and no one knowed where you went or what happened. We all wondered and worried about you. We searched 'round everywhere for you, didn't know if you was dead or alive. Then the ol' bitch Dory told us all your stuff was gone, so we suspected you just run off. No one really blamed you."

Jenny nodded. "Yeah, I'm truly sorry about that. It's a long story. I'll try to give you a quick version."

She covered the highlights of her escape, then told her things she'd never before told her, about the abuse she and Michael had suffered from Dory and Old George. She finished by telling her about how she'd found out about Michael's raping her. She discussed her grandparents, college, the mountains, Durango, and the real reason why she was back in California, to see her father.

Annie sat, listening, without a word. Jenny finished her saga. They both just sat for a moment. Jenny's untouched tea had gone cold.

Finally, Annie spoke. "That's just horrible, Jenny. I knew there was all sorts of shit going on with that Dory woman. I remember your father beating her, once severely. Two guys stopped him that time, or he might o' killed her. He caught her fucking Michael when he was only, like, fourteen, as I recall."

"Holy shit! I remember that. I was there. I saw it all, what Dory and Michael were doing, and Daddy coming in and finding them."

"As I recall, anyways, he would o' like kilt her if he weren't stopped."

"So what sort of stuff was it with Dory, other than that she was a total bitch and sexually abusing me and my brother?"

"You never knew? Dory brought up four or five whores from Oakland with her. Then this's a place to buy drugs back then. There're always men around … and women coming by to buy drugs or spend the night with a woman or a man; they weren't exclusive. There was sex and drug parties all the time. You didn't know?"

Jenny remembered those nights and what went on in the yurt when she and Michael were supposed to be sleeping.

"Yeah, I guess I do. I just thought it was people from here all getting together."

"Oh no! They's all outsiders: Sacramento, Frisco, other places. They paid money, lots of it, for a good ol' time of gettin' laid, stoned, or other stuff. Dory, that bitch! I hated her and those other bastards. A lot of us wanted them gone, but there's threats made. We's all scared, so's we just looked the other way. There's a lot of outside money involved, big money from Sacramento and Frisco; more'n we could mess with. We figured that the mob was involved, maybe Vegas types."

"Holy shit, Annie. That's all crazy. I never knew, but it all makes sense. She stopped her abuse toward me after I threatened to kill her one day."

Annie nodded. "She was a piece of work, that one. I's going to leave a number of times but never did … had some good friends here, and we's just wanted to stay the hell out o' the way, below the radar. That's until the feds rolled in one day. They swooped in one day … about a year after you'd gone. Got all 'em bastards. Searched every one of our places, mine too. Most everyone was cleared 'cept for Dory's crowd. Somehow that bitch Dory had conveniently disappeared right 'fore it happened. All the others're busted."

"Is that when my father was arrested?"

"No, he's arrested 'bout two weeks before. We's all figured he and the other guys spilt the beans about the operation. Where's he now?"

"Prison, San Luis Obispo. He's doing good and should be out pretty soon, from what I was told. Looks older but looks good, clean, sober, healthy."

"That's good. Always thought he's a good man. Sure got in with the wrong crowd when he come here with that bitch Dory.

"And Michael, poor guy, hung around for two years after. Some of the guys finally took him to Sacramento, kicked him out, and told him to never come back. He'd gotten real mean and nasty to all the women, figured he's miss'n Dory. Guess he somehow thought she was in love with him or somethin'. Maybe he just liked bangin' her, and, hell, none of the girls here'd ever gave him the time a day. Just got hateful, nasty mean to everyone. It was good riddance."

"Ever hear what happened to Dory?"

"Heard a few years ago that she's runnin' a call-girl ring outta Oakland. Dory—the article said Doreen Crawford— was found in an alley all beat up with two bullets in the back o' her head. Somebody saw it in a newspaper. Guess the cops thought it was an execution. I couldn' give a shit. Well fuckin' deserved."

Annie got up and made them some more tea. Jenny wished she could've had a glass of wine or a beer after all that had been said, but she enjoyed her tea.

"Oh yeah, you'll probably be happy to hear that Old George died three years ago. Nobody much liked him either. Buried him on the other side of the hill. Nobody misses him much. You weren't the only one he showed his pecker to. He's a sad old man."

"So the place looks really nice. You're actually growing food?"

"Yeah, after the 'big bust,' we's able to get more serious. Had to. No money coming in after them bastards was gone. So we went to growin' veggies, became a real 'farm.'" She chuckled at her little joke. "Got some bigger fields the other side a the creek. Lots a work, but we're part of the community-sponsored agriculture movement, where we sells shares up front for a year's worth of veggies. That does real well for us. We deliver big loads a veggies inta Sacramento every week most a the year. Now's we gots that grow dome. Didja see it when ya come in? We's also got booths at the Sacramento Farmers' Market. All 'n all, we make enough to keep ourselves fed and clothed. It's a good life, really. Main reason I come here fifteen years ago. It was like that until Dory and her crew showed up. Do ya think ya wanta come back?" she asked with a grin. "Love to have ya."

Jenny noticed for the first time that Annie had several teeth missing. She felt a pang of sadness run through her, but noticing those missing teeth suddenly became too much for her. She felt sick to her stomach and couldn't breathe. She needed to leave. She'd heard enough, more than enough. She looked at her watch and said she had to get back to San Luis tonight. She wrote down her contact information for Annie and told her to stay in touch, knowing she never would.

"Thanks for everything, Annie, for being my only friend

when I was a little girl, for your schooling me, and for all you told me today. It fills in a lot of blanks. It was wonderful to see you and how well everything looks here. You take care of yourself."

"Thank ya, yourself, for comin' by an' seeing ol' Annie. Come back anytime. Love ta see ya anytime yer around these parts."

Jenny got up, gave her a hug, and left. She didn't look back, leaving behind the sad memories of her childhood.

As she drove, her mind drifted to Dory and how she was found, beaten and murdered. Not too long ago, she would've smirked and said, "Couldn't happen to a better person, that bitch." But now all she felt was sadness, wondering how frightened she must have been, what her childhood was like, what her parents were like; did she even have parents or anyone to love her, nurture her, raise her? She thought how she could've ended up like her if not for her grandparents.

Then her mind drifted to Michael, and she thought of how close they'd been when they were children and how he'd changed to become so hateful and angry. She thought of him committing suicide, how confused, frightened, desperate he must have been. The lump in her throat turned to tears, and she realized that maybe she could forgive both of them for the abuse, for the heartache, for everything.

CHAPTER 50

She arrived back at the little hotel late in the afternoon. After dinner, she spent the rest of the night writing in her journal, processing the bittersweet experience of seeing her father and visiting Annie at the Farm.

She went to see Julian early the next morning and told him where she'd gone and about her conversation with Annie.

"So now you know it all," he said, "all the crap I was involved in and the other stuff. I'm sorry you had to find out. I didn't know about Michael being thrown out. God, Jenny, it's all such a mess, and I'm to blame for everything that happened to you kids. I can never forgive myself ... never." He hung his head and wiped his eyes.

"Daddy, I forgive you. You have to forgive yourself and let go of the guilt. It's okay. I love you. We've the rest of our lives to live. I want to live mine and want you to live yours, to be father and daughter. I have a lawyer working on getting you to be able to serve your parole with me in Durango. Nothing certain, no promises, but we're working on it. It'd be really nice to have you close by. It's been so great to see you. I want to have my father around."

"Thanks, Jenny. It was so wonderful that you came. Thank you, thank you. I take it you're heading back?"

"Yeah, it's time. I need to get home. I have some people I need to see. It was great to see you, Daddy. I do love you, and I forgive you for … for … everything. Please, please find it in your heart to forgive yourself. I have all your contact information, and I promise I'll keep in touch."

"When will I see you again?" he asked.

"Soon, I hope. We'll talk soon." She blew him a kiss, turned and left, her head bowed, tears running down her face. What she wanted more than anything was to hold him close and never let him go. She felt she had some closure and, at long last, actually felt some peace.

She made it to Kingman, Arizona, for the night after driving across the Mojave Desert. The stark emptiness added to her sense of peace. She looked forward to being home in her little house and felt an overwhelming warmth and love for her adopted community. She'd found people she could trust, people she could love, people she called friends, people who loved her. She felt she finally, really, had a home.

As soon as she reached her motel, she called Chris and told him she was on her way and would be back tomorrow. She wanted him to come out to her place as soon as he could after work.

That night she dreamed she was on her favorite ridge at eleven thousand feet, looking out over the vast, shimmering mountain landscape, arms hugging herself, enjoying a clear bright sunrise unfolding over the San Juan Mountains.

A NOTE FROM THE AUTHOR

If you enjoyed this book, I would be very grateful if you could write a review and publish it at your point of purchase. Your review, even a brief one, will help other readers to decide to enjoy my work.

If you want to be notified of new releases from myself and other Alkira Publishing authors, please sign up to the Alkira Publishing email list. In return you'll get a free e-book of short stories and book excerpts by Alkira Publishing authors. You'll find the sign-up button on the right-hand side under the photo at www.alkirapublishing.com. Of course, your information will never be shared, and the publisher won't inundate you with emails, just let you know of new releases.

ACKNOWLEDGEMENTS

I wish to thank my wife, Julianne Ward, for her patience and encouragement. Also, I wish to thank my publisher, Tahlia Newland, for all her amazing help, encouragement, and patience to get me through this project.

ABOUT THE AUTHOR

Ed Lehner, a retired professor of graphic design from Iowa State University, has journaled and written poetry for over forty years and, more recently, novels, such as *The Awakening of Russell Henderson,* and a short story collection, *Grandpa's Horse. San Juan Sunrise* actually came unexpectedly when he was recovering from pneumonia in 2015. The story began as a poem, then morphed into a short story and just kept growing and growing until, to his surprise, he brought it to closure. He lives with his wife, Julie, and Emma the cat in Durango, Colorado. He can be reached at www.elehner.com.

www.ingramcontent.com/pod-product-compliance
Lightning Source LLC
Chambersburg PA
CBHW051246210726
48287CB00002B/378